Second Chance Sunsets for their Lonely Hearts

STAND-ALONE NOVEL

A Western Historical Romance Book

by

Ava Winters

Disclaimer & Copyright

Table of Contents.

Second Chances and Sunsets for their Lonely Hearts.....1

Disclaimer & Copyright...............................2

Table of Contents. 3

Let's connect! 5

Letter from Ava Winters 6

Prologue 7

Chapter One...16

Chapter Two...26

Chapter Three 35

Chapter Four..44

Chapter Five..52

Chapter Six 62

Chapter Seven 69

Chapter Eight...77

Chapter Nine 87

Chapter Ten 96

Chapter Eleven 104

Chapter Twelve 113

Chapter Thirteen 124

Chapter Fourteen 133

Chapter Fifteen..141

Chapter Sixteen..149

Chapter Seventeen......................................158

Chapter Eighteen.......................................164

Chapter Nineteen..173

Chapter Twenty 182

Chapter Twenty-One..190

Chapter Twenty-Two..199

Chapter Twenty-Three 208

Chapter Twenty-Four..217

Chapter Twenty-Five..226

Chapter Twenty-Six 235

Chapter Twenty-Seven 243

Chapter Twenty-Eight...251

Chapter Twenty-Nine 260

Chapter Thirty...268

Chapter Thirty-One 278

Chapter Thirty-Two 287

Chapter Thirty-Three 296

Chapter Thirty-Four 303

Chapter Thirty-Five 311

Chapter Thirty-Six..315

Epilogue 327

Also by Ava Winters 331

Let's connect!

Impact my upcoming stories!

My passionate readers influenced the core soul of the book you are holding in your hands! The title, the cover, the essence of the book as a whole was affected by them!

Their support on my publishing journey is paramount! I devote this book to them!

If you are not a member yet, join now! As an added BONUS, you will receive my Novella **"The Cowboys' Wounded Lady"**:

FREE EXCLUSIVE GIFT
(available only to my subscribers)

Go to the link:
https://avawinters.com/novella-amazon

Letter from Ava Winters

"Here is a lifelong bookworm, a devoted teacher and a mother of two boys. I also make mean sandwiches."

If someone wanted to describe me in one sentence, that would be it. There has never been a greater joy in my life than spending time with children and seeing them grow up - all my children, including the 23 little 9-year-olds that I currently teach. And I have not known such bliss than that of reading a good book.

As a Western Historical Romance writer, my passion has always been reading and writing romance novels. The historical part came after my studies as a teacher - I was mesmerized by the stories I heard, so much that I wanted to visit every place I learned about. And so, I did, finding the love of my life along the way as I walked the paths of my characters.

Now, I'm a full-time elementary school teacher, a full-time mother of two wonderful boys and a full-time writer. Wondering how I manage all of them? I did too, at first, but then I realized it's because everything I do I love, and I have the chance to share it with all of you.

And I would love to see you again in this small adventure of mine!

Until next time,

Ava Winters

Prologue

Columbus, Ohio

April 17, 1869

"Kerouac, Peter, please step forward."

Peter shuffled to the counter, accompanied by a guard who towered over him and looked to weigh three hundred pounds of solid muscle. Heavy shackles weighed his hands down so they hung below his hips and stooped his shoulders. He thought the shackles an unnecessary precaution, considering that the officer at the counter sat behind massive iron bars that would probably survive a twelve-pounder shell. Besides, if Peter had any thoughts of violence, the presence of the giant standing next to him would likely preclude any chance of acting on those thoughts.

When he reached the counter, the officer set three objects in front of Peter. The first, a corroded bronze locket, was the only one of the three that Peter actually cared for. The silver dollar next to it was useful, but not very since it was the only one he had.

The third item was something Peter hoped to never see again.

"Thought you didn't give those back," he said to the officer.

His voice, gravelly from lack of use, sounded strange in his own ears. Behind him, one of the other prisoners slated for release–Big Bob–by the sound of his voice, scoffed. "Would you look at that? He can speak."

Peter ignored him. Big Bob talked a lot, but that was all he did. In two years, Peter had heard Bob talk the ears off of everyone—whether they listened or not—about what a dangerous man he was, but Peter had never seen him do anything to prove it. And anyway, Peter didn't much care if people respected him or not. Respect never saved anyone's life. It never brought anyone back from the dead.

"The State of Ohio returns all belongings to the inmate upon release," the officer said.

Peter stared at the item. "Well, I don't want it."

"What you do with it after you leave this prison is your concern," the officer said. "But it's your responsibility, and it's leaving here with you."

Peter was more than ready to be rid of the prison and its smell of death and decay. He'd had enough of death, but the object resting on the counter next to the locket and silver dollar was an agent of death, and as long as Peter had it, death would follow him wherever he went.

Peter sighed and nodded acknowledgement. The officer nodded to the giant standing next to Peter. With surprisingly gentle hands, the hulking man removed Peter's shackles. Peter rubbed feeling back into his wrists as the officer stepped back, tossing the shackles into a pile to be put away later.

"Peter Kerouac, you are hereby discharged from Columbus State Prison," the officer behind the counter said. "Please collect your belongings and go with God."

If Peter were still able to laugh, he might have chuckled at that. He had a rather different view of God than the benevolent, loving being the ministers extolled. He reached forward and took the locket and the dollar, then turned to leave.

"Mr. Kerouac," the officer said, betraying some annoyance. "You must take *all* of your property."

Peter stared at the ivory-handled pistol, a Colt Army revolver. There were many like it, ivory handle notwithstanding. It was the standard-issue sidearm for the Union Army, and many operators decorated their handles with ivory after the war. Peter's had been embellished by One-Eyed Jack Preacher, despite his name no more a servant of God than Peter himself.

He lifted the weapon. The cold steel chilled his hands, and as that chill spread through his body, a coppery taste came to his mouth. The remembered smell of rust and blood filled his nostrils, overwhelming the mustiness of the prison. He shoved the weapon in his pocket, eager to take his hands away from its chill.

Behind him, he heard Big Bob call, "Bye, Pete! Catch you on the other side!"

Peter ignored the catcall and the laugh that followed. He would wager his remaining dollar that Bob ended up back in custody before the end of the week, probably trying to rob a stagecoach, and definitely drunk.

He walked through the hallway to the gate of the prison. The officers at the gate opened it as he approached. He stepped outside into the air and was free.

He walked.

He didn't have a destination, so he just walked toward the city. He was free, but that caused him more problems than solutions at the moment. He had no money, no home, no friends, and no family.

The war had done for his friends. He served all four years of the conflict and whether by poor luck or the whim of a God who was not so loving as people liked to believe, he found himself in the middle of the worst of the conflicts the war offered. Bull Run both times, Vicksburg, Sharpsville, Gettysburg—he had survived them all.

Jeremiah hadn't. Sampson hadn't. Carter hadn't. Garth hadn't. The new friends Peter shared smokes with while they waited for the latest knucklehead in charge of the Army to send them back to the maelstrom didn't survive either. Only Peter.

He shuffled his way toward the rising sun toward the city ahead of him. Like all cities, it was loud and dirty and full of selfish, short-sighted people who lacked the ability and the inclination to see life past the limits of the world they'd created for themselves.

A wagon passed by as he walked, and he glanced at the occupants as they passed him. A family of five, the parents smiling as the kids excitedly related some tale of the sort that consumed children when they had the chance to tell it.

Peter was the youngest of three children. His sisters were both older than him, but didn't hold that against him the way so many siblings did. They were like aunts to him, always there to comfort him when he cried, lift him when he was down and encourage him when he was unsure of himself, even after they married and moved out of the family home.

His parents were every bit as wonderful as his sisters. His mother was kind and gentle and beautiful and his father was strong and brave. He loved his family. The four of them were the most important people in his life.

Until Penelope.

A soft smile flickered briefly across his face as he thought of Penelope: her bright green eyes, her golden hair, her soft laughter, the warmth of her body when they danced the night before Peter left for the war.

"I'll wait for you," she promised him.

And she had. She had refused all other suitors, until a stray bullet flew into the hospital tent where she worked and took her life while she tended to his comrade's injuries.When he returned home, his one comfort, his one reason for living, was that his family would be waiting for him with open arms, but that wasn't to be either. Their letters, nearly constant when he left to go to war, dried up suddenly about four months before the war ended. He tried to tell himself there was no reason to be alarmed. They were probably busy. Perhaps one or both of his sisters were with child. That would require far more of his parents' attention than a son who was soon to return home from a war with little real fighting remaining.

He told himself this right up until he arrived home to see Jacob McNally, the banker, putting a for sale sign on the door and learned that his parents had died of food poisoning. Four years of miraculous safety from the war, and spoiled meat had taken them from him before he even had a chance to say goodbye.

He went to his oldest sister Agatha's place, and learned from a tearful neighbor that Agatha and Sarah Lee, his other sister, had died in a cholera outbreak the previous winter.

And just like that, everyone Peter had ever loved was gone.

He had considered himself lucky. His friends had died, but he had survived. Against all odds, he had survived a war that had killed a million Americans.

He wasn't lucky. He knew that now. He had survived, but all joy in life had died with his family.

Church bells tolled ahead of him, marking the hour as noon. He looked up and realized he was in the city now, milling through crowds of people dressed in far nicer clothes than the faded canvas he wore and moving in and out of well-maintained shops. The facades here were wooden. In a mile or so, they would change to red brick.

He stared at the church bells and a flash of anger ran through him. He balled his hands into fists and thought—not for the first time—that if God did exist, He was a cruel, malicious being who punished people who didn't deserve it.

His anger faded almost as soon as it came. He did deserve it. He had gone to prison because he deserved it.

He should have served ten years for riding with the O'Malley gang, but the judge pitied him and sentenced him to only two. Peter had never used the weapon that he now carried in his pocket, so he was sentenced as an accomplice, not a perpetrator.

He guessed he should be grateful for that, but it was hard to be grateful for anything when the life he was released to was no life at all.

He shivered in spite of the sun's warmth and continued along his journey. The people he passed gave him a wide berth, perhaps because of the handgun visible in his pocket. It wasn't exactly illegal for him to carry the weapon, but the general and often accurate belief was that people who carried a handgun with them everywhere they went were up to no good.

His stomach rumbled, and he realized that if he was going to survive at all, he needed work. His silver dollar would buy him a drink and a meal, but after that, he'd be on his own.

He looked around and saw a saloon a few hundred yards ahead of him. It lay just outside the city proper and so was a wood plank building like all of the others in this suburb. He decided to stop here. The crowd here might be rough, but he doubted he could afford a meal in one of the nicer bars in the city.

He walked inside and sat at the bar. As was typical of places like this, everyone stopped what they were doing to take the stranger's measure. Evidently, despite the handgun in his pocket, they saw enough to decide Peter wasn't a threat but he wasn't a target either because they returned to work without paying him a second glance.

Peter ordered his drink and his meal. The serving girl offered him a pitying smile and returned with a steaming bowl of hearty beef stew and a glass with a generous pour of whiskey.

"Thank you," he said softly. His voice still sounded strange in his ears. "I don't suppose you folks are hiring."

"Um, I don't think so," the girl answered. "I can ask Mr. Byron if you want, but he just let our last bartender go. That's why I'm here behind the counter instead of out front making the guests feel comfortable."

She blushed a little as she said that, and Peter imagined that pretty blush on those youthful cheeks underneath bright green eyes had made many a guest feel very comfortable indeed. Peter didn't care one way or another what this woman did for money, and nothing she offered could comfort him. "That's all right," he said, "If you have a newspaper I can read, that will work for me."

"I can do that!"

She trotted away and returned a moment later with a stack of papers. "Mr. Byron only reads the funny bits. The want ads are usually in the back. I do hope you find something Mr..."

It took Peter a moment to realize she was asking for his name. "Kerouac," he said.

"Kerouac," she repeated. "Well, good luck, Mr. Kerouac."

He finished his drink and set the glass on the counter. He looked into the bottom of his glass and saw a tired, disheveled man who looked a decade older than his thirty-three years. His face was turned down in a frown and his eyes wore a haunted look that spoke of a lifetime of pain and loss. If there was any anger in that face, it would be very dangerous-looking indeed. But there was no anger remaining, only grief.

Not wanting to focus on his grief, Peter began to read through the ads.

There wasn't much. Like the rest of the nation, Columbus was full of veterans desperate for work, and four years after the war ended, most of the available jobs were taken. Peter looked through newspaper after newspaper. He finished his meal and his drink and was just about to give up when he came across an ad for a ranch foreman in Montana Territory.

He nearly dismissed it, but just before he tossed the paper onto the pile with the others, he paused.

There was nothing for him here, nothing but memories of death and suffering. There was nothing for him in Montana either, but at least there, he would be far away from a life that had brought him nothing but pain.

Then again, he had no money. He would have to work his way west, and that could take weeks. By that time, the...what was it? He looked at the ad again. The Gutenberg Ranch might have found another foreman.

Well, being broke in Stevensville, Montana was the same as being broke in Columbus, Ohio. It wasn't as though he had any plans. He only needed enough to get from one day to the next. If the foreman position was taken, maybe they would hire him as a ranch hand.

As long as he could fill his days with work, he could avoid using his revolver one last time. It was the most he could expect, but it was just a shade better than nothing.

He called for the serving girl and asked for a pen and paper. He wrote a response to the ad, and with the permission of the serving girl took the paper with him when he left.

He headed toward the post office. If memory served him, and assuming the city hadn't changed greatly in the two years he was imprisoned, it should be a mile or two into the city proper. He would mail his letter, then see if he could find work while he waited for an answer. Worst case scenario...

Well, the worst case had already happened. This might not make life any better, but it couldn't make it any worse.

Chapter One

Stevensville, Montana

May 19, 1869

Lydia sighed and rubbed her temples. The numbers were...well, they were what she expected them to be. Not good, in other words.

She and her mother sat in the modestly furnished parlor of their modest home in their modest ranch, which wasn't so much a ranch as a homestead on which her father had decided to raise cattle instead of grain. They were supposedly looking through the ranch's finances together, but as usual, it was Lydia who looked through the numbers while her mother offered platitudes meant to encourage her. Lydia found them far more annoying than encouraging.

Realizing that her endless stream of "things will look up," and "it's not so bad," and "we'll be all right," weren't having the effect she hoped, her mother said "I'll make some tea, dear."

Mary Gutenberg was a strong, stout woman of fifty-two. Age had lined her face and grayed her hair, but had not yet robbed her of her energy, and she got up from her chair without a hint of discomfort.

Lydia forced a smile as she thanked her mother. She managed to keep it until Mary turned the corner into the kitchen. Then she sighed and looked back at the ledger.

The numbers were still bad.

It had seemed like such a good idea. Everyone was doing it. Everyone who wasn't involved in the fighting, at least. The Union government, fearing the Confederate States would settle the Western territories and steal their resources away from the Union, offered struggling families the chance of a lifetime. One hundred sixty acres of farmland in any of the western territories. All they had to do was stake a claim and make profitable use of the land within five years.

Her parents, of course, had leapt at the chance. Nevermind that Lydia was months away from marrying. Nevermind that at twenty-five, Lydia was unlikely to have a chance with anyone else, especially moving away from Baltimore to Montana Territory. Nevermind that she could actually have loved him. Nevermind...

She sighed and shook her head to clear her thoughts. It didn't matter. They were here now, and Lydia had chosen to come with them. She could have stayed, and she didn't. That was her fault, and she couldn't blame her parents for that choice.

And she didn't hate the ranch itself. She actually rather liked it. Quaint and small and modest as it was, she liked it. There was something beautiful about getting to spend her mornings smelling the crisp clean air as she tended to the garden and her evenings gazing up at the stars—far more numerous and colorful than they were over Baltimore.

If only her father had even the slightest skill at ranching.

"Would you like sugar, dear?" Mary called from the kitchen.

"No thank you, mother," Lydia called back.

"Suit yourself," Mary replied.

Lydia listened to the sound of her mother busying herself in the kitchen. Her father was at the stable, probably learning nothing in spite of Eugene Flister's well-meaning attempts to show him the proper way to re-shoe a horse.

Lydia's lips thinned and her shoulders tensed. Greg Gutenberg was a loving husband and a wonderful father, but he was a terrible rancher. What had possessed him to leave his job as a clerk and travel thousands of miles from the city where Lydia had grown up so he could play at being a rancher, Lydia would never understand.

It didn't help that he was hopeless at it. The government had given them five years to make something of this ranch. That five years would be up in six months, and with nothing to show for it but mounting debt from which they would soon have no protection, it seemed likely that they wouldn't get any more years.

Mary returned with the tea and handed a cup to Lydia. Lydia forced a smile back onto her face, but thirty years of practice hadn't yet given her the skill to fool her mother. Mary smiled sympathetically and said, "Don't worry, dear. It will all work out."

Lydia sighed. "I don't see how," she said, gesturing to the open ledger. "We're already over a thousand dollars behind. When the homestead protection ends, Mr. Smith will almost certainly seize the ranch and everything on it. Unless..."

She caught herself just before saying what she meant to say, and instead finished with, "Unless some miracle happens."

"Well, we don't know that for sure," Mary said. "John has proven willing to work with us so far."

She wasn't entirely sure her mother knew why John was willing to work with them. Lydia was, and it sent a shiver of revulsion over her. "He hasn't had a choice, Mother. If he tried to collect from us now, we could prosecute him for breaking the law under the Homestead Act. In six months, he can do whatever he wants. The ranch will technically be his property by then."

"You're thinking quite a few steps ahead, dear," Mary said in an infuriatingly calm voice.

"Well, someone has to!" Lydia cried out. "You're too busy insisting that everything will somehow miraculously work out for us, and father—"

The door opened just as she said that, and Mary shot Lydia a sharp warning glance. Lydia stifled her words just as her father walked inside with Eugene Lister.

"I just don't understand how prices can rise so fast," Greg complained, arms gesticulating wildly as usual. "Land's sakes, it's like they expect us all to strike gold."

"It's a shame," Eugene said in his thick Texas drawl. "A real shame."

"It's more than a shame," Greg ranted, taking off his boots and hat. "It's criminal!"

"Hello, dear," Mary said, loudly enough for her voice to carry over her husband's complaints.

Greg's eyes snapped to Mary and Lydia. He reddened in embarrassment and said, "Sorry you had to hear that. It's nothing to worry about. I'm just grousing is all."

Lydia wondered why her father bothered to dissemble when she and her mother were responsible for the books. It's not like they didn't already know that finances definitely were something to worry about.

"How did the shoeing go?" Mary asked.

"Oh, fine, fine," Greg said. "Took a little work, but Eugene says that with a little practice, I'll have it down in no time."

Eugene smiled and nodded, but Lydia could see in his expression that he didn't share Greg's confidence.

Lydia sighed and stood. She needed to do something with her hands or she would go crazy. "Would you two like some tea?" she asked.

"Oh, dear, I can—" Mary began.

Before she could stand, Lydia said, "No, no, it's all right, Mother. I insist."

She walked to the kitchen. As soon as she was out of sight of the parlor, she pressed her hands to her temples and took several deep breaths to calm herself. When the urge to scream had passed, she began to make the tea.

She didn't hate her father for not being a rancher. She knew that he was only trying to do what he thought was best, but...well, it wasn't best! They were never wealthy back home, and they would never have been wealthy, but they had a roof over their heads and food on the table. Sure, there was fighting, but by the time they left, the fighting was far from Baltimore and the war was drawing to a close. The danger they faced on the road was worse than the danger they faced remaining at home.

She supposed it would have paid off if they had been successful, but they weren't. That's why they needed a foreman. They needed someone who actually knew how to run a ranch, not three well-meaning people who hadn't the faintest idea what they were doing. Lydia had sent an advertisement for a foreman, but she had received no response so far. If only they had advertised three years ago. There were thousands of former soldiers desperate for work then and willing to travel to find it. Now, there were very few people willing to uproot themselves to come work for a ranch in Montana.

Actually, no one at all was willing to uproot themselves. Lydia had placed the ad three months ago and not received a single response.

She brought the tea to the parlor and plastered on the fake smile she would wear while her father talked to Eugene about all of the big plans he had for the ranch and Eugene listened with a pitying expression and her mother pretended there was nothing wrong at all. She handed cups to the other three and prepared to sit when she heard a knock on the door.

She opened it and saw a smartly dressed young man in the uniform of a courier. "Letter for Miss Lydia Gutenberg," he said crisply.

He handed her the letter, pivoted sharply, and marched to his waiting horse. Lydia stared at the envelope, not daring to hope that it was what she thought it was.

She brought it inside, and when her parents saw what she was holding, their eyes widened with excitement.

"What is it, dear?" her mother asked.

"Is it a response to your ad?" her father added.

Eugene said nothing, but his eyebrows lifted in anticipation as Lydia opened the message.

It was a letter from Peter Kerouac expressing his hope that the position of foreman was still open and announcing his interest in the position if it was. Lydia finished reading the message and handed it to her parents.

When they finished reading, they handed the message to Eugene. "What do you think?" Greg asked.

"Well," Eugene said, "he has no experience, and that could be a problem. It might take him a while to learn, and if he don't learn right or he don't have the head for it, it might be a drain on your finances that you don't need. On the other hand, if he works hard, it might be useful to have him if only for a pair of young, strong hands."

"What would you do?" Mary asked.

"Well, I don't rightly know," Eugene said, "I would say hire him, but I've grown up on a ranch. I know I can run one, and that means my perspective is different."

He didn't say so out loud, but Lydia knew that what he wasn't mentioning was that the Gutenbergs didn't know how to run a ranch, and he wasn't sure if bringing in someone with no experience was a good idea or a bad one.

The conversation fell silent and after a moment, Lydia realized they were all looking expectantly at her. She took a breath and said, "Well, he sounds humble and hardworking. He says he prefers to work sunup to sundown and is partial to manual labor. I would hire him, but...well, experience really was the only reason I was looking for a foreman. If it were just a hand we needed, we could find one in town. We need someone who knows how to run a ranch, not just someone who works hard."

"Then again, there haven't been any other responses," Mary offered.

"That's true," Lydia admitted. She sighed. "I need to think about it. We can all think about it, then discuss our decision over breakfast."

"Good idea," her dad said. "Let it roll around in here a little bit."

He tapped the side of his head, and Mary rolled her eyes but smiled lovingly as she did. Lydia hoped desperately that things would work out with Peter. Her parents needed help, not to mention Lydia herself.

And that name, Peter.

"Well," her dad said, trying and failing at a jovial tone. "He has the right name."

Her mother said nothing, but Lydia could see the grief behind her eyes as she sipped her tea.

She thought of her brother Peter. Had it been twenty years since he died? She used to love caring for him. He was the younger child and her parents doted on him, but Lydia had never felt a moment's jealousy. She doted on him too. She used to walk him to and from school and sit next to him in church. She used to play hide-and-go-seek with him and leapfrog and blind man's bluff. She used to love the way he laughed, his whole body shaking with mirth.

And then he had died. The doctors weren't sure if it was pneumonia or fever. He was healthy one day, then the next he had a cough and a severe fever. He declined slowly over the next three weeks, then deteriorated all at once over another week. Then he died.

Everyone said it was an act of God, just another tragedy in a world full of tragedies, but Lydia knew better. She had taken him swimming the day before he got sick. He was shivering when they got out, and his lips were blue with cold, but he was smiling and laughing, and Lydia didn't think anything of it until he started coughing and complaining that his head hurt.

She felt her vision swim and blinked away the tears that came to her eyes, not wanting the others to see her cry. She stood and brushed her skirts back into place. "Well, I'm going

23

to wash for dinner. Mr. Flister, thank you for helping us again."

"Oh, I almost forgot," Eugene said, "Dotty asked if you could have dinner with us. I know it's short notice, but we'd love to have you if that's all right."

By Dotty, he meant his daughter, Dorothy, Lydia's best friend. Her only friend for that matter, but the bright, happy Dorothy would have been Lydia's best friend even if she were surrounded by companions.

Lydia smiled. "Of course, Eugene. Thank you so much."

Later, after dinner, she told Dorothy—she hated being called Dotty—about Peter—the respondent, not her brother—and asked her thoughts.

"Hire him!" Dorothy said immediately, her soft brown eyes lighting up with excitement. "Pa can teach him how to run a ranch, and if he works hard and has a decent head on his shoulders, he can help you turn your ranch around! Besides, he's around your age. What if he's handsome?"

Lydia rolled her eyes. Dorothy was twenty-one, nine years younger than Lydia and every thought she had was of romance, it seemed. She didn't blame her. At that age, Lydia herself had still believed in the handsome prince that would one day sweep her off her feet, and Dorothy looked the part of the princess with round cheeks, hair that framed her face in soft curls, and a ready smile that lit up the room whenever she showed it.

Still, Lydia had advertised for a foreman, not a mail order groom. "I think there are more important things to consider than romance, Dorothy," she told her young friend.

"Of course," Dorothy said, "I'm only saying, he might be able to fix the ranch *and* rescue you from a life of solitude and despair."

"Since when am I living in solitude and despair," Lydia asked. "I have you, don't I?"

Dorothy sighed in exasperation. "You need to stop acting like you're too old for love, Lydia."

"What are we talking about now?" Lydia asked. "I thought we were talking about a prospective employee."

"And I already said, hire him," Dorothy replied. She grinned mischievously. "I'm just saying, you shouldn't rule out the possibility of more than a working relationship with him."

"You're incorrigible," Lydia said with a laugh.

"And don't forget it," Dorothy confirmed.

Back at home, Lydia thought of the advice she'd received and decided to write Peter back. She wasn't at all hopeful that Dorothy's dream of romance would come true, but they really could use all the help they could get.

She took a piece of paper and smoothed it out on her bedroom table. She picked up her quill pen, dipped it in her inkwell and began to write.

Chapter Two

Columbus, Ohio

June 18, 1869

Peter read through the novel, losing himself in the world of Calaveras County and their notorious jumping frog. He had read enthusiastically since he was a child, but the habit had grown voracious when he was in prison. He had nothing to do there but work and think, and thinking was too painful, so he started to read. The church in Columbus would bring copies of the Bible to the prison, and that was the first book he finished cover to cover. The following year, the library had brought a number of other books that were too worn or faded to circulate anymore. Peter had read no fewer than a dozen the last year, but his favorite was Mark Twain.

He had read *The Notorious Jumping Frog of Calaveras County* three times and was halfway through his fourth reading while he waited for the arrival of Twain's new novel *Innocents Abroad or The New Pilgrims' Progress.* If it was half as good as *Jumping Frog,* Peter was sure he would enjoy it.

Hard work was the most effective method of pushing back the despair that hovered over Peter like a cloud, and he lost himself in work as much as he could, but he couldn't work constantly. He needed rest like everyone else, and when he needed rest, a few hours away from the real world lost in the witty fantasy of Twain or Dickens was enough to fill the hours between work and sleep without allowing that cloud to descend on him.

He hadn't yet received a response from that ranch in Montana. He knew that mail took time, but he was beginning to think his efforts were in vain. It wasn't really a surprise to him. The ad was three months old when he read it. They had surely filled the position by now.

He sighed and put the book away. He couldn't focus on it now.

He was staying in the church, sleeping in one of the pews at night and cleaning the church as payment. The pastor and his wife took pity on Peter, but Peter didn't want pity. He wanted to work. He wanted to make his own way, not rely on the kindness of strangers. Mostly, he just wanted to leave. He wanted to be far away from the memory of his pain and loss and build something somewhere else.

No, he didn't want to build something. There was no point in building anything, not when it could be taken away at a moment's notice. He just wanted to work himself to exhaustion every day and fill the space between work and sleep with books. As long as he wasn't stuck in the memory of the tragedies that had befallen him, he would be happy. Or if not happy, at least content, and that was good enough.

He stared at the ceiling and closed his eyes, but before sleep found him, he felt a gentle tap on his shoulder. He opened his eyes to see Isaiah Blake, the pastor's oldest son, smiling down at him. Isaiah was twenty years old, but already tall and strong and wise as his father. It was widely known that he would assume leadership of the church when his father retired.

"There's a letter for you, Peter," Isaiah said.

Peter took the letter and when he read it, his eyes widened in surprise. It was the Gutenberg Ranch. He had been accepted. He told Isaiah the news and the younger man beamed. "That's wonderful, Peter!" he said. "Congratulations!" His smile softened a little, and he added, "This means you'll be leaving us, doesn't it?"

Peter nodded and looked away. "'Fraid so," he said. "Thank you all for your kindness."

"It was well worth it," Isaiah said, "You're a good man, Peter. You deserve good fortune."

Peter nodded and even managed a smile, but he didn't respond other than that. Isaiah was young, too young to have served in the war and too far from the fighting to have suffered as Peter had. He could afford to believe that being a good man was enough to earn good fortune.

Peter knew better.

The pastor's family threw a going-away dinner for him that night. It wasn't really a party. The only people in attendance were Pastor Blake, his wife and three sons, Peter, and Jeremiah Canton, the ancient drifter who sometimes helped Peter sweep up after Sunday service in exchange for the occasional warm meal.

Peter said his goodbyes and endured the awkwardness of the parting, and early the next morning, he took the first train west.

***

July 15, 1869

Peter looked out the window and marveled at the landscape passing him by. Montana Territory was a huge expanse of land, several times bigger than Ohio, and the geography was as vast and varied as the territory. The train passed through winding canyons lined with peaks that stretched upward as far as the eye could see, so high that they remained snowcapped in spite of the warmth of summer.

The train passed through broad forests full of towering pine and larch and aspen. Peter gazed in wonder at their massive trunks. He thought he had seen tall trees before, but the trees here seemed to reach all the way to Heaven itself!

He felt like he was in the middle of one of his stories, traveling through an unknown land in search of freedom and adventure. He watched the land pass him by, and for the first time in a long time felt something akin to happiness.

At last the forests and mountains gave way to grasslands, and Peter got his first glimpse of the land he would spend the next several years—if he was lucky—working and living on. The plains grew tall and stretched from horizon to horizon. Everything seemed larger than life here. Even the grass was taller, reaching nearly to the window of the train car at times.

Peter hoped the ranch would still be waiting for him when he arrived. In his response, he mentioned that as he had no money it might be a few weeks before he arrived so he could earn his fare across the country, but he wasn't sure if the Gutenbergs had received his message or if they accepted that he would be a while joining them.

He had sent two other letters. One from Minneapolis, Minnesota a week after leaving Columbus and one from Yankton, North Dakota the week before, alerting them of his progress and telling them he was still interested in the position should it remain open when he arrived. He could only hope he wasn't too late.

And now finally, nearly four weeks after leaving Columbus, he was going to arrive at his destination. The train crested a small ridge and Peter saw the town of Stevensville for the first time.

It wasn't much of a town. Peter could see the entire scope of it from ten miles away. It stretched maybe three miles north to south and a mile east to west, and like all small towns, it was little more than a cluster of shops and official buildings lining the main street surrounded by scattered residences. There was a church on one end of Main Street, and as they drew closer, Peter could make out the five-pointed star of the sheriff's station and the jail behind. It was small, barely enough for two or three cells, Peter figured, and that was good. This was a quiet town.

Beyond the town, Peter could see the homesteads. Most of them were small, with modest houses and barns and fields populated either with pasture for cattle or sheep or with grains—corn, wheat and barley. A few of the homesteads were vast ranches with large buildings and stables that housed probably dozens of horses, but most were small. Family farms.

Peter felt a twinge of pain but pushed it away. He wasn't here to dwell on his past. He was here to forget it.

The train's brakes squealed as the engine pulled to a stop in front of the pine plank platform. The station was one of the newer-looking structures in the town and the wood was still smooth and clean, lacking the chips and warps and caked dust that would come with years of use.

Peter stepped onto the platform with his bag and looked around. The rest of the town, at least from what he could see on the platform, was much what he expected: wood-plank buildings of varying degrees of age and condition, dirt roads with a small crowd of people on foot and horseback making their way through the saloon, the general store, the livery and the post office.

He pulled the letter from his pocket and read the address of the ranch. It wasn't really an address but a list of directions. *Go east from the station two miles, then turn north and ride another mile.*

Peter wasn't sure if Miss Gutenberg meant for him to follow a road or simply use the sun to guide him. He decided to ask the ticket taker at the station and see if he could get more specific directions.

The ticket taker was an older man with thin wire-rimmed glasses and a reedy voice. He looked a healthy sixty, though Peter supposed that any kind of sixty that existed above ground was a healthy sixty.

The ticket taker looked at the letter and nodded. "Yes, I know them. Miss Lydia means for you to take the farm-to-market road. That's the road on the east side of the station. The road on the west side leads into town. Follow that and two miles up, you'll see the spur she's talking about that leads up to her homestead."

"It's just her?" Peter asked.

The ticket-taker smiled. "Her and her parents. There are a lot of homesteaders up in that area. They're one of the first ones. Came here when Lincoln offered to give the land for free on account of fear the Rebs would find it first."

Peter listened to him ramble a moment, but when the older man paused for breath, he took the opportunity to tip his hat and say, "Much obliged to you."

"And to you," the ticket taker replied. He shook his head and muttered half to himself, "Lord knows the Gutenbergs need all the help they can get."

Peter wondered at that but decided to reserve judgment until he reached the ranch. He picked up his bag and started to walk.

A mile past the station, he was suddenly struck by how empty the land was. Of course, it wasn't entirely empty. The town was behind him, the railroad to his left and a smattering of ranch houses visible to his right. Still, he had never been anywhere so open. Columbus wasn't the largest city in the world, but you could fit all of the buildings Peter could see into one block in downtown Columbus. He looked out across the endless expanse of blue and breathed deeply of the clean air.

He could live here.

He reached the ranch an hour later, and when he reached it, he realized he would have his work cut out for him. He had expected the ranch would need help, but he wasn't prepared for the state of affairs into which he now walked.

The ranch buildings were dilapidated. They were poorly constructed and even from a distance, he could see cracks and splinters in the uneven wood planks. The house looked in slightly better shape, but several warps in the roof and the walls showed that the wood hadn't been weatherproofed with pitch or turpentine. If he hadn't seen a few dozen cattle grazing in the pasture in front of the homestead, he would have assumed the place was abandoned.

As it was, the cattle he saw were thin and in questionable health. They regarded him apathetically and their movements seemed slow and labored. Peter wasn't a rancher—his father had been a cabinet-maker—but he had seen cattle before, and these were not healthy cattle.

He turned down the footpath to the ranch, and when he entered the courtyard, he came face to face with the most beautiful woman he'd ever seen in his life. She stood a few yards from him, smiling in a way that seemed coy and demure at the same time. Her hair was thick and raven-black and fell over her shoulders in waves that framed a face with noble cheeks, breathtaking blue eyes and full lips. Her figure was lithe without being too thin and curvy without quite being buxom. She was the picture of beauty, as though Venus herself had appeared before him.

She might not be in the first flush of youth any longer, but she wasn't old. Not by a long shot. In fact, Peter thought she was probably a few years younger than him. But her eyes held a wisdom and calm that few young women had, and the corners of her eyes betrayed lines that suggested she was no stranger to hardship.

Peter stared at this angel, and it was a long moment before he found his voice. "Yes," he finally said, "Yes, I'm Peter." His brow furrowed. "Were you expecting me?"

The angel smiled a little wider and said, "I was expecting you eventually, yes. I figured since you consulted the letter in your hand before approaching the ranch that you must be my new foreman, and that, I'm assuming, is my acceptance of your response with directions to the ranch."

Peter nodded in confirmation, and the angel extended her hand toward him and said, "I'm Lydia Gutenberg. It's a pleasure to finally meet you."

"Pleasure," Peter agreed, shaking her hand. Her touch was cool and soft, but her grip was firm and strong.

After a moment, she smiled slightly, and Peter realized he was still holding her hand. He flushed slightly and looked away as he released it. "Is the position of foreman still open?" he asked.

Her slight smile widened. "Yes," she said, "The position is still open. May I infer that you're still interested?"

He nodded. "Yes, ma'am."

His voice sounded thick and clumsy in his ears, and he was acutely aware of his awkward limbs and lanky form. Next to this picture of beauty, he felt like an ogre.

"Well, Mr. Kerouac," Lydia said, "Allow me to welcome you to the Gutenberg Ranch."

He nodded again and said, "Thank you," then allowed the angel to lead him inside.

Chapter Three

"Okay, draw your needle through here," Dorothy said.

Lydia concentrated and slid the needle through the fabric. The needle went through easily, but the thread fell out of the hoop and hung loosely from the plain cotton sheet that would eventually be a quilt if Lydia could ever figure out how to decorate it.

Dorothy laughed and covered her mouth. Lydia thought with a slight touch of jealousy that Dorothy appeared particularly youthful and pretty with her cheeks colored with mirth.

Dorothy quickly stifled her laughter and said, "You need to tie the thread to the hoop, Liddie. You can't just stick it through and hope it stays."

"Liddie?" Lydia said, "So should I call you Dottie now?"

"Eww," Dorothy said, grimacing. "Okay, fine, Lydia. Please don't call me Dottie."

"That's what I thought," Lydia said.

Dorothy set her needles down and planted her hands on her hips in false anger. "Do you want me to show you how to embroider a quilt or not?"

"Yes, please, your majesty," Lydia deadpanned. "Forgive this poor wench for her—now don't you start!"

Too late. The word *wench* was enough to send Dorothy into peals of laughter and seeing her friend overcome was enough to start Lydia giggling herself.

She loved these afternoons with Dorothy. She hadn't felt like...well, like a girl, since leaving Baltimore, but spending time with Dorothy made her feel young again. The younger woman's bubbliness and persistent happiness cut through Lydia's worry and exhaustion and made her believe for a moment that all truly was right with the world.

When their laughter calmed, Lydia made a show of exaggeratedly tying the thread to the hoop while Dorothy watched closely, arms folded. When she finished, Dorothy nodded and said, "All right. Well done."

She instructed Lydia on the basic hoop stitch and taught her a basic pattern she could practice with. While they worked, Dorothy said, "So, how is the handsome new rancher doing?"

Lydia felt heat creep up her cheeks and hoped it wasn't visible to Dottie. It had been a week since Peter's arrival and already the change at the ranch was significant. The cattle pens were completely repaired, and the stables and barn cleaned and organized. The cattle themselves were on a schedule, penned at night to provide warmth and protection from wolves and out to pasture during the day. Every other day, a portion of the herd would be rotated through the pens for a health inspection. Peter had no ranch experience, but what he didn't know he learned from Dorothy's father, who mentioned to Lydia when she arrived earlier that Peter was the hardest working man he'd ever seen and a natural leader.

Lydia said as much to Dorothy and Dorothy grinned. "He sounds like an excellent catch, Lydia."

The heat in Lydia's neck brightened to incandescence, and this time, she was certain her blush was visible. "I did *not* hire him as a mail order groom, Dorothy," she said. "I hired him to help the ranch."

"Of course," Dorothy said, "A[...] blossom between the two of yo[...] it to Providence."

Lydia rolled her eyes. "[...]

"You are young," Dorothy [...] need to stop talking as thou[...] spinster."

"I didn't say I was old," Lydia proteste[...] assuming that my lack of interest in marria[...] a belief that I'm unmarriageable."

I didn't claim that you thought yourself unmar[...] Dorothy countered. "But it's interesting that you t[...] way."

Lydia put down her needle and stared at her friend in exasperation. "Won't you ever stop?" she asked.

"Of course not," Dorothy replied. "You're like a sister to me, Lydia, and I can't bear to see my sister unhappy."

"We were talking about Peter, yes?" Lydia said. "Why don't we keep talking about him?"

She appreciated Dorothy's determination that she should find love and happiness, but sometimes her dogged refusal to leave the subject frustrated Lydia. She didn't think of herself as old and decrepit, but she *was* past her youth, and she needed to be sensible. She had a failing ranch and incomp— struggling parents to support. She didn't have time to think of love, and if she did, she certainly didn't have time to think about the man whose purpose was not to woo her but to help her get her business in order.

thy knew how crucial it was for the ranch to
if they failed, at least Dorothy wouldn't have to
Lydia to marry anymore.

ran through her at that thought. Before Dorothy
ak again, Lydia picked up her needle and thread
, "Anyway, Peter hasn't spoken more than four words
ince he arrived. He talks to my father, and he's polite
and my mother, but when he isn't working, he's mostly
s room. Even at meals, he keeps his head down and
ks only when spoken to."

"Well, a man doesn't need to be a conversationalist,"
orothy said, "I for one would love to marry a quiet man who
wouldn't feel a need to interject his opinion into everything I
have to say."

I'll bet you would, Lydia thought drily. Aloud, she said, "He
is a hard worker, though. He's up before me, and you know
I'm up at dawn every morning. He works until sunset, and
your father says he's completed the work of five men this past
week."

"Yes, he mentioned that to me," Dorothy said. "He also
mentioned that he seemed to have eyes for the lady of the
house."

Lydia stopped sewing again to stare at Dorothy. "Your
father said that Peter was attracted to my mother?"

Dorothy stopped her own embroidery and returned a frank
gaze to Lydia. "Yes, Lydia," she said seriously. "He told me
that Peter was swooning over your married mother. Clearly,
he couldn't have meant that Peter was attracted to you."

Lydia sighed. "You really aren't going to let this go, are
you?"

Dorothy offered a s.
you to be happy, Lydia
that because you aren't
ever want you."

"I'm aware that men wa

Her lips curled downwa.
had made his desire clear
interested in marriage right .

"I think you're just saying
get your heart broken," Dorotl

"Not everything is about love　　　, Dorothy," Lydia replied, a little tartly. "When you　　old er, you'll realize that."

Dorothy looked away and said nothing for a moment, and Lydia felt a stab of guilt. She sighed and said, "I'm sorry, Dorothy. I shouldn't have said that. I just..."

"It's all right," Dorothy said. Her smile returned. "Okay, Lydia. If you insist, I'll let it go for now. But not forever. I may be young, but when a woman blushes when she speaks of a man, you don't have to be old to know that she likes him."

Lydia shook her head and lifted her needle and thread with a tolerant smile, knowing she was once more going to have to endure Dorothy's unceasing attempts to marry her off, despite her assurance that she would drop the subject.

"And anyway, it's not a bad thing that he's quiet," Dorothy said.

"Yes, you've said that already," Lydia replied.

Dorothy went on as though she hadn't heard Lydia. "Strong, quiet men are always the most passionate underneath the surface. And he *is* strong, isn't he Lydia?"

AVA WINTERS

Her eyes took on a dre
needle and thread dow
never seen a man
before."

Eugene an
days ago
physic
jum

amy expression and she set her
n and stared ahead wistfully. "I've
wrangle a steer with his bare hands

d Peter had been working with the cattle a few
Eugene was teaching Peter how to perform a
l inspection and one of the steers had bolted. Eugene
ped out of the way to dodge its hooves, but Peter had
grabbed the young animal by the horns and with a mighty twist, wrestled the animal to its knees. The frightened steer had calmed then and allowed the two men to perform the inspection.

Dorothy and Lydia had watched while this happened and Dorothy had released a soft cry and reddened like an apple. Lydia recalled this and asked, "Would you like me to ask him about you? Perhaps he would enjoy an afternoon with someone who can do all the talking for him."

"No," Dorothy said, "Nice try, but he's all yours. I've already decided."

"Have you now?" Lydia replied.

"Of course!" Dorothy said. "He's perfect for you!"

"I'm sure he is," Lydia said tolerantly.

"Don't patronize me, Lydia Gutenberg," Dorothy said. "Here, let me show you the cross stitch."

An hour later, Lydia had thoroughly botched the embroidery job on the quilt and was heading home with a promise from Dorothy to help her again on her next visit. The sun was low in the sky but there was still an hour of daylight left, and Lydia would be home in half that time.

As she walked, she thought of Peter. He was strong, as Dorothy had said, and Lydia was old enough that she didn't feel the need to pretend that his strength didn't affect her. He was hardworking, and that was something Lydia valued far more than strength. Most of all, though, he had a sharp mind. He had no experience but he learned quickly, as Dorothy's father had said. Not only had he learned the manual labor, he had quickly determined the problems with the ranch's operations and found ways to address them.

He was dedicated to the success of the ranch as well. Since arriving, he had worked tirelessly, sunup to sundown every day. For the first time in her life, Lydia had met someone who rose earlier than she did.

Lydia hadn't shared the extent of the ranch's financial straits, not wanting to frighten Peter away, but she had made it clear that they needed things to turn around immediately.

Just how immediately, she also hadn't said.

Five months. Five months and the ranch's protection under the Homestead Act would be void. Five months, and her only options would be to sell the ranch and hope that she had enough left over after paying the bank to purchase a modest home for her family in town where she would have to find work as a serving girl or cleaning girl at the saloon or boardinghouse. If she was fortunate.

Or she could marry John. That was the other option.

She shivered and cleared that thought from her mind. She wasn't there yet, and anyway, it looked as though Peter might actually be able to help them turn things around. He had to.

She was so preoccupied with her thoughts that she wasn't paying attention to where she was walking. She heard Peter's gruff voice call out, "Hold on!" and looked up just in time to walk head on into him. She cried out and stumbled, but his strong arms wrapped around her shoulders and held her steady until she could regain her feet.

He *was* strong, she thought. How he was strong.

She looked up into his deep-set brown eyes. In the light of the late afternoon sun, they seemed to smolder under his brows. She felt her breath catch in her throat a moment before finally blinking and saying, "I'm so sorry. Excuse me."

"That's all right," Peter said, pulling his gaze mercifully from her own. "My fault. Had my head in the clouds."

He shuffled awkwardly and Lydia wondered that he could be so strong and sure of himself one moment and so awkward and fearful the next. "That's all right," she said, "I guess we were both a little distracted. Where are you going?"

Peter gestured toward the Flister Homestead. "I told Greg I'd have dinner with him tonight," he said. "He's going to teach me about selling cattle."

"Really?" Lydia said, "How wonderful! Are our cattle ready for market?"

"Not yet," Peter said, "Greg reckons it'll be about a month before they can sell, but he's going to talk to me about it in the meantime so I'm ready when it happens."

"Oh," Lydia said, trying not to let her disappointment show. "Well, enjoy your dinner."

Peter nodded. "I will. Thank you, ma'am."

"Lydia," Lydia said.

"Pardon?"

Lydia smiled. "It's Lydia. Not ma'am. If we're going to live in the same house, we might as well use each other's first names."

"Oh," Peter said. He reddened a little and nodded curtly. "Thank you, Lydia."

"I'll see you at home, Peter," Lydia said.

"See you there," Peter replied.

He started off, but after a couple of steps, turned and said, "Do you want me to walk you home?"

Lydia started to refuse, but stopped herself and instead said, "Thank you, Peter. That's very kind of you."

Peter shuffled into step beside her and escorted her the remaining half-mile to the ranch. They said nothing along the way, but Lydia was acutely aware of his deep brown eyes and strong hands as they walked.

Chapter Four

Peter knelt in front of the stream and laid the soiled canvas shirt into the water. The shirt sank promptly to the bottom and rather than getting clean, picked up fresh muck from the stream bed.

An image flashed through his mind of a torn shirt covered in blood at the bottom of a small, fast-moving stream known to the Union Army as Bull Run. Peter stood above the body, blood dripping from his knife as he gazed at the expression of shock forever frozen on the man's face.

He gasped and lifted the shirt from the stream, twisting in an attempt to wring out the dirt. Instead of helping, that only made the dirt sink in deeper.

He took a breath to clear his thoughts and tried once more to wash the shirt. He was about to give up when he heard a voice behind him. "Mind if I join you?"

He turned and when he saw Mary approaching, he reddened and held the shirt in front of him.

Mary smiled and said, "I've seen a man's chest before, Peter. You needn't worry about your modesty. Besides, you're young enough to be my son."

Her smile faded slightly when she said that. But it returned a moment later, and she said, "May I?" and reached for his shirt.

Peter handed her the shirt and watched as Mary walked ten yards farther upstream where a small waterfall over a pile of rocks offered clean, fast-moving water. She lowered the shirt into the stream and with practiced expertise quickly scrubbed the dirt free of the shirt. "Do you have a blanket?" she asked Peter.

Peter blinked and flushed slightly. "Oh," he said, "Uh, no. I didn't think of that."

"Well, then hold out your arm," Mary said.

Peter held out his arm and Mary draped the shirt over it. "Do you have anything else to wash?" she asked.

"Oh, um...my pants." Peter said. "Not the ones I'm wearing, just..."

He reddened and Mary smiled at his embarrassment. But she was kind enough to ignore the slip as Peter walked back to the soiled canvas pants that lay on the dirt where he had first started washing. "Miss Mary, you don't have to trouble yourself," he said.

"If it were trouble, I wouldn't trouble myself," Mary said. "Hand me the pants, please."

Peter handed them over and Mary stooped and with the same expertise began to wash the dirt and dust away. As she worked, she said, "How are you liking it here so far, Peter?"

"Well enough," Peter said. He flushed immediately and said, "I mean. I didn't mean—"

Mary looked up with a tolerant smile. "Young man, you need to get out of the habit of apologizing for everything you say. I asked you how you liked it here, and you gave a fair answer. There's nothing to apologize for."

Mary's kindness and honesty reminded Peter of his own mother. He felt a rush of newfound affection for the older woman and said, "Thank you kindly. I like it here. It's good work, honest work, and you folks seem to be decent people. I appreciate you taking me in."

"We appreciate having you," Mary said. "How are you liking your new cabin?"

When Lydia pointed out that the two of them lived in the same house, Peter felt embarrassed. It didn't seem proper to him to share a roof with an unmarried woman, and besides, he preferred to be alone most of the time. So, he had converted the woodshed into a small cabin, moving the wood and tools to the barn.

"It's fine," Peter said. He shuffled his feet and said, "I want you to know I wasn't unhappy with my room. I just—"

"What did I tell you about apologizing?" Mary interrupted, standing from the stream and wringing out the pants.

"Oh," Peter said, "Right."

"Lydia and I are very appreciative of you," Mary said, draping the pants over Peter's arm. "We were in quite a fix before you arrived, as I'm sure you know."

Peter only nodded.

"Well, with you here, we have some hope for the future," Mary said. "So thank you for that. Greg appreciates you too, by the way. He has a harder time accepting help because he feels it's a sign of his own failure, but he's glad to have you even if he seems gruff sometimes."

Peter hadn't noticed any gruffness from Greg, though he allowed that the older man's occasional scowl and terse manner of speaking could come across that way. As for the failure..."It ain't a failure to struggle with a ranch," Peter said. "It's hard to build a life out here so far from everything."

"That's what I tell him," Mary said, "But you know how men are. Any time something goes poorly they take it as a sign they aren't strong enough or capable enough or intelligent enough or something. Every bad thing on Earth is a personal failure to them."

Peter shuffled his feet awkwardly, not sure how to respond. Mary noticed his awkwardness and smiled. "I'm sorry, Peter," she said. "It's not appropriate of me to speak this way. I only wanted to tell you that Greg appreciates you too. I should have left it at that."

"No trouble, ma'am," Peter said. "I'm grateful for the opportunity."

Mary sat on a rock near the stream and gazed out across the plains beyond. "I had a son named Peter," she said, her voice dropping. "He was a lot like Greg. Towheaded, brash, exuberant, full of energy. He had the biggest dreams you ever heard of, even for a child." She laughed and said, "He was going to fly. He told me that one day. 'Ma,' he said, 'One day, I'm gonna build a machine that can fly in the air like the birds.'" She laughed again and said, "That boy wouldn't have cared if the Heavens themselves stood against him. When he wanted something, he went for it. He was a good boy."

Peter didn't say anything. He wasn't sure if he should ask Mary about Peter's death or let the older woman make that decision herself. He shuffled his feet a moment, then stopped, realizing he had shuffled more often than he had stood still. He swallowed and instead of asking about Peter, said, "I had sisters. Older. They cared for me like aunts until I went to war."

"Did you lose them too?" Mary asked softly.

Peter nodded. His throat tightened a little. "Yep, sure did. They got sick while I was away. Died afore I got back. Parents too."

Mary turned a compassionate gaze to Peter. "I'm so sorry," she said. "It's a horrible thing to lose a family."

"Yes," Peter agreed. "It is."

Mary smiled. "Well, maybe we can be family to each other to help ease the pain of what we've lost."

Mary's words reminded him of a sermon Pastor Blake had given back in Columbus. He had read from the Epistle to the Romans, chapter eight, verse twenty-eight, *And we know that all things work together for good to them that love God, to them who are called according to his purpose.*

Pastor Blake's sermon focused on the loss and hardship sustained by so many families during and after the war and encouraged his flock to believe that God had a plan for them and that God would reward the temporary hardship and suffering his followers endured. "We may not understand His calling," he said. "But we must have faith that He sees what we can't see, and He has a plan for each and every one of us."

Peter didn't consider himself a lover of God, but maybe the minister was right. Maybe God really did have a plan for him. Maybe that was why he had been brought to the Gutenberg family.

The thought frightened him, though he wasn't sure exactly why. He felt a rush of claustrophobia . His shoulders tensed and a cold sweat broke out on his brow. He needed to leave now. He cleared his throat and nodded at Mary. "Thank you, ma'am. For the wash."

"Of course, dear."

Peter nodded once more, then turned and walked quickly away. He flushed slightly in embarrassment at his rudeness, but he couldn't shake the feeling of being trapped, of being stuck under the weight of grief and loss.

He realized now why the thought had frightened him. The Gutenbergs saw him, in a way, as their salvation. He couldn't be that for them. He couldn't manage their grief on top of his own. He could help around the ranch, but he couldn't be part of their family, and they couldn't replace the family he had lost. Lydia, beautiful though she was, couldn't replace Penelope. Peter couldn't replace her brother.

If God had a plan for him, He had once more forgotten to include Peter in the process.

He reached his little cabin and walked inside, closing the door behind him. He sat heavily down on the rough pine chair he had made for the cabin and breathed a heavy sigh.

He stared blankly at the wall until his breathing slowed, then stood and walked outside to hang his clothes. The sun was low on the horizon, and it occurred to Peter that he should have washed his clothes in the morning and left them to dry while he worked rather than washing them after work was over. It also occurred to him that he would need to find more work to do around the ranch to avoid days like this where he finished early and had nothing to occupy his time. Maybe he could work on repairing the barn. He didn't like to think ill of his employer, but Greg really didn't know about carpentry. The barn was one bad storm away from collapsing completely–not an issue in the warm, calm summer but a serious problem come winter.

Yep, that's what he would do. He would complete his chores and while he waited for the cattle to be ready for sale, he would shore up the barn and possibly the stable depending on how quickly he could get the work done.

Thus decided, he headed inside and picked up his book, *Robinson Crusoe*. Peter kept the novel carefully wrapped in a cloth and tucked in his pillow. Peter considered the novel one of his most prized possessions, second only to the locket he kept next to his breast.

The novel was a gift from the librarian in Columbus, who remarked that she had never seen a man so interested in reading as he. Peter had loved everything he'd read, but this was his favorite so far. The style was simple, even more so than Twain, but its clean prose and straightforward narrative allowed Peter's imagination the freedom to construct the world around Robinson and his friend and companion Friday, picturing himself in Crusoe's place.

He opened the book and began to read. He was at the part where Crusoe was teaching Friday English and planning to convert him to Christianity. As the novel recounted Robinson's trials in reforming the native, Peter felt his anxiety fade and eventually disappear.

The beauty of novels was their predictability. Things always worked out in the end. Whatever trials the protagonist faced, the ending was always a satisfying one. Even Dickens, who tortured his characters perhaps more than anyone Peter had ever read, generally left them better off than they began.

Peter wasn't sure yet if things would work out for Robinson yet, but he seemed content enough with his circumstances, all things considered, and since Friday had met Robinson escaping from cannibals, Peter imagined it could hardly get worse for him.

Real life, of course, wasn't a novel. There was no benevolent stranger to rescue Peter from his demons. They would follow him the rest of his life, and when Peter could no longer bury himself in hard work and reading, the only end waiting for him lay at the end of his revolver, hidden on a shelf in the back of the small closet he had built for himself.

He read on, but as he paged through the book, his thoughts slipped from Crusoe and Friday—a Christian at last thanks to Robinson's diligence—and turned to Lydia. They had spoken little in the week since he arrived at the ranch, but he had stolen the occasional glance at her when she worked in the small garden behind the house or sat with her mother on the porch. If not for Penelope, Peter could see himself with a woman like Lydia.

But Peter had already fallen in love, and the only memory he had left of her was her faded portrait in the locket that now hung around his neck. He had nothing left to offer anyone else.

Chapter Five

Lydia whisked the eggs briskly, whipping them into the batter with rapid circular motions that frothed the yolks. Her mother glanced over from where she peeled potatoes for dinner and said, "Slow down, Lydia. You want to fold the batter, not whip it into a foam."

Lydia slowed her movements and found with some irritation that her mother was right. The batter quickly smoothed, and the air bubbles generated by her frenzied motions slowly disappeared.

"There you go," Mother said. "Slow and steady. Patience is key when you're baking."

"To hear you talk, patience is the key to everything in life," Lydia said.

"So it is," Mary agreed. "Nothing is gained by running around anxious all the time."

Lydia looked up from her dough. "Is there something you wanted to say to me, Mother?"

Mary looked up sweetly from the potatoes and said, "Nothing you haven't ignored many times before, my dear."

Lydia rolled her eyes but couldn't help smiling. She and her mother had honed their banter over many years, and what might seem like a squabble on the outside was in fact a very personal expression of their love, made all the more personal by the fact that few would recognize it as such.

Besides, she was in a good mood today. With Peter helping her father with the ranch, Lydia was able to keep up with the household chores, so she no longer felt worked to the bone, nor did she have to rely so much on her mother for the backbreaking that kept the house running.

Of course, that didn't make a difference in their finances. Only five months remained until their protection under the Homestead Act ended. Five months until the bank could begin the process of default and foreclosure. Five months until John Smith...

She sighed and began to spoon dollops of cookie dough onto the baking sheet. So much for her good mood.

"I have to say, dear, you have quite the eye for men."

Lydia started, accidentally flinging her spoonful of dough so it pasted itself on the wall. Coming on the heels of her most recent thought, her mother's comment was like a slap to the face.

"Careful, dear," Mary said lightly.

Lydia turned to her mother, red-faced with embarrassment and exasperation. "And why, dearest mother," she said, "would you say that?"

"Why, because of Peter," Mary replied.

Lydia's flush deepened. "Oh," she said. "Of course.

"Who did you think I meant?" Mary asked.

"Nothing," Lydia said, "no one. I'm glad you like Peter."

"What's not to like?" Mary said. "He's so strong and hard-working. Handsome too."

"Don't you start," Lydia said, placing the last of the cookies onto the sheet and opening the oven. "I hear it enough from Dorothy."

"Hear what, dear?"

Lydia sighed. As she carefully slid the baking sheet into the oven, she said, "You know, Mother, it's quite frustrating when you put on that innocent act and pretend you don't know what I'm talking about."

Mary smiled and said, "You're right, dear, I'm sorry. I do tease you a lot, but that's only because you remind me so much of your father."

Lydia straightened and closed the oven door. "Why thank you, Mother," she said drily. "Just what every daughter wants to hear."

Mary burst into laughter at that comment, and in spite of herself, Lydia laughed too. When her laughter subsided, she said, "On a serious note, yes, Peter seems to have done well so far."

Mary lifted her eyebrow. "Seems to?"

"Not everything everyone says has a double meaning, Mother," Lydia said. "I mean what I said. Peter seems to be doing well."

He was. The cattle were filling out and gaining energy. Their coats were clean and healthy, no longer mangy or flea-bitten. The stable was clean, as were the pens, and the fence around the ranch had been completely repaired. Even the grass was growing better thanks to Peter's decision to rotate the herd so they grazed only a quarter of the pasture at a time. Lydia could almost believe that she might get to keep her home after all.

But he was too quiet. He had been here only a week, and Lydia didn't expect for him to be a member of the family already, but he could be a little more sociable. At the very least, he could join them for dinner.

"Daydreaming, dear?" Mary asked with a smile.

"Just thinking, Mother," Lydia replied. "He's a little quiet, isn't he?"

"No quieter than Eugene is."

"True, I suppose, but Eugene has dinner with us when we invite him."

"Would you like to invite him to dinner?"

"I have invited him," Lydia said. "I made it clear to him that he was welcome anytime, but he's only joined us for that first meal."

"Well, he values his privacy," Mary replied. "There's nothing wrong with that."

"No," Lydia admitted, "I suppose not."

"I think he's grieving," Mary said.

Lydia turned to stare at her mother. She had a special talent for delivering shocking statements as though she were merely remarking about the weather. "Why would you say that?"

"I spoke with him earlier while he was washing his clothes," Mary said. "I mentioned that he shared your brother's name, and he told me he lost his family as well."

"Mother!" Lydia snapped. "You shouldn't have pried into his past!"

"I didn't pry," Mary protested, "he told me!"

"Still, it's none of our business," Lydia said. "And why did you tell him about Peter?"

"Well, he shares your brother's name," Mary said. "I didn't see the harm in it."

"He shares the Apostle's name too," Lydia said. "Perhaps next time you can read to him from the Bible instead."

"Lydia, what on Earth has gotten into you?" Mary asked. "There's no cause for you to be this angry."

"I just..." Lydia bit her lip and took a breath to calm herself. "I just don't think we need to share those details with someone who is, after all, a stranger."

"Well, what do you want from him?" Mary asked. "You want him to join us for dinner every night, but you want him to remain a stranger?"

"I want..." Lydia didn't finish.

What she wanted was to stop spending every waking moment of her life recalling her dead brother. She hated herself for that thought, but she couldn't help it. She felt guilty enough for Peter's death without being reminded of it.

She couldn't say that out loud, though, because her guilt wasn't her mother's fault, and her brother's death had nothing to do with the Peter who now lived in their old woodshed.

Mary stood and pulled Lydia into an embrace. Lydia endured the embrace, knowing that it would be pointless to tell her mother she didn't need a hug right now.

"I know you're worried about the ranch, dear. I don't blame you. But take heart. Peter really seems to be making a difference here. That's all I was trying to say."

Lydia pushed gently away, smiling so her mother would know she wasn't upset. "I know, Mother. I'm glad he's here."

***

Lydia wasn't the only one glad he was here. Her father unleashed an almost endless string of praise for him at dinner that night. Any jealousy he might have felt when Peter first arrived seemed to have quickly faded as Greg's ranch slowly transformed from a dilapidated hovel to an actual functioning operation.

"It's no wonder we beat the Rebs with men like that on our side," he said in his booming voice. "I told Eugene when we first moved here, we'll win this war because we understand the value of hard work. We don't feel a need to eat off the backs of others. We make our own way in the world."

"Yes, of course, dear," Mary said.

"And he's so good with the cattle," Greg continued. "He says he's never worked on a ranch before. I say he's finally found his true calling. You should see him with the animals! It's like he can speak to them!"

Lydia, of course, had seen Peter with the animals. She felt a flush creep up her cheeks as she recalled the way he'd wrestled that frightened steer to the ground. For the first time, she considered that he had not only overpowered the animal but also calmed it almost immediately.

"And he has to be the best carpenter I've ever seen." Greg laughed and continued, "I asked him about the stable the other day, and he got all red-faced and stammered around. I think he thought I was embarrassed at the poor work I did. 'Well, hey, that's all right,' I told him, 'I have a real woodworker here now.' Honestly, Lydia, I couldn't be more happy for you. You really know how to pick them."

Lydia's lips thinned. "Yes," she said, "I'm happy for *us* too."

Her father continued to extol Peter's praises, oblivious to Lydia's reaction to his comment. Mary cast a sympathetic glance at Lydia before asking Greg what he thought about the rumors of gold in British Columbia.

Greg immediately began ranting about those foolish prospectors who threw away their lives chasing shadows and rumors. Lydia offered her mother a grateful smile for turning the conversation away from Peter and herself, but her own thoughts remained on the quiet stranger who once more had spurned their offer of a meal.

After dinner, Lydia cleared the dishes and put the leftovers in the icebox. The cookies she and her parents hadn't eaten sat on the counter to be taken to the Flisters in the morning. Her parents retired early, but Lydia couldn't sleep, so she wrapped herself in a shawl, made herself a cup of cocoa, and headed to the porch.

That was one aspect of living in Montana that Lydia would admit was better than living in Maryland. The view at night was beyond breathtaking. It was almost as though by traveling across the country, they had arrived at an entirely different world. Lydia often spent her evenings gazing in wonder at the scattering of yellows and blues and brilliant whites that filled the sky from end to end.

She sat on the porch swing and looked up at the stars, letting their soft but brilliant light soothe her troubled mind. The moon was barely a sliver on the western horizon and Lydia hadn't bothered with a lantern, so the stars were even brighter tonight than usual.

Lydia looked up into the night, but though the stars were particularly radiant tonight, her attention was quickly pulled away by a light from the woodshed. She looked for a moment to confirm what she saw. It was the soft flickering of a candle in Peter's cabin.

She looked at the light and wondered what on Earth he was doing up so late. Despite her parents' belief that he was salvation incarnate, Lydia was still unsure of him. He was, as her mother and Dorothy made sure to point out at least once a day, very strong and hardworking and yes, Lydia had to admit, very handsome, but he was also very reserved and quiet, almost...she didn't want to say secretive. After all, he could simply be private, as her mother believed. Still...

She watched the flickering candle for a moment, then decided to see what he was doing up so late. She told herself her concern was nothing more than an employer's concern over the habits of an employee, but the truth was she was simply curious. Peter was a mystery, and Lydia had always loved mysteries.

She headed inside and took a few cookies from the cloche on the counter, wrapping them in a napkin and pouring some milk into a mug. She headed with the milk and cookies to the shed, grabbing the lantern from the porch and lighting it. It was awkward going with the milk and cookies in one hand and the lantern in the other, but she managed to make it to the little makeshift cabin without dropping her burden or falling over.

She knocked on the door and a moment later, it cracked open. When Peter saw her, he opened the door wider. "Evening, ma'am," he said in his deep, husky voice. "Is everything all right?"

"Yes, everything's fine," Lydia said. "I just thought you might like some cookies."

She offered the milk and cookies, feeling suddenly foolish. What must he think of her, walking all the way over here this late at night?

If he suspected her of impropriety, he didn't show it. He nodded and said, "Thank you kindly," reaching forward and taking the milk and cookies.

He made as though to close the door, and Lydia quickly said, "What are you doing up so late?"

And now she felt incredibly foolish. What was she, his mother? She nearly apologized and left, but Peter showed no sign of irritation and no more than his usual awkwardness. "Reading," he said, "I like to read."

"Really?" Lydia said, "That's wonderful. May I ask what you're reading?"

"*Robinson Crusoe,*" he said.

"Oh, how wonderful!" Lydia said. Had she said that already? "I loved that book when I was a girl. I won't tell you my favorite part. I don't want to spoil it for you."

She smiled at him, and he shifted his feet in uncomfortable silence. After a moment, Lydia tried again. "I'm partial to Edgar Allen Poe myself. Have you read him?"

Peter nodded. "Mmhmm."

"Most people prefer his short stories, but I just loved *Arthur Gordon Pym,*" Lydia said.

She peered past Peter as she spoke, but saw nothing inside his cabin save his cot, his chair and table and the open book laying facedown on the thin straw mattress.

"Well," Peter said, "I oughta turn in. Early day tomorrow."

"Aren't all days early?" Lydia said with another smile.

Peter shifted his feet again and once more offered an eloquent, "Mmhmm."

"Well," Lydia said. "I'll leave you to it, then. Enjoy the cookies."

"I will," Peter said. "Thank you, ma'am."

"It's Lydia," she said, "I might not be young anymore, but I'm not a ma'am yet."

"Oh," Peter said. "Sorry."

"No need to apologize," she said, "Good night, Peter."

"Good night, Lydia."

She turned and started back toward the house, cheeks flaming. Behind her, she heard the door to Peter's cabin close.

Well, now she had gone and thoroughly embarrassed herself. What was she thinking? Interrupting the poor man when he was only trying to enjoy his book before bed. And that comment about not being old enough to be a ma'am. No wonder everyone thought she was interested in him.

Was she interested in him?

Of course not! My, what a foolish thought.

"All right, Lydia," she muttered under her breath. "Time for bed."

She snuffed the lantern and hung it outside the door. Just before heading inside, she turned back to Peter's cabin.

The light in his window was out. She felt a touch of disappointment, though she couldn't say exactly why.

She took a breath and released it, then walked inside.

Chapter Six

Peter started sawing back and forth, but after a few strokes, he stopped and said, "Would you mind holding it a little steadier, sir? No need to push down on the plank, just hold it."

Greg smiled at him and said, "Well, I'll hold it still, but you have to promise to stop calling me sir. My name's Greg."

"Greg," Peter repeated dutifully.

He forced a smile that he hoped wasn't as awkward as it felt and continued to saw at the plank.

"What do you think?" Greg asked. "You think a half dozen more horses will be enough?"

Considering that he was the only employee the Gutenbergs had, Peter thought the four horses the Gutenbergs already owned were more than enough. But first-name basis or not, he didn't want to directly contradict his boss, so he said, "I think maybe half that will be fine."

"Just three?" Greg said, "Well, you're the expert."

Peter was far from an expert, but considering the state of the ranch when he arrived, he might as well be.

"I think a new stable is a good idea," Greg offered. "The old one's falling apart. I was going to just add a few more stalls, but what do you think about just building a new one?"

"That's a good idea," Peter said. "It'll be easier to do than to try to fix the old one and won't take any longer."

He didn't add that the stable, like the barn, was so shoddily constructed that they would need a new stable for the horses they had. The rotting, cracking and flaking building they now had wouldn't survive the coming winter. Peter wasn't sure how harsh the winters were in Montana, but they wouldn't have to be very hard to overwhelm the ranch's buildings. The house, at least, was solid enough that it would only take some minor repairs and some turpentine to weatherproof it.

"We should see if Eugene can help us," Greg said, "He helped me build the house, you know."

Ah. That made sense.

"That's a good idea too," Peter said. "We could use an extra pair of hands."

"Maybe I'll run over there after lunch," Greg said, "See if he has some time this afternoon."

Peter finished sawing through the plank, taking the length of pine and setting it to the side behind him. Pine was a soft wood, and it would require some treatment to be strong enough to construct the stable, but it was light and strong and if tempered properly and treated to prevent rot, it would stand for the rest of their lifetimes.

Peter lifted another length of pine and nodded at Greg, who dutifully planted his hands on either side of the plank and held it steady while Peter worked.

In addition to being easily worked with, pine was also abundant and cheap, since the plains where Stevensville lay were surrounded on all sides by pine forests. After salvaging the usable wood from the old building, they wouldn't need to buy much lumber. In fact, Peter thought he could simply procure the lumber himself. He judged the nearest stand of pines to be a half day's journey east. He could travel there, harvest some lumber and return with a wagon load within the next day. He reckoned three such trips would be enough for the stable and maybe another four for the barn. It would take time, but time was something they had in abundance.

Or so Peter thought until Greg spoke again. "I have to say, Peter, you couldn't have come here at a better time. If you'd come a month later, we'd be bankrupt."

Peter hesitated for the briefest of instants before resuming sawing. "That so?" he said, keeping his tone casual.

"Oh yes," Greg said. "See, we came here on the Homestead Act. You're familiar?"

"Yes, I'm familiar," Peter said.

"Well, we were given five years to make profitable use of the land," Greg said, "During that time, we can't be sued for default on our debts and the bank can't foreclose. Well, we have five months of protection left. After that, no more help from Uncle Abe. Or I guess it's Uncle Ulysses now."

Peter managed to maintain his calm as he finished sawing through this plank and set the two lengths of trimmed pine next to the others, but he was alarmed by this news. He wondered how he could manage to ask about the ranch's financial state without overstepping his bounds, but he didn't need to worry for long, because Greg's effusiveness continued to offer Peter a wealth of unwanted but very much needed information.

"I really hope the cattle are ready for sale as soon as you and Eugene hope they are," he said, "If we don't make some money soon, we have maybe a month or two after the protection ends before we're in default and the bank forecloses." He smiled at Peter. "Not to worry, though. With your help, we can pull through."

Peter nodded and offered another smile, then stood and said, "Well, I think that's good for now. We can start again after lunch."

"I was hoping you'd say that," Greg replied gratefully, stretching his arms over his head and groaning. "Don't ever grow old, Peter," he said. "Time is not kind."

"No," Peter agreed. "It isn't."

"Why don't you come to the house and join us for lunch?" Greg said. "We'd love to have you."

Peter shook his head. "Thank you, but I'd like to look around at the site for the new stable and test the ground. Make sure it's solid."

It was a weak excuse, but the inexperienced Greg fell readily for it. "Good thinking," he said, "We don't want to start building only to have to tear the whole thing down again."

"No," Peter said wryly. "We wouldn't want to do that."

Greg left, promising to bring Peter a sandwich when he returned. Peter nodded thanks, then headed off to pretend to look at ground that he already knew was more than adequate.

It was just his luck to find a job only to learn that he wouldn't be able to keep it. Of course he would only find this out after moving halfway across the country to a town half the size of an average neighborhood in Columbus. If jobs were scarce in Columbus, Peter could only imagine how much trouble he'd have finding work in Montana.

He wanted to feel angry at the Gutenbergs for misleading him, but he couldn't. Greg was clearly in over his head, and Mary didn't seem aware of how desperate their situation was.

Lydia probably had an idea. She was smart, and he recalled Greg mentioning that she was the one responsible for the books. She was the one who had advertised for a foreman, but she had placed that advertisement four months ago, and it wasn't her fault that the only respondent took so long to find her.

Then again, it was telling that no one else had tried for the job.

He sighed in frustration, removing his cap and running his hand through his hair. If the ranch folded, he had nowhere to go. He supposed he could strike west for California or Oregon and find work in one of the ports. He wasn't a sailor, but he was strong and comfortable with hard work. He could find employment as a dockworker, he was sure.

But what would happen to the Gutenbergs? Greg was too old for anyone to hire him, especially considering his almost complete helplessness with almost any kind of work. Mary was kindly and might find work as a nanny or schoolteacher if they managed to make it to a larger town or a city, but that wasn't likely. Even in those professions, youth was preferred.

Lydia would be their only hope, and the only work available to a woman in these parts was as a serving girl or cleaning woman. That paid enough that Lydia could survive, but she wouldn't be able to support her parents. He knew Eugene would put them up for as long as he could, but Eugene wasn't wealthy, and he had a daughter of his own to provide for.

Well, Peter couldn't really help them. He had no money himself. He could give back most of the wages he had been paid and work his way west until he found a new home, but he doubted a few weeks of modest wages would make any appreciable difference to them.

He was trapped, and so were the Gutenbergs.

He returned to the new woodshed he had built and where he and Greg now worked on the wood for the new stable just as Greg arrived with a sandwich. Greg continued to talk effusively while Peter ate, but thankfully, he didn't return to the subject of money. After Peter finished eating, Greg asked if he would join him on the ride to the Flister Ranch.

Peter didn't have a good reason to refuse. Well, he did. He would get more work done faster without Greg "helping" him, but he couldn't very well say that to him, and he didn't feel right about lying a second time, so he agreed and followed Greg to the wagon.

"I hope you don't mind the wagon," he said to Peter. "Riding on horseback is getting harder for me these days. Don't ever grow old, Peter. Time isn't kind."

Peter decided not to mention that Greg had said that already.

The first half of the twenty-minute drive to the Flister homestead was spent in surprising silence. Evidently Greg had finally burned himself out.

The real reason for his uncharacteristic silence was revealed to Peter when he said, his voice low and subdued, "I don't know what to do if the ranch doesn't make it, Peter. This is all I have. This is all my family has. I..." he lifted a hand and dropped it. "I brought them all this way and promised them a better life, and I really thought I could give it to them. Now?"

He sighed and turned to Peter, forcing a smile. "I'm sorry, Peter. You don't need to hear me ramble on. Besides, you're here now. We'll be okay."

"Yes," Peter said with confidence he didn't feel. "We will."

Greg brightened at Peter's statement, and Peter wasn't sure how to feel about that. The Gutenbergs were putting altogether too much faith in him. He knew that faith was born of desperation, but that didn't make him feel any better about it. What was he supposed to do, fix everything by himself in the next few months?

Well, he had all but said he would to Greg just now. So much for moving West. Now if he left, he would be breaking a promise. Maybe that wasn't exactly true, but it was close enough to make Peter feel obligated. Why had he said that? Why couldn't he have said, "Don't lose hope," or "Keep your head up," or better yet, just nodded?

They reached the Flister Ranch, and when Eugene came out and smiled at Greg with real affection, Peter felt a glimpse of hope.

Eugene knew how to run a ranch. He had already helped Peter a lot with managing and caring for a herd of cattle. He clearly cared for Greg and Peter knew that Lydia and Dorothy were close friends.

Peter couldn't save the ranch by himself, but with Eugene's help, they had a chance. A small chance, barely any chance, really, but more than no chance.

He could try. He *would* try. If there was one thing he knew he could do, he could work tirelessly. If they managed to save the ranch, that was good. If not, well, Peter could figure something out.

Unless he stayed. Maybe he could start his own homestead. He could stake out some land past the homesteads already here. He knew how to raise a small herd of cattle now. He wouldn't be wealthy, but maybe he could help at least a little. Then the Gutenbergs would have two friends on their side. Then he wouldn't have to leave Lydia behind.

His face flamed at the thought, and to distract himself, he focused on the conversation between Greg and Eugene. Try as he might to immerse himself in their discussion about pine as a construction material, he couldn't shake the image of Lydia's blue eyes glowing by lantern light.

Chapter Seven

Peter released the last of the cattle and sighed, wiping sweat from his brow. His chest heaved with exertion, and he thought that while it lasted, this ranch work was apt to be the best job he'd ever had. He hadn't felt this tired since the war.

He and Greg had just finished branding the herd, which meant he had just finished branding the herd while Greg fought mightily to be of use and failed utterly. Peter didn't mind. The exertion had him feeling the closest to content he had felt in years.

He headed to the spring to wash up, stopping by his cabin for a change of clothes. The ones he wore now were covered in sweat—both his and the cattle's—soot, and dust. Thanks to Mary, he now knew how to wash them properly. Though since he would be washing himself too, he traveled a good half-mile further upstream than he did with Mary.

He picked a spot sheltered from view of the homestead and the surrounding homes by a small stand of juniper and stripped out of his soiled clothes. He started to wash and only after he had entered the stream did he realize he had forgotten a blanket, a towel and soap.

He chuckled and thought to himself that he was as hopeless at domestic stuff as Greg was at running a ranch. He supposed he just wasn't used to creature comforts. Soap was a rare treat in the army and utterly nonexistent in prison, except for the day of his release, since the need to inconvenience a prisoner was outweighed with the need not to overwhelm the law-abiding citizens of Columbus with stench.

Well, he had survived a war and a prison sentence. He could survive a few moments of being wet in the warm summer sun.

It was August today, he realized. He had been on the ranch seventeen days.

That was nothing in the scheme of things. He had spent longer than that encamped by the Potomac while he trained for war.

Images flickered across his mind's eye, eclipsing the sunny day for a moment. Marching for hours through soggy swamps and spending nights shivering in the freezing rain. Creeping up on an enemy camp, knowing what he had to do next.

He blinked and shook his head to clear the memory, but another, far worse flashback came to him.

"When you stab a man," Sergeant Bentley said, *"stab him through his neck, not his gut or his chest. You stab him through his gut, he has time to scream for his friends to come help him. Stab him in his neck, he don't even have time to gasp."*

The grizzled old veteran's eyes glittered hard as diamonds beneath hooded brows. Peter could only speculate how many men he'd stabbed in just the same way.

Peter stood suddenly, lifting his shirt from the stream. That life was behind him. He had a new life now. He could be happy here.

Guilt flooded him the moment he thought of that. Greg and Mary were wonderful people, but they weren't his parents. Lydia was beautiful, but she wasn't Penelope. He wasn't here to be happy, he was here to survive.

And on that note, "here" was still very much in danger. They needed at least three more months to finish preparing the ranch for winter, and that was assuming they had the ranch long enough to make it to winter. Even as industrious as he was, he couldn't sell the herd and repair the ranch by himself. Eugene could help, but he had his own ranch to prepare for winter.

He didn't need to think about being happy. He needed to think about finding a way to keep the homestead afloat.

He finished washing and stepped ashore. The sun was warm, but the breeze that blew chilled him, and he promised himself he wouldn't forget a towel next time.

While the sun dried him, he washed his clothes. The spot he selected was right next to a large rock, so he laid his clothes there to dry since he didn't have a blanket.

When he was finished, he decided he was dry enough to dress and gratefully pulled on the canvas shirt and pants. He made a mental note to ask Mary to make some canvas pants for Greg. The cotton clothes he wore were ill-suited to hard work, and several of the pants were torn and threadbare. Mary didn't need to buy cloth. Potato sacks would work just fine. A good scrubbing with a horsehair brush would soften the fabric enough to be comfortable. Well, wearable, at least.

He chuckled to himself. So he knew how to prepare sackcloth pants for wearing, but he didn't think to bring soap with him to wash. It was funny, the skills you picked up in life and the ones you didn't. He wondered what skills Greg had left behind to try his luck as a rancher.

He realized he liked the older rancher. The man was hopeless at his chosen profession, but he was a dogged optimist, and his gregariousness was far less annoying now than at first.

He frowned slightly as he remembered the rare moment of anxiety Greg showed on the road to Eugene's house. Greg was an optimist, but not foolish enough to believe his optimism would save him.

He believed Peter would save him, or at least hoped so desperately enough that it might as well be belief.

Peter sighed as he headed back to the ranch. He wanted very much to be the man who could work a miracle and save the Gutenberg ranch from destruction, but like Greg, he wasn't foolish enough to be truly optimistic and he was no longer foolish enough to hope, either. In his experience, hope was as useless as optimism.

But he did hope, and the hope concerned him because it meant he had something to live for.

Something to lose.

He needed to take his mind off things. He could do more work on the new stable.

The horses were kept outside for the moment, while Peter and Greg demolished the old stable and salvaged what they could to start construction on the new one. So far, they had salvaged enough of the load-bearing wood for the major beams of the new stable and enough planks for half a wall. Peter anticipated they would end up with maybe a third of what they needed and have to harvest the rest.

He reached the ranch and started toward the stable. He passed by the house, and noticed Lydia sitting on the porch swing with her head buried in her hands and an open book next to her on the swing.

He hesitated, trying to convince himself that it would be better to leave her alone than to interrupt her, but she was clearly upset, and he couldn't stand that.

He didn't like knowing that he couldn't stand that, but there it was.

He shook his head. He was overthinking it. It wasn't a sign of infatuation to attempt to help an upset woman. He was being polite, that's all.

He walked up to her and cleared his throat. She snapped upright, eyes wide, and Peter lifted his hand. "Sorry, ma'am— Lydia. I just...I...Well, I noticed you were upset."

"I'm all right, thank you," Lydia replied, politely but with enough of an edge that Peter knew she wasn't happy with the interruption.

Peter shuffled uncomfortably, but now that he was on the porch, he could see that the open book next to Lydia was the ranch's ledger. He felt a rush of sympathy for Lydia. It wasn't right that she should have to bear the financial burden of her father's mistake. It wasn't Greg's fault either. He had tried, and, as happened far more often than people liked, he had failed despite the fact that he was a good, honest, hardworking person.

Still, Lydia shouldn't have to shoulder this alone. "Mind if I take a look?" Peter asked. "Might help me. As foreman, I mean."

"How would this help you as foreman?" Lydia asked.

She smiled, but Peter could see hesitance in her eyes. He said, "Well, I should know how much money we have, and how much we need so I can make decisions. The cattle should be ready to sell soon, but if we sell too many, we won't have enough to replenish our numbers for next season."

Lydia chuckled. "Well, Peter, you can assume that we need to make as much money as possible and spend as little money as possible. I hope you've warned Father about buying those extra horses. Heaven knows he won't listen to me."

Peter hadn't spoken to Greg. He felt somewhat guilty for choosing to avoid confrontation earlier.

"I'll talk to him right now," he said, "I'm just heading over to the stable."

"Ah yes," Lydia said. "And how much wood do you think we'll need to buy for that?"

"Won't need to buy it," he said. "I can harvest what we need from the forest."

Lydia stared frankly at him. "The forest that's ten miles away."

"Nearer fifteen," he said.

Lydia pursed her lips, and Peter quickly said, "But yes, that forest. I can ride out early, harvest some wood and have it back by lunchtime the next day. I figure three trips for the stable and four for the barn. Maybe one extra to shore up the house."

Lydia's face adopted an unreadable expression. "You'd single-handedly harvest a full ton of wood from a forest a half day's ride from here so you can build us a new stable and barn."

Peter nodded. "Yes, ma—Lydia."

She chuckled. "You're a strange man, Peter."

"Yes, ma'am, I suppose I am," Peter replied.

"Well," she said, "I'll be honest with you, Peter. Things are looking bleak, but the more I talk to you, the less bleak they look."

Peter felt his face flame at the compliment. He hoped Lydia didn't notice, but judging by the small smile that played at her lips, he thought that she did.

"Thank you, Lydia."

Her smile widened. "Well, listen to you. You actually remembered to use my name this time."

His flush deepened, and he decided it was time for him to leave. "Well, if you need help with the ledger—"

"I'll let you know," Lydia said.

Peter nodded and tipped his hat, then left the porch. After a few dozen steps, he turned around to see Lydia still watching him as he walked toward the stable. His face flamed once more, and he tipped his cap at her again and continued on.

He saw Greg working on stacking the planks Peter had cut, a task that was nearly impossible to do incorrectly. Greg waved and grinned as he approached. "Got most of them stacked up neat," he said. "Should be able to start on that wall you were talking about."

"We'll make the frame first," Peter said. "We need that to measure how large the walls will be."

"Right," Greg said, "Good thinking."

Peter nodded and shuffled his feet. He always did that when he was nervous. It made him a terrible card player. "Greg," he said finally, "I need to talk to you about something."

"Sure," Greg said, "What is it?"

"Well," Peter said, "It's about the horses."

"What's wrong with the horses?"

"Nothing," Peter said, "I just mean... I don't think you should buy more horses, Greg."

Greg blinked. "Well, why not?"

"Well," Peter said, "Greg, I hope you won't consider me rude for saying this, but we can't afford it. I mean you can't afford it. I mean the ranch can't afford it."

"Oh," Greg said.

He flushed a little, and Peter felt his heart sink to his feet.

"Yes, of course," Greg said, "You're right. We need to save money. Got a big deadline coming up."

He flashed a smile, but this one faded almost as quickly as it arrived. Peter felt about two inches tall, but it had to be said, no matter how much it hurt the old man's feelings.

He cleared his throat. "I'm gonna talk to Eugene about helping me sell some of the herd. If I can make a little money, we might be able to pay enough of the debt to delay default a couple months. It only buys us a little time, but that might be enough to sell some more and chip away at it until you're caught up. It won't be quick, but it could work."

Greg smiled again, and this one stayed. "Sure. Good thinking, partner."

Peter offered a far less enduring smile than Greg's and felt the weight of responsibility that came with Greg's statement.

So now he wasn't a foreman, he was a partner. Well, that was no surprise. Mary had already called him family.

He nodded to Greg and said, "Right. Let's get to work."

As he sectioned off more of the wood, he hoped desperately that he could save the Gutenberg Ranch.

But he knew better than to believe it.

Chapter Eight

Lydia smiled softly to herself as Dorothy talked nonstop at Mary about her latest embroidered creation. Mary mentioned that she knitted, and Dorothy's eyes had widened in excitement.

For the past hour, she had gone on and on about needles, stitching, thread, and thimbles. Mary listened with her usual unflappable patience and eventually said, "You might like a career as a clothier or a seamstress, Dorothy."

Dorothy laughed and said, "Oh, no such luck for me. Who will run the ranch when father's gone?"

"Don't say that," Lydia scolded her softly. "Eugene has many years ahead of him."

Dorothy shrugged. "Sure, but when he goes, I mean. You never *really* know when."

Lydia turned toward her friend. "What's wrong, Dorothy? Why are you worried about losing your father?"

"I'm not worried about losing him," Dorothy said, "I just accept the possibility that it might happen."

"What brought that thought to your mind, dear?" Mary asked.

"Well, it's my mother's birthday today," Dorothy said. She would have been...let's see...forty-four today. No, forty-six." She smiled. "Wow. Time really flies."

"Oh, Dorothy," Mary said, "I'm so sorry."

Lydia offered her friend a sympathetic smile.

Dorothy laughed again and said, "You two are sweet, but I'm all right. She died six years ago. I've done all of my grieving already." Her smile faded. "Still, I do miss her a lot some days. Like her birthday."

"We should bake a cake," Mary said. "Celebrate your mother's birthday."

"Mother," Lydia began, "I don't think—"

"Oh, what a wonderful idea!" Dorothy exclaimed. "We can bake a chocolate cake! That was her favorite!"

"Where do you propose we get the cocoa powder?" Lydia asked.

"Mr. Hemsworth always has cocoa powder in August! He has a second cousin who works at a shipyard in California. He unloads cocoa shipments and the captain always lets the dockworkers have a bag of cocoa beans. Oh, please say we can, Lydia."

Lydia smiled and chuckled a little. "You're an adult, Dorothy, you don't need my permission to bake a cake."

"Oh, but you know we can't do it without you," Dorothy said matter-of-factly.

"She's right, dear," Mary said.

Lydia rolled her eyes. "Well, of course I'm going to help you."

"Yay!" Dorothy exclaimed. She threw her arms around Lydia and planted a kiss on her cheek, nearly knocking them both off the bench.

"Will you get off me!" Lydia laughed. "You clumsy oaf!"

"I'll forgive you your rudeness since you're helping me bake a cake," Dorothy said with a grin.

Lydia shook her head, but smiled as she said, "I swear you'll be the death of me one day."

They reached town ten minutes later, and Lydia drove straight to the general store, the urgency of the new plan for cake overwhelming the urgency of new shoes for the horses. She would have to apologize to Peter and head to town herself tomorrow.

They had flour, butter, eggs and cream at home, so all they needed was sugar and cocoa powder. When Lydia saw the price of the cocoa powder, she balked. But old Mr. Hemsworth apparently had a sweet spot for Dorothy, who he said reminded him so much of his daughter Maud. So they got the cocoa powder for free, and Dorothy ended up paying for the rest of the ingredients anyway.

Lydia felt a sharp stab of embarrassment when Dorothy bought the ingredients. She was the youngest among them, and it was her mother's birthday. Lydia wished she could have bought the ingredients, but though she had the money, she knew it was better to save it.

She hated being poor. She knew it wasn't fair to her parents to feel this way, but she did. She hated that she was right on the edge of losing her home. She hated that her friend had to shoulder the financial burden of her dead mother's birthday cake.

She knew she was overreacting, but knowing that didn't make her feel any better.

The three of them started toward the livery. The proprietor, Mr. Sorley, was also the blacksmith and the farrier. It looked like Lydia would get her horseshoes after all.

"Is everything okay?" Dorothy asked.

Lydia realized her feelings were showing on her face, so she forced a smile and said, "Yes, sorry. I was just distracted."

Dorothy smiled mischievously. "By thoughts of Peter?"

Well, now she was. "Yes, by thoughts of Peter," she said resignedly. It wasn't worth trying to deny it, even if it wasn't true. Well, mostly not true.

"He really *is* handsome, isn't he?" Dorothy said.

Lydia sighed. "Mother, will you introduce Dorothy to Peter when we get home? She seems quite captivated by him."

"Oh, I would never do that to you, dear," Mary replied with an angelic smile.

Dorothy giggled, and Lydia sighed. "You two are terrible together. I'm sitting in between you on the ride home."

Dorothy giggled again, and Mary grinned, making herself appear at least a decade younger.

"Seriously, though," Dorothy said. "How are you two getting along?"

"Well, we're eloping next week," Lydia deadpanned. "We have a little cabin in the mountains of British Columbia waiting for us. We're going to live off the land and pan for gold and be oh so happy."

"How wonderful!" Dorothy said.

"Congratulations, dear," Mary offered.

Lydia rolled her eyes. She opened her mouth to offer another witticism but stopped when she saw John Smith.

He stood in front of the bank, talking with a squirrelly little man Lydia recognized as Gordon Meecher, the bank's manager. John owned the bank, but rarely bothered to show up to work, leaving most of the day to day to Gordon.

"He's just a beauty, isn't he," Mary said, a touch of venom in her voice.

"So you see him too," Lydia said.

"At least he doesn't see us," Dorothy said.

Lydia snapped the reins and drove them past the livery without stopping. She could send Peter for the shoes tomorrow. "That filthy man," she muttered.

"I heard his wife didn't die," Dorothy said, grinning. "She just shaved her head and pretended to be a boy so she could travel to California and join a ship's crew to get away from him."

"I heard worse than that," Mary said.

So had Lydia. Behind John's kindly exterior was a venomous and violent mind. He had been married three times before, and only one of those women still lived. The deaths were officially ruled to be accidents, but John's neighbors said they could hear screams from his house the night before John's most recent wife was found dead.

"Well, forget about him," Dorothy said. "Let's go make a cake and eat way too much of it."

"Good idea," Lydia said.

She snapped the reins again, and the two old mares pulling the wagon looked behind at her as though to say, "Good luck getting us to move any faster."

As the town receded behind them, John's image slowly faded from Lydia's mind. It didn't matter what happened. He wouldn't get what he wanted.

Lydia pulled toward the Flister homestead, but Dorothy said, "Oh, would you mind if we celebrated at your home? It's just...well, I don't know how Father would react. He's not at your home today, is he?"

"No, I don't believe so," Mary said. "Peter said he and Greg should be fine on their own today."

"Oh good," Dorothy said. "Thank you. I just don't want Father to be upset."

"Does he not talk about her?" Lydia said.

"He does," Dorothy said, "But he doesn't talk much on her birthday. Just sits in his chair and stares. He gets very morose too."

Lydia thought of Peter's behavior and Mary's confession that he had told her of the loss of his family. It could explain why he was so aloof and quiet. She couldn't imagine carrying that kind of grief with her.

Except she could. She thought of Peter—her brother. His laugh, his inquisitive stare, his lopsided smile, the way he would snuggle with her.

"Lydia, are you sure you're all right?" Dorothy asked.

"I'm all right," she said, smiling at her friend. "I was just thinking about my brother."

"When's his birthday?" Dorothy asked.

"Next week," Lydia said. "The tenth."

"Well, we'll bake a cake for him too. What did he like?"

"Cornbread," Lydia replied.

"Cornbread?" Dorothy asked, wrinkling her nose.

"Oh yes," Mary confirmed. "He would sneak it at night. I would find him in the morning asleep with molasses all over his face. Half the time, I wouldn't say anything and just let him think he got away with it."

Lydia giggled as she recalled his dazed expression every time he woke up after one of his late-night snacks. "You know what?" she said. "I could use some cornbread."

"Well," Dorothy said, "On the tenth of August in this Year of Our Lord Eighteen-Sixty-Nine, we shall make the best cornbread known to mankind. I shall even charm Mr. Hemsworth into giving us some molasses."

"Blackstrap," Mary said. "That was his favorite. Heaven only knows why."

"The blackest of straps," Dorothy promised.

The three women laughed as they continued toward the Gutenberg homestead, thoughts of John driven from their minds in light of their new plans.

***

Lydia had to admit. This was one exceptional chocolate cake. Dorothy's mother had been a fantastic baker.

"I am afraid I'll have to shamelessly steal this recipe," Mary said.

"Go ahead," Dorothy replied. "Mother never kept it a secret. That's how I know it."

"Well, it's delicious," Lydia added, "and I have most definitely eaten too much of it."

"So have I," Mary agreed. "Not that I'm going to deny myself a third helping."

She reached for the knife and cut herself a generous slice. Lydia tried to abstain, but in the end, the allure of the confection was just too powerful. She cut herself another slice and promised it would be the last sweet thing she ate before her brother's birthday.

"Say, you two," Dorothy asked, "I've been meaning to ask; where are you from?"

"Baltimore," Lydia replied. "You know that."

"No, I mean originally," Dorothy said, "For instance, my family's from Ireland. Where are you from?"

"Oh," Lydia replied. "Um, Holland, I believe."

"Prussia," Mary corrected. "Friedrich Gutenberg was a Hessian soldier in the American revolution who fell in love with an American woman and defected to the colonies' cause."

"Oh, how wonderful!" Dorothy corrected. "I hear Prussia's just beautiful, especially in the winter!"

"Well, I'll take your word for it," Lydia said. "I don't imagine I'll ever go."

"But don't you want to know about your origins?" Dorothy asked.

Lydia shrugged. "I'm happy here." If she could only watch the garden bloom and the herd grow without the threat of foreclosure looming.

"Have you ever been to Ireland?" Mary asked.

"No," Dorothy said, "but I'd love to visit someday."

"Well, I suppose I would enjoy the chance to visit Prussia one day if I ever have the chance," Lydia said.

"It's settled!" Dorothy said. "The three of us shall tour Europe as soon as possible. We shall see Ireland and Prussia and France and Spain and England!"

The three of them laughed and continued fantasizing about an adventure that was almost certainly beyond their reach. Still, there was some comfort in dreaming, even when there was no possibility of those dreams coming true.

Lydia glanced out the window and caught a glimpse of Peter trudging off to his cabin. She thought of her mother's revelation that Peter's own family was lost. He was alone here.

No, he wasn't alone. He might think he was, but he wasn't.

Lydia stood and said, "Will you excuse me one moment?"

She cut a slice of cake and grabbed a plate and fork.

"Where are you going?" Dorothy asked.

"I'm going to offer Peter some of this cake," Lydia said.

Dorothy smiled mischievously. "Ooh, what else are you going to offer him?"

Lydia reddened. "Well, not my hand, if that's what you're implying."

"Ooh, how scandalous," Dorothy teased, ignoring her.

"You're horrible, Dorothy," Lydia said. "I'm only being kind."

She left before Dorothy or her mother could tease her further. When she reached the cabin, she knocked. A moment later, Peter opened.

"Would you like some cake?" she asked, handing him the slice.

"Oh," he said, "Well, yes. Thank you."

"You're welcome, Peter," she said.

He took the cake and after an awkward silence, Lydia said, "You might consider eating with us sometime. It would save me needing to walk here every time I bake."

He nodded seriously, and she said, "That was a joke, Peter."

"Oh," he said. He offered what Lydia decided was a decent effort at a smile, all things considered, and said, "I'll join you for dinner tomorrow night, if you'll have me."

She smiled, and her smile widened when she saw a flush come to his cheeks. "I would like that very much," she said.

"Thank you," he said again. "You're very kind."

"You deserve kindness," she said.

The light was already dimming as the sun dipped below the horizon, but Lydia could have sworn she saw the blush deepen. It looked good on him.

Chapter Nine

"Peter, for heaven's sake, take a break," Greg said. "We have five months to catch up on our debts, not five minutes."

Peter looked up from his work. "Well, I'm hoping to sell some of the herd tomorrow. If we can attract a buyer, we might be able to sell more of the herd before too long, and when the Homestead Act protection ends, you can pay off enough of your debt to avoid bankruptcy."

"You're splitting logs for stable fencing," Eugene pointed out with a smile. "That doesn't have anything to do with sales."

"Oh," Peter said. "No, I guess not."

Greg chuckled and said, "From what Eugene says, the herd is as good as sold."

"Oh yes," Eugene agreed. "The cattle you're offering are perfect for the Double Bar S's needs. They don't need size, they need hardiness."

Peter had agreed to meet with representatives from the Double Bar S ranch to sell fifty head of breeding stock. That sale, if it went through, would offer little more than a drop in the bucket compared to the ranch's needs, but if the sale went well, the Double Bar S might agree to buy another fifty head. That would cut their herd in half but leave them enough money to avoid bankruptcy while they replenished the herd's numbers.

"Where are they from anyway?" Greg asked.

"Arizona," Eugene said.

"And they want cold-weather cattle for that?"

Eugene patiently explained that it wasn't the ability to handle extreme weather that mattered but the ability to thrive on sparse grass and a greater proportion of grain in their diet. Greg listened intently, but Peter could see he was having trouble following.

That didn't worry him as much as it had before. In the month since he'd arrived, the ranch had slowly but surely improved. The new stable was fully constructed from the outside and two more weeks would be all they needed to finish the inside. The barn would probably take another two months, and after that, Peter could move on to the house. If they still had a ranch come winter, that ranch would be more than ready for whatever weather the colder months brought.

It no longer seemed so much of a stretch that they might have a ranch. Peter had accomplished much more than he expected to in the short time since he'd been here. He had a lot to be proud of. If his parents could see him...

His smile faded, but thankfully Eugene interrupted his thoughts before a depression could settle over him. "Say you two, I was hoping I could ask for a favor."

"What's that?" Peter asked.

"There's this boy in town, Micah. He's been sweet on my Dotty for a while now. He's coming today to talk to me about courting her. I was hoping you two could join us for dinner and tell me your thoughts."

"Oh, I don't know," Peter demurred. "I don't want to embarrass Dorothy."

"No need to worry about that," Eugene said. "She'll be dining with Miss Lydia and Miss Mary today. I arranged it so that it would only be us men."

Peter had no idea what kind of help he could offer Eugene, but Eugene had sacrificed much of his time and energy to help Peter, so he didn't feel right about refusing. "All right," he said, "I'll be there."

"Of course!" Greg agreed. "Say, why don't we leave now?"

"Oh," Peter said. He looked at the pile of wood he intended to carve into rails for the stables and said, "Well, I was hoping—"

"Peter, for heaven's sake," Greg interrupted. "You do the work of ten men every day. The work will still be there when we get back. Take one afternoon off to help your friend mercilessly judge his daughter's suitor."

Eugene burst into laughter at that, and a moment later, Greg joined him. Peter smiled slightly. "Well, all right."

The three of them stopped by the house to let Mary and Lydia know the plans. Lydia crossed her arms, clearly displeased at the interference, but when Eugene explained that he was afraid Dorothy's heart would overwhelm her mind in this case, she sighed and said, "Well, I suppose I can understand that. Please be kind to him," she said. "And to her."

"I will," Eugene said, "That's why I'm asking for help before I tell him to stay away. I know I might be a bit biased, so I want an objective opinion."

Mary and Lydia shared a glance and Peter said, "If he's a good boy, humble, hardworking and kind, then I don't imagine any of us will object. Eugene just wants to make sure he finds the best for his daughter."

"You mean if he's like you?" Lydia said, smiling softly.

Peter felt heat and cold war for preeminence in his body. Heat won, and he averted his gaze from her so she wouldn't see the flush that crept into his cheeks.

He wasn't so lucky with Eugene and Greg.

"Say," Eugene said, "Lydia's not being courted by anyone at the moment, is she?"

"Why no," Greg said with a grin. "I don't believe she is."

Peter snapped the reins, urging the wagon faster. He didn't feel comfortable talking about Lydia when she wasn't there, and he definitely didn't feel comfortable with the direction he knew the conversation was headed.

"Peter," Eugene said, "Have you ever thought about marriage?"

"No," Peter said stoically, "can't say I have."

That wasn't the truth, of course, but he didn't want to talk to them about Penelope, and he definitely didn't want to give them any room to talk about him and Lydia.

"You know, Lydia likes you," Greg said.

Peter's cheeks flushed even deeper. He rather suspected Greg was right. She always made sure to sit near him when they ate dinner together, and on those nights he chose to work late rather than eat with them, he could count on her waiting for him at his cabin with a plate of food and a glass of milk. He noticed her watching him from the porch sometimes as he worked, and he could tell that she admired his strength.

Then again, that didn't necessarily mean she liked him. The meals could easily be explained by politeness, and she could admire his strength as something useful in a ranch employee, not as a quality she wanted in a husband.

"I'm glad to hear that," he said to Greg, "I enjoy working for her. And for you."

Greg laughed. "All right, Peter, I'll stop teasing you. I'm only saying that if Lydia ever did choose to marry, I'd be happy for her to find a man as strong and honest as you."

Peter offered a curt thank-you and urged the horses faster again.

They reached the Flister ranch just as the sun began its journey to the western horizon in earnest. "Micah should be here in an hour or so," Eugene said. "Would you two like coffee while we wait?"

"I'll never say no to coffee," Greg said. "Thank you kindly."

Peter nodded his acceptance, and Eugene made them a fresh pot. They talked about cattle while they waited, and Eugene reiterated his belief that Peter would succeed in his sale tomorrow. Peter appreciated the encouragement. Even more than the encouragement, he appreciated the trust both men showed in allowing him to make the sale on his own.

They had accepted him so completely already.. At dinner, they would talk to him as though they'd known him for years and didn't seem to mind that he talked little. Even Lydia seemed less unsure of him as the days went on. He felt almost like part of the family

That thought prompted memories that Peter would rather not deal with at the moment, so he was grateful when hoofbeats interrupted them. A moment later, Eugene ushered a foppish-looking man of about twenty-five into the parlor.

Introductions were made, and Peter noted that Micah's handshake was rather weak. He wasn't sure if that meant anything, but combined with the dandy's togs and general air of the young man, it wasn't the best of first impressions.

"Thank you for having me, Mr. Flister," Micah said. "As you know, I'm quite fond of your daughter."

"As she is of you," Eugene said.

"Really?" Micah asked. "What did she say?"

"Just that she's fond of you," Eugene said cryptically.

"Well, that's excellent," Micah said. "Because I've been considering courting her. Officially, I mean."

Eugene nodded. "Well, how can I help you, young man?"

Peter expected that this was when Micah would ask for Eugene's blessing. Instead, Micah peppered Eugene with questions about Dorothy. Can she cook? Fairly well. How is she with chores? Knowledgeable enough. Are her tastes expensive or cheap? Well, that depends, I suppose, on what you might consider expensive or cheap.

Peter's misgivings deepened as the conversation went on. Micah appeared far more concerned with Dorothy's suitability as a wife than his own suitability as a husband, a fact he seemed to take for granted—and worse, seemed to expect Eugene to take for granted.

"What kind of work do you do, Micah?" Peter asked.

Micah turned to him in shock, clearly not expecting Peter to question him. Peter met his gaze and was displeased to see Micah's own falter almost immediately.

"Well," the young man said, "I have some investments left me from my uncle. It's not the world's largest fortune, but it's a tidy sum. More than enough to support a woman of modest tastes."

"And when that sum runs out?" Peter said, "How do you make a living?"

Micah blinked. "Oh, well. I'm studying for business."

"What kind of business?"

"I...I'm not sure," Micah answered, reddening. "I suppose I'll figure that out soon enough. My father is a blacksmith of some skill. I could learn the trade from him. Or perhaps I could learn ranching from Mr. Flister. I'm not partial to sheep myself, but I imagine it's not much different from cattle."

"Do you have experience with cattle?"

"Well...no."

The four of them fell silent a moment. Then Greg asked, "What do you look for in a wife, Micah?"

Micah brightened immediately, grateful the conversation had turned away from his suitability. "Oh, well, she must be beautiful, of course," he said, "and Dorothy certainly is beautiful. She has a form that would make Venus herself blush with envy!"

Eugene narrowed his eyes slightly and Micah blushed himself, though Peter doubted it was envy that prompted it.

They finished dinner, and before Micah left, he turned expectantly to Eugene. "So? May I have your answer?"

"I'll give it to you in time," Eugene said evenly.

Micah blinked and seemed about to express offense, but a glance at Peter's stoic expression quelled whatever statement he wanted to make. He bowed stiffly and walked out.

Eugene waited until his hoofbeats faded, then said, "Well, what do you two think?"

Greg shifted uncomfortably. "Well, he seems nice enough. He seems to like Dorothy. I suppose there's no harm in allowing them to see each other."

"Do you think he'd make a good husband?" Eugene asked.

"Well," Greg said, keeping his eyes averted. "I think it's hard to tell from a first meeting."

Peter didn't feel comfortable being put in this position, but he felt less comfortable allowing someone as self-centered and immature as Micah clearly was to call on Dorothy. He cleared his throat and said, "I think he's a bad fit, Eugene."

Eugene turned to Peter. "Think so?"

"I think so," Peter said. "He acted as though it should be taken for granted that he's a good fit for Dorothy, and when I asked him about what he did for a living, he clearly hadn't given it any thought. He seems to expect that his uncle's fortune will sustain the two of them. He might be wealthy, but if he isn't hardworking, then Dorothy will have to be. Wealth without hard work doesn't last. Besides, I can't imagine Dorothy would be happy with a lazy man."

"So you think he's lazy," Eugene said.

"Lazy and altogether too self-important," Peter said. "I hope Dorothy doesn't like him too much."

"I don't think so," Eugene said. "She just likes being liked, I think. To tell you the truth, I didn't get the best impression from him either. Thank you for being honest with me, Peter. I know it's a mite uncomfortable, but I appreciate it."

He smiled at Peter, and Peter offered his own in return. He did feel uncomfortable, especially since Greg reddened with guilt at his own dishonesty, but he appreciated that he could offer Eugene valuable input.

His appreciation diminished when Eugene's grin turned mischievous and he said, "Say, since we're all being honest with each other, Greg, what would you want in a husband for Lydia?"

Greg grinned. "Well, I wouldn't mind someone tall and strong and hardworking, maybe a little awkward, but very honest."

Peter sighed and resigned himself to enduring continued teasing from his friends for the rest of the evening. It wouldn't bother him so much if he wasn't attracted to Lydia, but he was. He could no longer deny it. She was beautiful and strong and hardworking herself and possessed of a sharp mind that Peter considered at least as important as strength. She would make a fine wife...

Penelope's image invaded Peter's mind suddenly.He cleared his throat and changed the subject. "Eugene, would you mind helping me with some tips for the sale tomorrow? I want to make sure I present the ranch well."

"Sure," Eugene said. "What do you need help with?"

He asked Eugene questions but couldn't manage to focus on the answers. He couldn't shake the conflicting images of Penelope and Lydia from his mind.

Later that night, though, as he tried and failed once again to immerse himself in his book, it was Lydia's image that carried him to sleep.

Chapter Ten

Lydia stood and groaned, planting her hands on the small of her back and arching backwards. She and her mother had just finished scrubbing the floors in the parlor, and Lydia's back was screaming in protest.

"You're much too young to be complaining about back pain, dear," Mary said.

Lydia cast a wry glance at her mother. "I didn't realize pain was something that belonged only to the elderly. Besides, I'm not that young."

"You're not old," Mary countered.

"Well," Lydia said, "I appreciate you saying so."

"Don't you believe me?" Mary asked.

"I'm younger than you," Lydia said.

Mary looked frankly at her daughter. "I won't be so easily put off by your thin veneer of rudeness, dear. I'm worried about you."

"Worried about me?" Lydia said, "Whatever for?"

"Well," Mary replied, "You carry yourself like you have one foot in the grave already."

"For heaven's sake, mother, I only stretched. It's not like I'm limping to a rocking chair and reaching for my needles."

"Was that an insult to my knitting hobby?" Mary asked indignantly.

"I thought you weren't so easily put off, Mother," Lydia replied.

"I'm not," Mary insisted, "But I am put off by your refusal to address the issue."

"What issue?" Lydia asked. "I'm fine. I was just stretching. My back is sore, Mother, that's all."

"Yes, but you still behave as though your life has already passed you by."

Lydia sighed. "Mother, can we not have this argument again? I'm not bubbly like Dorothy. I've never been that way."

"Stop trying to distract me, dear, I'm your mother."

"Then stop trying to solve a problem that doesn't exist!" Lydia cried. She lowered her voice. "Mother, I understand that I have a lot of life ahead of me. If I seem preoccupied, it's only because I would like that life to be spent here and not in a poorhouse somewhere."

"Well, we're not in the poorhouse yet," Mary insisted. "Peter has sold fifty head of cattle. That will protect us from bankruptcy."

"No, Mother, it won't," Lydia said. "Not unless he makes another sale and probably three or four more after that."

"Well, it's a start," Mary said, "and we owe that start to you for finding Peter."

"Well, thank you," Lydia said. She wasn't sure what Peter or the sale had to do with her age, but she was grateful the conversation was no longer an argument over her happiness.

"Peter is an excellent man, isn't he?" Mary said.

Well, so much for that. "He's an excellent employee," Lydia agreed.

"And so strong and kind too. And handsome, don't you think?"

"All right," Lydia said, heading for her room. "I'm not having this conversation again."

"There's no need to rush off," Mary said, "Besides, I'm headed to nap anyway. I only bring this up because I care about you."

"And what does Peter have to say about this?" Lydia asked. "Does he know that you're not-so-secretly hoping the two of us marry?"

"Of course, dear," Mary said. "Your father has been steadily reminding him almost since he started here."

"Wonderful," Lydia said. "Maybe he should leave the poor man alone and you should leave your longsuffering daughter alone."

"That's exactly what I *don't* want to leave you," Mary said. "A life lived alone is no life at all."

"Thank you for that bit of wisdom," Lydia said, "now can that be the end of it?"

"For now," Mary said. "That's the best I can promise."

"I'll take it," Lydia said. "Enjoy your nap, Mother."

Mary sidled off to bed, and Lydia sighed. She really was exhausted after the day's chores, despite her mother's insistence that it was some kind of act designed to make herself seem old.

She decided to go over the books again. She had spent the past week poring over the numbers trying to see how much the ranch needed to make to avoid bankruptcy, but so far the only thing she was sure of was that Peter's sale, although helpful, wasn't enough by itself.

She sat on the porch and went through the numbers with a fine-toothed comb, but something still didn't add up. According to her calculations, they would have to sell the entire herd thrice over to avoid bankruptcy. She just couldn't believe it was that bad. If it was, then they might as well give up now.

Or she might as well agree to John's demands.

She couldn't do that.

She looked up and saw Peter carrying an armload of lumber to the stable. According to her father, it would be finished by the end of the week and they would move on to the barn.

She hesitated before calling him over, but she supposed this was a good question for a foreman. If worse came to worst, he would be unable to offer any new insight, but it was worth a try.

"Peter!" she called.

Peter stopped and turned toward her.

"When you're finished bringing that to the stable, would you mind helping me with something?"

"Of course, Miss Lydia."

Lydia smiled wryly at him as he resumed his journey for the stable. He still wouldn't call her Lydia. It was always Miss Lydia. Well, at least he wasn't calling her ma'am anymore. That was something.

She chuckled and shook her head. Her mother wanted him to marry the man, and he couldn't even use her first name without some sort of title beforehand.

He returned a few minutes later, holding his hat in his hand. She looked him up and down, and felt color come to her cheeks, as it often did when she saw him. He really was a fine figure of a man. She recalled the way his arms felt that afternoon a month ago when she had run into him on the road. It was a brief touch and could hardly be called an embrace, but she recalled the warmth that spread through her at the contact as though it happened yesterday. If circumstances were different...

But they weren't different. She had a ranch to run, and she needed Peter's help with the ranch, not with her heart.

"Are you any good with figures, Peter?" she asked.

"Fair," he said. "I used to help the purser with pay when I was with the Third Ohio."

"The Third Ohio?"

"In the Army."

"Oh, right," she said, "Well, I was hoping you could help me with the ranch's books."

His eyes widened a little. She remembered that earlier occasion a few weeks ago when he had come across her working on the books. At the time, she wasn't sure yet if she could trust him with their finances, but now she not only trusted him but very much hoped he could help her make sense of this.

"Of course, Lydia," he said.

It was a small thing, but she felt her cheeks warm when he used her first name without "Miss" in front of it.

She led him inside and sat on the couch. He hesitated a moment, then joined her. She was acutely aware of his closeness as she opened the ledger and set it in between them.

"I've been looking through the numbers trying to determine how much money we need to avoid foreclosure. It's...well, as nearly as I can see, it's impossible, but that doesn't make sense. According to these numbers, it's not possible for the ranch to make enough money to pay off our debt or even to pay off a portion of it. I can't believe that we're in such a terrible situation that there's not even a chance at success."

Peter nodded. "You're right. We're in a pickle barrel for sure, but not one we can't crawl out of."

Lydia smiled, partly because she found the pickle barrel analogy adorable and partly because she noticed that he said "we". He considered himself a part of the ranch as much as Lydia and her family were. That was good.

"May I?" he asked, reaching for the book.

"Of course," she said.

He picked up the book and looked through it carefully. While he was preoccupied with the ledger, Lydia studied his face. It wasn't youthful, but it wasn't aged either. The only lines were soft crinkles at the corners of his eyes, but his expression carried a weight far beyond his years. She was sure that his experiences in the war and the tragedy that befell his family were to blame.

She wanted more than anything to find a way to ease that burden. The strength of her desire was so powerful as to be nearly frightening. Was this what it was to fall in love with someone?

She dismissed that thought as ridiculous. Sure, she found him attractive. Any woman would acknowledge that. There was no emotional connection though, at least not a romantic one. She recalled Timothy's courtship in Baltimore, when her stomach filled with butterflies and she felt giddy and almost out of sorts in his presence.

Her stomach didn't flutter around Peter, and she didn't feel anything she could describe as giddiness. Rather, his presence imbued her with a peculiar sense of calm, as though as long as he were here, she was safe.

Maybe that was why her parents liked him so much for her. Heaven knows safety was something that seemed in short supply for them these days.

"I see what the issue is," Peter said, interrupting her thoughts. "May I show you?"

Lydia smiled. "Well, it won't be much use to me if you don't."

He reddened slightly, but a ghost of a smile played across his lips. Maybe there was a butterfly or two in her stomach after all.

"Here," he said, pointing to the bottom of the column where Lydia tallied the ranch's expenses. "This number is what you think you need to stay out of foreclosure, right?"

"That's right."

"Well, actually," he said, "That's the number you need to pay off your debt entirely. In fact, you only need to come up with ten percent of that number to avoid foreclosure."

"Really?" she said, eyes widening. "That's all?"

"That's all," he said, "Thirty percent would be better. That would take you out of default entirely, but ten percent will be enough to delay foreclosure by another three months."

"That's wonderful news!"

"It's not everything we need," Peter said. "Like I said, thirty percent would be better, but if we get one more sale before the Homestead Act expires, we'll have enough to make it until next season, and if these sales go well, we have a strong chance at attracting more business."

Lydia stared at the numbers, her heart pounding. Did she dare to hope? Could they actually be free of their debt? Could *she* be free of John?

She heard hoofbeats and looked up through the parlor window. Her blood ran cold when she saw the approaching wagon.

"Who's that?" Peter asked, frowning at the richly appointed coach. "Someone you know?"

"He's from the bank," Lydia said, not wanting to share more. "Will you wait for me inside, please?"

Peter frowned and seemed about to protest. "Please, Peter," Lydia said. "Please let me handle this."

He sighed, clearly unhappy with her request, but he nodded and said, "All right, Lydia."

She clasped his hand and said, "Thank you."

He laid his other hand on top of hers, and the brief contact allowed her to summon the strength she needed for the coming encounter. She stood, squared her shoulders and walked out to the porch just as the owner of the coach descended and approached her.

"Good afternoon, Miss Lydia," he said in his cultured voice. "It's lovely to see you, as always."

"Hello, John," Lydia replied. She didn't return the pleasantry. She didn't feel it.

Chapter Eleven

John walked to the front of the porch and smiled expectantly at Lydia. "Aren't you going to invite me inside?"

"No," Lydia said, "I've already told you you're not welcome here."

John's smile faded for a moment, and in that moment, Lydia could see the rage that boiled underneath. But he recovered quickly. "Now there's no need for rudeness. We're friends."

"We're not friends, John," Lydia said.

"No? You wound me, Lydia. After everything I've done for you and your family—"

"Everything you've done?" Lydia laughed bitterly. "John, you've done nothing but position yourself to profit on our foreclosure."

"That's not true, and you know it," he said. "If that were true, then I already would have—"

"You would have done nothing, John, because we're still protected under the Homestead Act. Am I to understand you're extending our grace period?"

John reddened when Lydia interrupted him, and Lydia felt a chill run up her spine. She thought of his previous wife, mysteriously lost the year before, and barely stifled a shiver.

"I've already told you that I will not only extend your grace period but pay off every cent of your debt," he said evenly. "I only ask for one thing in return."

"I've told you before," Lydia said. "I will not marry you."

"And why not?" John asked, the veneer of politeness cracking. "Am I not a suitable husband?"

"We've been over this, John," Lydia said, "I don't care to repeat myself."

John's smile disappeared entirely. "You're mighty arrogant for a woman on the verge of bankruptcy."

Heat crept up Lydia's neck. Her lips thinned, and it was only with great effort that she maintained her calm as she said, "For now, that's true, John."

"Well, unless you've miraculously come into money in the three months since we last spoke, I can't see how your circumstances have changed."

"Your blindness is not my problem, John," she said. "The answer is and shall always remain no."

"Listen to me, you little brat!" John hissed, stepping toward her. "Your ranch belongs to me. Your family belongs to me. You belong to me. You can hide behind your Homestead Act a while longer, but sooner or later, you'll have to accept it. You can either do that willingly and enjoy a pleasant marriage while your parents retire in comfort, or you and your parents can experience firsthand what happens to people who scorn me!"

Lydia felt a chill at his words. She knew full well what happened to people who scorned John Smith.

She also knew full well what happened to people who married John Smith.

She took a breath. "John, leave my property."

"*Your* property?" he shouted. "Ha! It's as good as mine already. And so are you."

He took another step toward her, and Lydia braced herself for his touch, but before he lifted his hand, she heard Peter say, "Miss Lydia asked you to leave, sir. I suggest you listen to her."

John's face paled. He took a step backward.

Lydia turned to see Peter standing next to her on the porch. His pose was relaxed, and his voice was calm, but there was a hardness in his eyes that she had never seen there before. He gazed steadily at John and the older man visibly shrank under his stare.

A moment later, John blinked, and, realizing what he had done, turned a shade of red so dark it was almost purple. His hands trembled impotently, but Lydia no longer felt afraid. Peter's presence was like the calm after a storm, and Lydia knew that it didn't matter how much John raged. He couldn't touch her with Peter at her side.

John laughed, a hoarse cackling sound that he no doubt intended to be intimidating but only sounded weak. "So this is your salvation? Some drifter you've taken in? He looks strong enough. He certainly is handsome. If only he could warm your wallet as well as your bed."

He sneered at Lydia, but his words had no effect on her anymore. "Are you finished, John?" she asked calmly.

He blinked and his eyes flickered in between Lydia and Peter. He offered another weak chuckle and said, "For now, Lydia. But I'll be back, and when I come back, it won't matter if your new man is here to save you or not."

He blinked again and his rage was masked once more by a polite smile. He bowed low, tipping his hat, and said, "Good day, Miss Lydia. Mr..."

Peter remained silent. A brief flash of rage crossed John's face, but it disappeared quickly, and with another tip of his hat, he spun around and returned to his coach. Once inside, his driver, who had spent the entire confrontation looking as though he desperately wished he were somewhere else, snapped the reins gratefully and drove away from the ranch.

Lydia waited until the coach turned onto the main road, then heaved a sigh. "I'm sorry you had to see that, Peter."

"Are you all right?" he asked.

Lydia didn't answer right away. She wasn't all right. Not by a long shot. John frightened her. She could pretend to be strong. She could pretend she wasn't affected by his threats, but at the end of it, she was on borrowed time, and she knew John well enough to know that he wouldn't rest until he got what he wanted...or made sure no one else could have it.

She nearly admitted her fear to Peter, but she felt suddenly embarrassed. She hated that John could affect her like this. She hated that her future was at the mercy of such a terrible man, and she was embarrassed that Peter, who had crossed the entire country to work for her, was now fully aware of the situation he had walked into.

"I'm all right," she said. She forced a smile and added, "I'm afraid John has a rather hard time taking no for an answer."

"You should file a complaint with the sheriff," Peter said.

Lydia laughed. Peter had no way of knowing how useless that idea was, but Lydia was well aware of how pointless it was to talk to Sheriff Ben Roberts about John's harassment. "I don't think that will solve anything, Peter," she said.

"He'll come back," Peter said.

Lydia blinked at the blunt statement. When she didn't respond right away, Peter said, "I'm sorry, Lydia, but I've met men like this before. He thinks he's got a right to your ranch and everything on it, including you. He'll still see it that way even if we do avoid bankruptcy and pay down the debt. He won't stop until he has you or he can't have you."

Lydia looked away and crossed her arms. "I don't mean to frighten you," Peter continued, "but we need to take steps to ensure he can't follow through on his threats."

She looked back to Peter. He was as calm as ever. No, calmer. He wasn't shuffling his feet or averting his gaze anymore. He was speaking confidently to her, not resorting to one-word responses and looking for the nearest way out of the conversation.

"You've grown mighty talkative lately," she said.

She didn't intend anything rude by the comment, but she was still shaken up by the encounter with John, and her voice came out harsh to her own ears. Peter apparently felt the same way, because he lowered his gaze and said, "I apologize, ma'am. I didn't mean to speak out of turn."

Lydia wondered how on Earth he could be more intimidated by her than by John. "There's no need to apologize," she said. "I guess...I guess I'm a little more worked up than I thought. But it's all right. He can shout at me until he's blue in the face. I'll never marry him."

Peter nodded, but he still didn't seem reassured. "Let's just forget about it," she said, "He can't do anything unless we go bankrupt, and from what you've told me, that's not at all a sure thing. Let's you and I both work on making sure we avoid bankruptcy, and that will take care of John."

She could see in Peter's face that he wasn't at all convinced that John would back off just because they avoided bankruptcy. In fact, he had explicitly stated as much only a moment ago. Lydia sighed and said, "Peter, please. Just...let's not talk about this."

"All right," Peter said. "Did you need anything else from me?"

"No," she said, "No, that's all right. You can go finish your work."

He nodded and tipped his hat. "Ma'am."

"Don't call me ma'am," she said, her voice once again much harsher than she intended.

She started to apologize, but that ghost of a smile crossed Peter's face again. "My apologies, Lydia. I'll see you at dinner."

He left the porch, leaving Lydia to wonder how she could have been so frightened only a few minutes ago only to feel completely safe a moment later. She stood on the porch for a long moment before it occurred to her that if Peter still saw her, she would cut a ridiculous figure standing there swooning like some kind of schoolgirl.

She needed some coffee.

She walked inside and started a kettle boiling. Her mother came into the kitchen a few minutes later and frowned. "Coffee? This late in the day?"

"Yes, Mother, this late in the day. Would you like some?"

Mary stared at Lydia a moment. "Why, Lydia, you look pale. Is everything all right?"

"Fine, Mother. I'm just tired. Hence the coffee."

Mary stared a moment longer. Lydia turned to her and put a hand on her hip. "Is that all, Mother?"

Mary smiled. "You're cranky today. Maybe you are getting old."

Lydia rolled her eyes and pointed at the kettle. "The cure for crankiness is brewing as we speak. Again, would you like some?"

Mary considered a moment. "Actually, I will take some. Just don't tell your father."

Lydia couldn't imagine what on Earth would be wrong with her father learning that Mother had a cup of coffee in the afternoon, but she decided not to ask.

At dinner, her father said, "I saw that John came by today."

Lydia glanced sharply at Peter, who shook his head slightly. She turned to her father and said, "Yes. How did you know that?"

"I just told you," he said, "I saw him pull up. Sorry I didn't come over to talk with you, but I was busy with the horses. Shoeing day."

He kept his eyes off of Lydia's when he said that. She glanced again at Peter, but Peter didn't meet her eyes either. Her lips thinned slightly, but she said, "Don't worry about it. He only stopped by to talk."

"How did he seem?" Greg asked.

Lydia hesitated a moment. "Fine," she said finally. "He asked about the ranch. I told him we'd hired Peter and made a sale."

"What did he say?" Greg asked anxiously.

Lydia chose her words carefully. "He expressed hope that we would find a way to avoid foreclosure."

"Ah," Greg said, "That's good."

They fell silent. Mary sipped her tea. Greg ate his food. Peter frowned. Lydia focused on her own meal. No one met each other's eyes.

No one spoke again until Peter stood and said, "Thank you for dinner, Lydia. It was delicious as always."

"You're welcome, Peter," she said.

He headed for the door, and Lydia asked, "You're not staying for dessert?"

He hesitated a moment, then said, "I think I'll turn in early tonight. I'm a little more tired than usual after today."

"Oh," Lydia said. "That's fine. I'll see you tomorrow."

"See you tomorrow, Lydia."

He said goodnight to her parents, then walked out the door. When he left, Lydia felt the tension in the room rise. Her parents continued to avoid eye contact with her and with each other.

Finally, Lydia had enough. She stood and said, "You know what, I'm tired too. I think I'll go to bed early as well."

"Sure," Greg said, "Good night, sweetheart."

"Good night, dear," Mary echoed.

Lydia returned the sentiment, then headed to her room. She changed into her night clothes and lay down on her bed, but it would be a long time before sleep came for her that evening.

While she waited for sleep, she thought of Peter standing strong and tall next to her on the porch. He was like a rock in the middle of a storm. She recalled how safe she had felt, how protected.

She held onto that feeling and finally, her eyes closed and she was able to rest.

Chapter Twelve

For the first time since arriving on the ranch, Peter found it difficult to concentrate on his work. He was carving the last of the rails for the stalls, but after an entire morning of work, he had finished maybe a dozen rails.

He couldn't stop recounting the encounter with John in his head. He wasn't exactly sure who John was. He guessed a banker or else a wealthy landowner. Maybe both. Whoever he was, he was clearly obsessed with Lydia. In his sick mind, he might believe he was in love with her, but it wasn't love in his gaze, only desire. Pure, glittering desire.

He had seen that look before. When he returned home from the war to find everyone he loved gone, he had started taking odd jobs around town, drowning himself with work to keep from going mad from grief. One day, while sweeping up at a saloon that hired him to clean, he heard a voice ask, "Do you want to spend the rest of your days as a washerwoman, or do you want to live like a king?"

Peter had looked up to see eyes that glittered with the same madness he saw in John's eyes. That was how he met Sean O'Malley, leader of the O'Malley gang and Peter's off-and-on employer for the next year.

Peter knew what Sean was the moment he saw him, but at the time, he didn't much care. If Sean killed him or he died in a confrontation with the law, so be it. He spent most of his nights staring at his revolver and wondering what would happen if he bit down on it and pulled the trigger anyway, so it didn't faze him that he was working for an outlaw gang.

Soon enough, though, he learned that the look on Sean's face wasn't reserved only for gold. He saw everything he wanted as his God-given right and would fly into a terrible rage if he was denied anything at all. Peter had never been the object of his wrath, but he had seen others suffer it.

John was much the same as O'Malley: convinced that whatever he saw and wanted was his. Lydia believed that if they fixed the ranch's finances, they would be safe, but one look at John told Peter that wasn't the case. It didn't matter if the ranch was bankrupt or wealthy beyond belief. John wanted it, and he wouldn't rest until he had it.

It wasn't just the ranch he wanted though, and that was why Peter had trouble concentrating. He wanted Lydia. Lydia knew that he wanted her, and she knew how dangerous it would be for him to get what he wanted, but she didn't understand how relentless he would be in his pursuit.

Men like that didn't stop unless they were stopped.

"Peter?"

Peter looked up from his work and saw Lydia approaching. "Morning, Lydia," he said.

She smiled, and Peter felt warmth spread from head to toe. It bothered him how easily she could affect him this way, but at the same time, he looked forward to these moments of sunlight that broke for a moment the clouds that filled his mind.

"What are you working on?" she asked.

"The rails for the stalls," he said, "I was hoping to have the stable finished in a day or two and start working on the barn. I'm a little behind, I suppose."

"Would you like some help?"

"Oh, that's all right," he said, "you don't need to trouble yourself, ma'am."

"What have I told you about calling me ma'am?" she said, folding her arms.

"Yes," he said, "I apologize. Um...Thank you, Lydia, I appreciate the help."

"Better," she said, smiling again. "What can I do?"

"Could you hold this steady?" he said, lifting one of the planks.

Lydia grabbed the length of pine and held it while Peter sawed. "I can't believe you've gotten so much done already," Lydia said.

"I was a carpenter by trade," he said, "or I would've been if the war hadn't happened. My father was a cabinetmaker in Columbus. He taught me a lot about woodworking."

He set the length of pine down with the others and lifted another plank. Lydia set down her own length and held the new plank.

"Did you do any carpentry during the war?" she asked.

"No, not much," he said, "just field repairs now and then. I was assigned to an infantry regiment, but we would rarely move without artillery and supply trains, so me and the others with backgrounds in woodworking and metalworking would help out whenever a wagon or a field gun split an axle."

He finished this plank and moved on to the next one. Lydia set her length down and said, "I'm surprised they didn't want to keep you where your skills were best suited to the war effort."

A series of vivid images flashed through Peter's mind. It just wasn't his carpentry the army valued most, and they had placed him exactly where his skills were best suited to the

118

war effort. He recalled the long days of cold and wet lying in wait for rebel supply wagons and scouting troops, his face covered in mud, his knife at the ready in one hand, his revolver in the other.

"Peter?"

He blinked and breathed in sharply.

"Are you all right?" Lydia asked.

He looked down and saw his knuckles turning white around the handle of the saw, which remained still atop the plank. He began to saw again and said, "Fine. Just a little tired."

"Well, let's take a break," she said. "You've been working hard. It's fine to rest a moment."

Peter wasn't even close to tired, and he didn't really want to take a break, but he couldn't tell Lydia the real reason for his pause, so he set the saw down, nodded curtly, and said, "Thank you."

They leaned against the wall and Peter was acutely aware of her closeness. He could reach over and put his arm around her if he could. He looked at her, and she smiled at him. Once more, the darkness in his mind dissipated as warmth filled him. Her lips were soft and full and inviting, and Peter felt his resolve slipping.

"Hey there, Pete, Lydia" Greg said, pulling Peter from his thoughts. "How's work going?"

Peter didn't care to be called Pete, but he didn't feel like pointing it out to Greg at the moment. "To tell the truth, I'm a little out of sorts today," he said. "Guess I must finally be gettin' tired."

"That so? Well, I don't blame you. You've been doing the work of ten men, wouldn't you agree, Lydia?"

"He's been working hard," Lydia agreed.

"Yes, I can tell," Greg said. He shuffled his feet and glanced at Peter.

Lydia smiled tolerantly at her father and turned to Peter. "Well, I should get started on the garden. I'll see you tonight, Peter."

"See you tonight, Lydia."

Greg waited until Lydia was out of earshot, then said, "Are you sure everything's all right, Peter? You look worried."

"Everything's fine," Peter said. "I just wanted to be a little bit farther along with the stable."

He didn't mention the real reason for his preoccupation. From what he saw at dinner the night before, none of the Gutenbergs wanted to acknowledge the danger John presented. Peter had his own feelings about that, but he didn't see how it could be helpful to argue with them over it.

"Well," Greg said, shuffling his feet. "I guess I better wait to ask you to break a horse for me then."

"No, sir," Peter said. "I can break a horse if that's what you need. I work for you. If you need something, I'll get it done."

Greg smiled slightly at him. "Peter, you're not just an employee. You're family. Maybe you don't see it that way yet, but it's true all the same."

Peter marveled that the man could vacillate so wildly between strength and timidity. It was as though there were two different Greg Gutenbergs and only chance would decide which Greg appeared at any given moment. "Well, thank you, Greg," he said, "All the same, I can break the horse for you."

"You have experience breaking horses?" Greg asked.

"No, but Eugene showed me a thing or two, and you've seen me wrestle steers. I figure I can tire him out and work my way forward from there."

Greg nodded. "That sounds like a plan. All right. He's in the pen. The dun horse–between the stamping and the squealing, you're not likely to miss him."

Peter glanced at the pen and quickly identified the horse. "All right," he said, "I'll take care of it."

"Thank you kindly," Greg said. He hesitated a moment, as though he were about to say something else, then seemed to think better of it. "I'm going to head inside for lunch. I'll see you later."

"See you later, Greg."

Greg left for the house and Peter headed for the pen. The stallion proved far easier to manage than Peter expected, probably because he was barely over two years, still strong but not stubborn the way an older horse would be.

Peter started by following him around the pen, keeping a safe distance but not backing any further away when the stallion reared and challenged him. When the colt was used to his presence, Peter approached more closely until eventually, he laid a hand on the animal.

For the next twenty minutes, Peter backed off as the colt reared and bucked, then approached again. When the animal had tired himself out enough, Peter leapt onto his back.

The colt reared and bucked, but it was already exhausted from the past hour and quickly gave in and allowed Peter to

121

remain on its back unmolested. Peter sat atop him for five minutes or so, then decided that was enough for today. He dismounted and patted the horse's cheek. "All right, boy," he said. "Go ahead and get some food and water. You've earned it."

The horse walked slowly to the trough at one end of the pen and drank deeply. Peter wiped sweat from his brow and headed back to the stable. The exertion had calmed him, and he thought he might be able to finish the rails after all.

When he approached the stable, however, he was distracted once more by Lydia. She worked in the garden on the side of the house, and she was absolutely beautiful. Peter could no longer deny that fact to himself. Rather, he could no longer deny that her beauty affected him. She looked like an angel. Her dark hair shimmered in the sunlight, and as she stooped to harvest carrots for tonight's dinner, her dress clung to her skin, revealing the curve of her hips and the gentle swell of her breasts.

She looked up and caught his eye and he turned quickly away, face flaming. He couldn't believe himself. He was a man, not a lovestruck boy. He should have more self-control than to gawk at his employer like that.

He thought of the way John looked at her. Once more, he found himself too distracted to work. He sighed and was about to head for his cabin when he heard footsteps approach.

He turned and saw Mary walking up to him, a basket in her hand. "Hello, Peter. Do you mind if I join you for lunch?"

"Not at all," he said. "Thank you."

"For the food or the company?" she asked.

Her smile was just the slightest touch mischievous, and Peter could see the family resemblance between her and Lydia. He returned a smile of his own and said, "Both."

Mary regarded him and said, "A smile looks good on you, Peter. I'm happy to see it."

He flushed slightly. "Thank you, Mary."

Mary set the basket down and retrieved two sandwiches with beef and cheese. She handed one to Peter and he bit into it gratefully. He hadn't realized until now how hungry he was.

Mary started on her own sandwich, but after a moment nodded over at the garden. "Lydia's really thankful for the way you stood up to John for her. I am too."

Peter looked toward Lydia, who was now pulling weeds. He recalled dinner the night before and said, "Forgive me for saying so, Mary, but the three of you seem mighty reluctant to face this situation."

Mary didn't respond right away. After a moment, Peter said, "I'm sorry. It's not my place."

"No, don't apologize," Mary said. "It is your place. I'm sorry we've kept you in the dark for so long." She sighed and said, "Well, you probably know by now that John has intentions toward Lydia."

"Yes," Peter said. "He was very clear on that subject yesterday."

Mary nodded. "I'm guessing he wasn't as polite as Lydia indicated at dinner."

"No ma'am," Peter said, "I don't mean to frighten you, but he was very confrontational."

Mary sighed. "I was afraid so."

"May I ask why you three haven't tried to put a stop to his behavior once and for all? Maybe reported him to the sheriff?"

Mary smiled sadly. "I'm afraid that the sheriff is intimidated by him. John is very wealthy and very well-connected."

Peter thought of the crazed lust in his eyes. In a man with relatively little power, that desire was dangerous. In a man with the kind of power Mary described, it was destructive.

"Ma'am," he said, "I'm worried that if we don't take steps to prevent John from acting against us that his behavior will grow more and more aggressive."

"Yes," Mary said, "I believe you're right."

Peter felt frustration grow and fought to keep calm. "Mary, I'm worried about Lydia. He intends to marry her, and he seems like just about the worst husband I could imagine."

Mary nodded. "I know. I'm worried too, Peter. I know I don't show it well. That's a family trait that Greg and I both unfortunately passed to Lydia. We're very good at keeping our head up and our shoulders square, but we're not always good at facing the right direction when we do."

Peter didn't reply. He understood that feeling very well.

"I told you that we had a son named Peter, right?" Mary asked after a moment.

"You did," Peter said. "I'm sorry for your loss."

"Thank you," Mary said. She sighed and added, "Well, I haven't told you that Lydia blames herself for his death."

Peter looked at her in surprise. "She blames herself? Why on Earth would she do that?"

"Well," she replied, "she took him to play in the pond behind our house one morning. Unfortunately, that morning happened to be in late fall. Peter caught a fever, and since he caught it just before winter, his fever never got better."

"Oh," Peter said, understanding, "and Lydia blames herself because she took him out to swim in the cold."

"Yes," Mary said.

"Well that isn't her fault," Peter said. "Why would she blame herself for that?"

"Because Lydia, like her father, believes herself responsible for everything that happens to the people she loves. Unlike her father, she also believes she should be infallible. She can't accept that her mistake was innocent and that she bears no blame for Peter's death. The way she sees it, she took him to the pond, so she is guilty."

She fell silent a moment, then said, "I'm afraid Greg and I haven't done much to help her with that. We...we moved here to escape Peter's memory."

She let the words hang in the air a moment. Peter said nothing. He had no idea what to say. He knew perfectly well that nothing he said could ease her pain.

"It's hard," she said. "To live in the same house your dead son once lived. To walk past his room and not hear his voice. To eat at the table and see his place empty. To work in the garden and not have anyone to scold for tramping little feet through your onions."

Tears welled in her eyes, and she said, "We couldn't do it anymore. Greg left his job as a clerk and went west under the Homestead Act. We told Lydia that we were seeking opportunity, but we weren't. We just couldn't live with his ghost anymore. Do you understand?"

125

"Yes," Peter said and meant it. "I do."

"Well," Mary said, "Lydia knows, but she doesn't understand. In her mind, this ranch is her responsibility because in her mind, our grief is her fault. She can't accept that this ranch will fail because she can't abide our suffering through her neglect. She suffers too, of course, and of course she isn't guilty of neglect, but she'll never believe that."

Mary looked at Peter and said, "I'm telling you this because if we don't find a way to save this place in time, Lydia will marry John Smith."

Her words hit Peter like a sledgehammer. He stared numbly at Mary and the older woman continued. "She will marry him knowing full well who he is and what he's capable of. I'm so sorry to ask this of you, Peter. You had no idea what you were getting into when you came here. But please. Please don't let her marry him. Do whatever you have to do to stop that. Anything."

Peter thought of his revolver, safely hidden in the closet of his cabin. He wondered if Mary knew of it and thought of it as well.

He hoped it wouldn't come to that. He hated that weapon with a passion so intense it was almost nauseating.

But when he answered Mary, there was no hint of dishonesty in his voice or his thoughts.

"I will," he promised. "I will make sure that John never lays a finger on your daughter. You have my word."

Mary sighed. Then she smiled. "Thank you, Peter. You're a good man."

Peter nodded politely, but he couldn't manage a smile. He wasn't a good man.

And if he had to be a bad man to keep Lydia safe, he would be.

Chapter Thirteen

Lydia smiled as she saw Dorothy approaching the house. Her friend waved exuberantly at her, and Lydia laughed. Her thoughts had been dark since John's visit two days ago, and she found she looked forward to this visit even more than she usually did.

Dorothy burst through the door and rushed to Lydia, carrying a basket in front of her. "Lydia!" she cried. "I know we're making cornbread for your brother's birthday tomorrow, and I know you swore you wouldn't eat anything sweet until then, but I made some of the queen cakes using the recipe you gave me, and oh goodness, you just have to try them!"

Lydia smiled and decided not to explain to Dorothy that— the recipe being hers—she knew exactly what they tasted like. Instead, she tasted one and allowed her eyes to widen in surprise. "Wow," she said, "That's good."

"Isn't it?" Dorothy said. "It's a good thing too. I've had the most horrible day."

She slumped dramatically down onto the couch and Lydia stifled a laugh as she sat across from her on one of the upholstered chairs. "I'm so sorry to hear that, Dorothy," she said. "What happened?"

"My father ruined my courtship with Micah!"

Lydia's brow furrowed. "Courtship? Ruined it? How? "

"Yes!" Dorothy said. "You know Micah Porter from town?"

"Yes," Lydia said, "I believe so. He's that—" She caught herself just before saying *dandy*. " That well-dressed boy whose grandfather is a merchant."

"His uncle," Dorothy corrected. "Yes, that's him. He was going to court me! He was going to ask Father for permission, and he did, and that horrible old man denied it! He told him to stay away and that I wasn't interested in a courtship with him. Imagine him thinking he can speak for me!"

Lydia thought of her brief interactions with Micah. She didn't say it out loud, but she agreed with Eugene. She wondered how she could explain that without hurting Dorothy's feelings.

"Well, maybe it's for the best. Did you really love Micah?"

"Well..." Dorothy said. She shrugged and finished with, "I might have loved him given enough time."

"Well, there you go. If you were really in love with him, you'd know without a doubt."

Peter's slight half-smile flashed vividly in Lydia's mind as she said this, and she continued quickly to drive the image away. "Besides, he's rather...well...is it rude of me to say callow?"

Dorothy chuckled. "Terribly rude," she said. "But terribly true." She sighed. "I suppose he wasn't necessarily the best choice for me for husband, but that doesn't mean he couldn't have courted me!"

Lydia smiled wryly at her friend. "Are you upset because you miss Micah or because you miss the picnics and love letters and being treated like a princess?"

Dorothy blushed. "Why do you say it like those are all bad things?"

Lydia rolled her eyes and Dorothy giggled. "Oh, whatever," she said. "So I like being showered with attention. I'm hardly the only woman who feels that way. And anyway, don't I have the right to decide who courts me?"

"Of course you do," Lydia said, "but think rationally about it. Micah's a...a very handsome boy." Lydia struggled to keep a straight face as she said this. Micah looked...well, he looked soft, and Lydia, for one, couldn't feel any kind of attraction to someone who looked like he'd never worked a day in his life. "But is he really someone you can imagine spending your life with?"

Dorothy pouted. "Well, no, but...it just feels so nice to imagine someone fawning over me and showering me with attention. Doesn't every girl want to feel like a princess, even for a little while?"

"Well, sure," Lydia said, "but wouldn't you rather feel that way receiving attention from a prince?"

"You know, if he were a prince, he'd probably be even softer than he is now," Dorothy said, "He'd have servants to do everything for him, and I'd have servants to do everything for me!"

Dorothy stood and flitted about with her nose pointed in the air. "I would be Princess Dorothy Flister, heir to the throne of Stevensville!"

"How wonderful for you," Lydia said, a patient smile on her face.

"You could be my chambermaid," Dorothy said. "I'd find you a lovely, strong man for your husband, maybe a tall, dark-haired, hardworking man who could serve as keeper of the royal stables. You know, a mysterious former soldier who—"

"Don't start with that," Lydia said, rolling her eyes. "We're talking about you, remember?"

"Well, we might as well talk about you," Dorothy said, "since my father and your own handsome prince seem bent on denying me my own chance at romance."

Lydia raised her eyebrow. "Peter objected as well?"

"He did," Dorothy confirmed. "He was the one who told my father that Micah was likely a stranger to hard work and hoping to live off of the income our ranch generates rather than earn his own way in the world. He even dared to suggest that most of his attraction to me was attraction to my money! Can you imagine that?"

Actually, Lydia could. She didn't want to tell Dorothy that, though. "I'm sure Micah was very enamored with you. Who wouldn't be?"

Dorothy rolled her eyes but smiled. "Well, thank you very much for that, Lydia." She sighed and sat back on the sofa. "I suppose you're all right about Micah. I mean, when I look past the feeling of being admired, I have to admit he's more of a boy than a man. I just hate feeling like my life is for others to decide and not me."

Lydia thought of her sudden departure from Baltimore and move to Montana. When she said, "I know what you mean," she meant it.

"Haven't you ever felt like this?" Dorothy said. "Not necessarily in love with a man, but in love with...I guess with being in love?"

Lydia thought of Timothy and smiled wistfully. Timothy, like Micah, hadn't been the manliest of men by any means. He was a banker and one of only modest success at the time he courted Lydia. Still, he showered Lydia with attention, calling her Milady and fawning over her like she was some fragile treasure to be protected and worshiped. He wasn't quite so self-centered or childish as Micah was, but looking back on his courtship with the experience of the past five years behind her, Lydia had to admit she wouldn't feel the same attraction to him now that she did then.

Still, it did feel wonderful to experience that first blush of love. "Yes," she said to Dorothy. "I remember it."

Dorothy's eyes widened. "Really? Have you been in love before, then?"

"I thought I was in love," Lydia said, "I suppose in that way, I was even more...fanciful...than you are over Micah."

Dorothy leaned forward on the couch, the prospect of a tantalizing tale of her friend's love life far more important than lamenting over her own. "Who was he?"

Lydia sighed, a touch wistfully. "His name was Timothy van Buren."

"Ooh, another Prussian!" Dorothy said, eyes twinkling.

"Dutch, actually," Lydia corrected. "Although like me, his family had migrated to America since before the War of Independence. Anyway, he was very handsome. He had the most enchanting green eyes and a soft, mellow voice that left butterflies in my stomach every time he spoke to me."

Dorothy gazed at Lydia in rapture, drinking in the story of Lydia's lost love with the rapture of a child listening to a fairy tale. Lydia blushed a little, finding she enjoyed a chance to be the romantic one for once.

"He met me at church one Sunday and introduced himself to my parents the same day. Well, he knew Father from the bank, since Father was a clerk at the same branch where he worked, but he formally introduced himself to them and asked permission to call on me.

"And just like you, I felt like the most important thing in his world. He would bring me flowers and chocolates and write me poems—"

"He wrote you *poems?*" Dorothy cried. She swooned, blushing and saying, "Oh, Lydia, how wonderful!"

Lydia laughed. "Well, it certainly seemed so at the time, but if I'm being honest, they weren't...Frankly, they were terrible."

"Lydia!" Dorothy giggled. "Were they really that bad?"

Lydia smiled ruefully. "Let's just say that even in the throes of my infatuation, I thought to myself that he would be better off leaving the arts behind and focusing on finance. I never told him that, of course. He had a terribly fragile ego. I think that's why I didn't miss him so much when we moved."

"I was going to ask," Dorothy said, "how the two of you reacted to that move."

"Well," Lydia said, "I won't exactly say we were happy about it. He had courted me for nearly a year by that point, and while the first blush of attraction was gone between us, we both anticipated a perfectly content marriage. When my family decided to move out here, I told him and offered him the chance to part on amicable terms. I gave him the option of asking me to remain with him as his wife, but to tell the truth, even though I was unhappy about my prospects of marriage being taken away, a part of me was relieved when he declined."

"My goodness, you sound so mature," Dorothy said. "You really didn't mind losing your chance at marriage?"

"Not entirely," Lydia said. "I didn't realize until very recently that I would be happier without Timothy than I would have been with him."

Dorothy grinned mischievously. "Did this realization possibly coincide with the arrival of a certain tall, dark and handsome stranger?"

Lydia sighed and reddened, partly because she was annoyed by everyone's constant attempts to insinuate a romantic connection between her and Peter, but mostly because she suspected Dorothy was right. Peter's arrival had, in fact, quelled the last of her romantic feelings for Timothy.

She wasn't about to admit that to Dorothy, however. "I just grew older," she said, "and realized that if I had stayed with him, I would be unhappy. He and I weren't compatible. I just liked feeling like a princess, and at twenty-five, I was already rather old for marriage..."

"Oh, don't say that!" Dorothy cried. "I'm only a few years behind you!"

"Right," Lydia said, smiling wryly and thinking about the difference in maturity and life experience between twenty-one and twenty-five. Then again, she had been just as enamored with Timothy as Dorothy was with Micah, so who was she to judge?

"My point," she continued, "Is that what we think we want when we're young is often not what we really want or what we need."

"No wonder you're still single," Dorothy said, shaking her head. "I pity the poor man who has to convince you he's worthy of your attention."

"What can I say?" Lydia replied. "I have high expectations for a husband, should I ever find one."

"I don't know," Dorothy said, "I feel like he'd have to be a tall, dark-haired soldier who traveled all the way from Ohio to fix your ranch and—"

"All right, *Dotty*," Lydia said, a slight smile hiding real exasperation.

Dorothy gasped and covered her mouth with her hand. "Oh, you horrible friend!" she exclaimed. "You know how I hate that nickname!"

"Well, maybe you'll finally stop bringing up the idea of a marriage between me and my foreman."

"Ah, I see," Dorothy said, nodding knowingly and adopting the mischievous grin again. "You prefer your men to kneel at your feet rather than stand at your side."

"I do not! And don't you have dinner to make?" Lydia said, reddening.

"I do, actually," Dorothy said, standing up, "and that's the only reason I'm leaving right now. I'm not letting go of you and Peter, though. Micah may not be right for me, but I'll bet everything I own that Peter is right for you."

Lydia rolled her eyes and dismissed her friend's claim, but when Dorothy left, she thought seriously about what Dorothy had said. The fact was that she was attracted to Peter. It wasn't the flighty, giggly, fluttering feeling she had for Timothy, but when she thought about a man to stand at her side for the rest of her life, she thought of someone almost exactly like Peter: someone quiet, strong, hardworking and maybe a little stubborn. Someone who could be happy with a nice, quiet life on a nice, quiet homestead and not feel the need for wealth or notoriety. Someone who was romantic and emotional, but who left those emotions in their proper place.

She thought of the first night she visited Peter at his cabin. She wondered if he had finished *Robinson Crusoe* yet.

She should get him a new book. She had several in her room that she felt he might enjoy. In particular, *Great*

135

Expectations seemed something he would enjoy. He seemed like a fellow who would appreciate Dickens.

She headed upstairs to get the book, and it wasn't until she returned downstairs that she realized her memories of Timothy had disappeared as quickly as they came.

Chapter Fourteen

Lydia wondered if she should wrap the book in something before she brought it to Peter. Should she bring it now or wait until evening when Peter was at home? Then again, if she did, would he see that as an attempt to court him? She really didn't want that. Whatever her attraction to him, she was in no place to consider marriage. Not with her family's future on the line, to say nothing of John's lurking presence.

She sighed and shook her head. She was being foolish. If he was going to take her gift the wrong way, he would take it that way whether he received it face-to-face or came home tonight to find it.

She finally decided to just take it to his cabin. That would at least avoid any awkwardness between them. She took the book and walked to the cabin, looking around for any sign of him. She couldn't see him from where she walked. He was probably working in the stable or the barn somewhere.

She reached the cabin and knocked on the door, just in case. When he didn't answer, she left the book on the porch and turned to leave.

She took three steps and stopped, turning halfway back toward the cabin.

He was so quiet, so private. She barely knew anything about him. She knew he was from Columbus, Ohio and had fought for the Union Army in the war. She knew that his family had died tragically, but she'd learned that from her mother, not Peter himself.

He was so closed off. She no longer mistrusted his intentions because of that, but he was a part of their family now, at least a part of their ranch. She wanted to know more about him. Didn't she have a right to know a little bit about her foreman's past?

Her conscience piped up then, stating loudly and clearly that she absolutely did *not* have the right to know about his past. He had proven himself nothing but honest and hardworking here, and she had no justification for prying into his private life.

She was curious, though. She wanted to know about him. She didn't know why, but the mystery of Peter Kerouac fascinated her as no mystery ever had before.

There was something behind that gruff, solemn exterior. She had seen glimpses of it, like the gratitude in his eyes when she had brought him dessert that one night a few weeks ago, or that ghost of a mirthful smile that crossed his lips when she scolded him for calling her ma'am. She was desperate to see that man come out, and since Peter showed no sign of allowing it, she might as well see what she could learn on her own. What he didn't know wouldn't hurt him, and besides, what harm could a brief look around the cabin do?

So, ignoring her better judgment, she opened the door and walked inside, carrying the book with her. She hesitated and realized she should at least leave a note with the book. He would know it didn't belong to him and know that it must be from Lydia. She should at least have some kind of justification for being in his cabin.

She found a quill and an inkwell on Peter's table and wrote on the inside of the book's cover, *From Lydia. For your next adventure.*

She looked at the note and reddened. It was a foolish note. What did that mean, anyway, *for your next adventure?* Lydia intended it to mean his next imaginary adventure, something he could immerse himself in when he was finished with *Robinson Crusoe*, but when she read it again, it just seemed silly and foolish. Romantic, even.

Well, it was too late now. She left the book on the table and looked around. The cabin was small and sparse, barely larger than her own bedroom. There was a bunk with a canvas sack filled with straw for a mattress and a blanket Lydia recognized as belonging to her mother. Probably she had given it to him when she found him washing his clothes in the stream a while back.

There was an extra pair of clothing hanging in the closet, a wooden chair for the table, and *Robinson Crusoe*, lying face-down and open on the bed. So he hadn't finished it yet. Or he was reading it again. Oh well, he would appreciate something to start on after he did finish.

There was a handgun in the closet, tucked carefully away in the corner of a high shelf where it wasn't visible from the rest of the cabin. Lydia left it where it was. She thought of the war and felt a rush of sympathy for Peter.

They had been blessed to avoid direct fighting in Baltimore, but Lydia recalled the aftermath of the fighting along Antietam Creek. She and many other young women were pressed into service as temporary nurses for the Union soldiers who were transported to Baltimore for medical care.

The men all wore blank, vacant stares. They rarely seemed to see what was in front of them, but their eyes were all filled with visions that Lydia knew were too horrible to speak of. Most of the men she treated were missing limbs or eyes or else had horrific wounds that would leave scars the rest of their lives.

Peter didn't have any physical scars, at least none that Lydia could see, but she knew that the mental scars such fighting left behind were often as damaging as the physical scars. That could explain why he was so closed-off and solemn most of the time.

It also explained why he kept his weapon but chose not to wear it or even look at it most of the time. If Peter were as gentle and kindhearted as Lydia suspected he was, then the things he would have had to do with that weapon probably scarred him far worse than anything else he might have suffered.

There was nothing else to be seen, and Lydia decided she had wasted her time. She felt a flush of guilt as she reconsidered how rude it was for her to walk into Peter's home uninvited. If he had walked into her room like this, she would have been very upset.

She shook her head and started for the door, but stopped when she saw another book. It lay half-hidden under the blanket and couldn't be seen from the front of the cabin. So he had books besides *Robinson Crusoe* after all.

She picked up the book, telling herself she simply wanted to be sure it wasn't *Great Expectations* so she didn't accidentally give him a copy of a book he had already read. Her conscience, however, wasted no time pointing out that she was only making excuses. The real reason was to satisfy her own curiosity.

She picked up the book and frowned when she saw there was no title. She opened it and realized it wasn't a book after all, but a journal. Peter's private journal.

She quickly closed the book and set it down. She had invaded his privacy enough. She wouldn't read his most private thoughts like that. She wouldn't.

She opened the door but stopped. Her conscience screamed at her to leave, but her curiosity screamed a little louder. After glancing around to make sure she wasn't being watched, she slowly closed the door and turned around.

She picked up the journal and began to leaf through it, guilt and curiosity warring in her mind.

The first entry was dated June 12th of that year. He had started the journal recently. It was short and to the point, like Peter's speech. He mentioned that the journal was a gift from Pastor Blake and that he still hadn't received a response from the ranch in Montana and thought it likely that they had filled the position already. Lydia smiled at that. By that time, her acceptance was weeks old, though for some reason it hadn't yet reached Columbus.

She flipped through the other entries. The next one was June 21st, and was mostly a discussion about how he would make his way to Montana now that he was accepted. The next few were on his journey and detailed the odd jobs he took to earn his way further west. So that was what had taken him so long. Lydia almost felt guilty for her own concerns with money, considering that Peter had only just managed to pay for his trip west by working his way to them.

She nearly put the journal down but came across an entry dated August 7th. Yesterday. She began to read, and when she did, her heart began to pound in her chest.

The prose in this entry was flowery and beautiful, very unlike the previous entries. He wrote at length of a woman with angelic features, a beautiful smile and a graceful figure the image of which alone was enough to keep him warm at night.

She blushed red at this. Could he be talking about her? It must be her. There was no one else it could be about. The only other women he knew were Mary and Dorothy, and he couldn't very well be talking about her mother. Dorothy was beautiful, but she showed no romantic interest in Peter, at least not romantic interest between *herself* and Peter. Besides, the few occasions Peter and Dorothy had interacted, he spoke to her as though he saw her as barely more than a child–which, Lydia admitted with a touch of guilt, was pretty similar to her own thoughts of Dorothy.

Maybe someone in town...but no, he had only been in town briefly and always on ranch business. He had never spent enough time in town to be courting anyone there, and even as private as he was, she couldn't imagine she would know nothing of his romantic interests if he had one.

Unless, of course, he felt that romantic interest was out of his reach. His boss, for example.

She continued to read, and as she read, her heartbeat quickened and her flush deepened. He wrote of her as though she were a fairy tale princess, some otherworldly goddess whose fairness surpassed mere mortal beauty.

She wondered if she should mention anything to him. Obviously, she couldn't say she had read his journal, but maybe...Lydia hadn't considered courtship, had, in fact, dismissed it in no uncertain terms when her parents or friend had brought it up. But if he felt *this* way about her, maybe he wouldn't mind a picnic lunch with her by the stream one of these days.

She smiled as she continued to read. It seemed her stomach could flutter after all.

"...and if I could live but one moment more, I would spend that moment with you, admiring your golden locks that burn bright as sunlight..."

She read that last part again. Sunlight.

Her hair was black as a raven's wing. Not at all golden.

So this woman wasn't her but some blonde woman he knew from before. A lover he met on his journey, perhaps? A woman he left behind in Columbus?

It didn't matter. What mattered was that this golden-haired woman wasn't her, and her foolish dream of romance between them was just that: foolish.

"What are you doing in here?"

Lydia jumped and shrieked. Peter stood in the doorway, frowning with confusion. Lydia stared at him in shock, her mouth working soundlessly as her face lost all of the color that had filled it only a moment ago.

Peter's eyes moved to the journal, still open in Lydia's hands. His eyes widened, then his frown deepened into a scowl as he realized what she was doing.

"Why were you reading my journal?"

His voice was dark and dangerous. It was different from any tone he had used before because it was filled with anger. Even when he had run John off of their porch and heard the man threaten him and Lydia with harm, he hadn't seemed so angry.

"I...I'm sorry," Lydia breathed. Her voice sounded thin and weak in her ears.

"You're sorry?" he said, "Lydia, that's my private thoughts. This is my home. I wouldn't walk into your room and read your own private journal."

"No," Lydia said, reddening again as she recalled thinking that exact thing only a few minutes ago.

Peter continued, his voice rising in volume as he spoke. "I understand that it's your property and I'm your employee, but I think it's reasonable for me to expect that I should have some privacy. Did you need something from me?"

"No," Lydia said, "I'm sorry. I was just..." She gestured to the copy of Dickens on the table.

Peter lifted the book, glanced at it briefly, then tossed it back onto the table. It bounced once and came to a halt near the edge. That dismissive toss hurt Lydia far more deeply than anything else he could have done. She felt tears well in her eyes, and when Peter said, "Please leave," she did so without another word.

She managed to keep her cool until she reached her room, but as soon as the door closed, she burst into tears and threw herself on her bed, weeping uncontrollably.

As she sobbed, her conscience showed her no mercy. This was what she deserved. What could possibly have possessed her to think Peter was interested in her? She was his employer, nothing more. For all her self-congratulatory comparison between her own maturity and Dorothy's childishness, she had allowed herself to believe in a dream of romance rather than accept reality.

And now she had poisoned the little trust she had gained. Now they couldn't even be friends, let alone anything more than that.

She pulled her blanket tightly around her shoulders and wept.

Chapter Fifteen

"A toast!" Dorothy cried. "To Peter Gutenberg! May his imagination and joy live on forever in our hearts!"

Lydia and Mary lifted their glasses, echoing the toast and drinking. Lydia grimaced as the wine passed her lips. She had never been much for alcohol, but Dorothy had spent her allowance on this bottle, one of only three left in the Stevensville General Store, and Lydia would have felt rude refusing it.

Mary wiped tears from her eyes after she drank, but her smile showed nothing but joy and gratitude. "Thank you, Dorothy," she said, "Thank you for everything."

"Of course, Miss Mary!" Dorothy said, coming around the table and putting her arm affectionately around the older woman. "You two helped me celebrate my mother's birthday. It was only right that I return the favor."

Return the favor she had. In addition to the wine, she had brought the bottle of molasses and a charming card for the other two to write notes to Peter. Strangely, she had bought a second card with an identical message.

"We have to burn the one for Peter, of course," she said by way of explanation. So the letter will rise to Heaven. The copy is for those of us still here on Earth."

In addition to the molasses, the wine and the cards, she had dressed in a lovely cotton gown as blue as a summer sky.. Her Sunday best, she proclaimed, but no less than Peter deserved on his big day.

Her cheerful exuberance had quickly removed the typical pallor of this birthday and soon Mary and Lydia were laughing and smiling along with her. Lydia was grateful for

145

Dorothy's presence. It normally fell to her to lift her mother's spirits today, but after the incident with Peter's—the current Peter's—journal, she wasn't up to the task of managing anyone else's happiness today.

The three ladies finished their wine—or rather Mary and Dorothy finished theirs while Lydia managed one more sip for politeness' sake—and moved to the kitchen to start the cornbread.

Mary and Dorothy chatted happily while they gathered the ingredients for Lydia, who by virtue of drawing the short straw was relegated to the task of mixing the batter. Lydia tried to focus on the joy of the occasion, but her mind was preoccupied with more depressing thoughts.

She hadn't spoken to Peter since he walked in on her reading his journal. He had excused himself from dinner the past two nights, and she expected he would excuse himself from dinner tonight as well. When they did run into each other around the ranch, he would nod and offer a coldly polite, "Ma'am," or "Miss Lydia," then move on without waiting for a response.

For her own part, Lydia didn't encourage conversation. She had no idea what to say to him. She supposed she could apologize, but she already had apologized. Besides, what would she say? Sorry that I, a thirty-year-old woman, somehow felt that my curiosity about you was worth invading your privacy without your knowledge, snooping through your stuff and reading your journal? Sorry that I lacked the courage to admit my interest in you and instead hoped that somewhere you admitted interest in me yourself so I wouldn't have to risk rejection? Sorry that I spend one moment deciding to ignore my feelings because the ranch is more important, then the next entertaining fantasies of romance?

And what would Peter say? Well, that was easy. She was his boss. He would accept her apology at least on the surface, but that didn't mean he had forgiven her intrusion. It didn't mean he would trust her, now or ever again.

She felt a hand on her shoulder and jumped, startled. Her mother smiled gently at her and said, "It's okay, honey. I miss him too."

Now Lydia felt even more guilty. This was her brother's birthday, and she had spent the day thinking about a man she had no business thinking of as anything more than an employee. She forced a smile of her own and hoped the guilt on her face translated only into grief. "I know, Mother," she said. "It's just hard. I feel confused and angry about everything half the time, and that just makes it harder."

She didn't mention that a lot of what she felt in the moment was guilt that the feelings she described were related to her feelings for Peter Kerouac and not any lingering sense of injustice over her brother Peter's death.

Mary squeezed her shoulder again and said, "We'll talk later, sweetheart. I think I know what's really going on."

Lydia suppressed the rush of fear that ran through her when Mary said that. She smiled and said, "Oh, I'm fine. Really."

"Later, dear," Mary said.

"Making plans without me?" Dorothy interjected. "Why, how terribly rude of you two."

She grinned and planted her hands on her hips in mock indignation. Lydia leapt at the chance to change the focus of attention. "Oh, I'm so sorry, Your Highness," she said with an exaggerated bow. "I forget that all attention is to be directed solely to your person at all times."

Mary burst into laughter at that. Dorothy reddened, but continued to grin as she loftily extended her hand for Lydia to kiss. "I'll forgive this slight once, Lady Lydia, but see to it you don't make the same mistake a second time."

"Of course not, Your Grace," Lydia said, offering another deep bow.

They finished the dough and started baking the cornbread. While the bread baked, they sat in the parlor knitting a quilt for Dorothy's eventual marriage. "Although when that will happen now that Father and Peter have run off my only suitor, only Heaven knows," she lamented.

"I'm sure you'll have another puppy nipping at your heels in no time," Mary said, "Lovely young women like you never want for attention."

"Did the young men follow Lydia around the same way?" Dorothy asked.

"No, not all of them," Mary said, "Lydia here was rather intimidating to young men. She had a sharp tongue and wasn't afraid to use it. Very few suitors would risk her wrath by attempting to court her."

"Well, there was Timothy," Dorothy said, casting a mischievous glance at Lydia.

"Oh yes," Mary said laughing, "I forgot about him."

"Of course you did, Mother," Lydia said, a trace of bitterness in her voice. "We were only planning to be married."

"Well," Mary said, flipping her hand dismissively. "You wouldn't have been happy with him anyway. He was a dandy if there ever was one. You need a real man, a strong, hardworking man."

"A ranch foreman, for example," Dorothy added.

Lydia sighed and stood. "I'm going to check on the cornbread."

She left the parlor, ignoring a surprised look from Dorothy and a slightly guilty one from her mother. She knew very well the cornbread had at least another ten minutes, but she no longer wanted to listen to them talk about her hopeless marriage prospects.

It hurt a lot to hear them talk about her as though she were already an old spinster. Dorothy didn't ask if men still courted her but if they used to when she was young, taking it for granted that Lydia wasn't young anymore. Her mother made light of the fact that she had few suitors when she was younger, suggesting that it was her own sharp tongue and insufferable personality that left her lonely. When Lydia pointed out that she was, in fact, nearly married to a man, Mary dismissed that interest as well.

She had just had it with people deciding they knew her feelings and thoughts better than she did!

The worst part was that they were both right. Lydia wasn't old, maybe, but she wasn't young either. She really had possessed a sharp tongue as a youth and the men who did express interest *were* quickly put off by her acerbic wit. She really wouldn't have been happy with Timothy and had admitted as much to Dorothy just two days ago.

Still, they didn't need to poke fun at her for it. She was so tired of everyone assuming that her feelings couldn't be hurt!

Her mother stepped into the kitchen with a tentative smile that faded when she saw Lydia's expression. "Lydia, dear," she said, "I'm sorry. I didn't mean to hurt your feelings. I really don't believe you would have been happy with Timothy, but I know you were very fond of him, and I know it was very hard for you to leave him behind. I'm sorry I laughed about it."

"I'm not upset about that, Mother," Lydia said, which wasn't entirely a lie. "I just... I hate that you still talk about me like I'm some... some child! And what business is it of Dorothy's that I didn't have many suitors? For that matter, what business is it of yours?"

"You're right, dear," Mary said contritely. "I'm very sorry."

Dorothy had wandered into the kitchen by then and gazed at Lydia with a similarly meek expression.

"And I've had enough of you two constantly engaging in these fantasies about me and Peter!" Lydia cried. Tears were welling in her eyes, which only made her angrier. "It's not happening! All right? He's not interested in me, and I'm not interested in him. I hired him as a foreman, and that's all he is, okay? He *works* for me! That's *all!* So enough of 'Oh Lydia, you need a big strong foreman,' or, 'oh, isn't he so handsome?' Yes, he's handsome. So is Reverend Whittier, but I'm not courting him either."

"I'm sorry, Lydia," Dorothy said, her lip trembling as she stared at her feet. "I didn't mean to upset you." She lifted a hand to wipe away a tear that formed in one eye.

Lydia sighed in frustration. She lifted a hand to her temples, but let it drop before it reached its destination. "It's all right, Dorothy," she said. "I just... I wish people could just allow me to live my own life without all of this pressure to think and act and feel the way everyone else wants me to think and act and feel!"

Dorothy nodded, her eyes still fixed on her feet. Mary retained her contrite expression, but there was a knowing gaze behind it. She turned to Dorothy and said, "Dorothy, honey, would you mind giving Lydia and me a moment?"

Dorothy nodded and shuffled away, looking as dejected as a kid caught eating the cakes her mother had saved for the church bake sale. Mary waited until Dorothy was back in the parlor, then stepped closer to Lydia.

"Is this about the money?" she asked quietly.

It was so much not about the money that it took Lydia a moment to realize what her mother was talking about. She sighed and this time didn't stop the hand that rose to her temples. "No, Mother," she said, "I'm not upset about the money. In fact, with Peter nearing another sale, I'm even less worried about that than before."

"So it's about your brother? Lydia, I understand that you're angry. Believe me, I spent years blaming God for his death. You remember I came home from church crying every Sunday for months. Even when I stopped crying, I still felt angry. How could God take away such a beautiful, perfect soul like his?"

Lydia opened her mouth to explain to her mother that believe it or not, it was possible for her to be upset simply about the fact that they were so dismissive of her feelings but stopped when she saw the expression on her mother's face. Once more, it wasn't Lydia's feelings she was concerned with. Her lips trembled as she said, "I used to look forward to seeing him come home from school every day. You were always so serious and practical, but Peter was just filled with such joy. He loved everything and everyone so much."

Lydia felt as though a knife were driven into her chest. Her mother might as well have said that she wished Lydia had died and Peter had lived. There was no explaining that to Mary, though. She seemed to take for granted that Lydia would feel the same way.

She forced a sympathetic smile and said, "I miss him too, Mother."

151

"I know," Mary said. She took a breath and squared her shoulders. "But we have to go on. For his sake."

"Yes," Lydia said, "For his sake."

The door opened and Lydia looked up to see Peter entering. He stopped when he saw the three women clearly in a state of distress. "Oh," he said, "I'm sorry. Miss Mary invited me to dinner for your brother's birthday. I see I'm too early."

He moved to leave, but Lydia quickly said, "No, please stay. We just finished baking cornbread. Please, join us."

He looked between the three of them, clearly wishing he could be anywhere else right now, but he eventually nodded and said, "All right. Thank you, ma'am."

"Don't call me ma'am," Lydia snapped, and this time, she didn't care that her tone of voice was harsh. Mary stiffened and Dorothy gasped, but Peter simply nodded again. "My apologies, Miss Lydia. You've said that before. I should have remembered."

Lydia still felt incredibly embarrassed about spying on him. She still felt wounded to learn his heart still belonged to whatever golden-haired beauty still wandered the halls of his past. She was still humiliated to know that he was right to be angry with her.

In spite of everything though, he remained the only person in her life who seemed genuinely to care about her feelings. She smiled at him, and there was no falsehood in this smile. "That's all right, Peter. Thank you."

It could just be her imagination, but she could swear she saw yet another ghost of a smile flash across his own face. "You're welcome, Lydia."

Chapter Sixteen

Peter shook Mr. Carter's hand and said, "Thank you, Sir. I appreciate your business."

Carter gripped Peter's hand firmly and smiled. "We appreciate it too." He released Peter's hand and added, "I hope you won't think me rude when I tell you I had some friends of mine examine the last batch you sold us. You'll be happy to know that they all agreed they were the hardiest bunch of cattle they'd ever seen. My foreman thinks they'll decrease losses from weather and disease by half."

"Well, I'm happy to hear that," Peter said, "and since your second opinions led you to buy another fifty head from us, I'll forgive the rudeness."

Carter laughed heartily and clapped Peter on the back. "Very well, Mr. Kerouac," he said, "I'm happy this worked out well for both of us. While I have you here, how likely is it that you'll be able to sell us another hundred head come spring? I understand your ranch is a small concern at the moment and it may take a while before you can replenish what you've sold."

"It won't be a problem at all," Peter said. "I'll have those hundred head fat and ready for you when spring comes."

"Outstanding," Carter said, clapping Peter once more on the back. "In that case, I leave you with my blessing and the hope that you have a warm and successful winter."

"You as well, Mr. Carter," Peter replied.

On the way home, Peter considered his promise to Carter. Spring was eight months away, and from what Eugene had told him, that should be more than enough time for them to raise enough cattle to maintain the herd and still meet the Double Bar S's demands.

If everything went well.

That was the problem. They had no margin for error. Examining the books had showed Peter there was a chance to save the ranch, but it was a slim chance, much slimmer than he had admitted to Lydia. This second sale all but guaranteed that they would avoid foreclosure when the Homestead Act protection ended, but that was all it did. They would need far more money to keep up with the installments on the debt.

Essentially, they needed to survive the winter without losing any of the herd to disease or exposure, and they needed to replenish the numbers they had sold to Double Bar S and keep the adult cattle fat and healthy enough to be sold in the spring. Then they'd need to find a way to replenish those numbers without losing a significant portion of the herd. There was just no room for any misfortune, now or for the foreseeable future.

Peter sighed. It was better, but it wasn't everything. They were crawling out of one hole only to find themselves in another hole to crawl out of.

Well, at least he had good news for Lydia today.

Things had been awkward between them since she read through his journal three days ago. The dinner the night before seemed to have eased some of the tension between them, but it would be a while before trust was rebuilt.

A part of him wondered if he had overreacted. Sure, it was wrong of her to snoop on his private thoughts, especially if she read his most recent entry, but was it helpful of him to berate her for it the way she did?

Another part of him insisted that he was well within his rights to react like that. She had snooped on his private thoughts and read things she had no right to read. If he had walked into her room and read her own journal, she would be livid. He would probably be out of a job. Just because she was his employer didn't give her the right to violate his privacy.

Still, he could have been more gracious. He could have calmly and politely asked that she respect his privacy instead of demanding that she do so.

He sighed and decided to put those thoughts out of his mind. There was nothing he could do about it now. He comforted himself with the knowledge that after last night, they were at least on speaking terms.

When he reached the ranch, he found Lydia on the porch looking through the ledger. She looked up at his approach and said, "Good afternoon, Peter. Did the sale go well?"

"Very well, Lydia," he said, carefully avoiding the mistake of calling her ma'am. "They bought the fifty head, and they want another hundred in the spring."

"Wonderful!" Lydia said. An exuberant smile flashed across her face, and as the sunlight gleamed off of her hair, Peter thought it really did shine like gold. That thought troubled him, but he couldn't put his finger on the reason at the moment.

Lydia's smile disappeared almost as quickly as it came. "That presents another problem though. Those hundred head represented half of our herd. Can we replenish those numbers by spring?"

Peter nodded. "We can, but it'll be a near thing. We need to think about keeping the cattle in the stable at night, or at least rotating them through every other night so they suffer less in the cold." He cocked his head. "Actually, I think we should keep the dams with their calves in the stable during the winter and leave the steers in the pens or the pastures. The steers are hardy enough they should be all right. The calves won't be. If we can keep them alive, then we can easily replenish our numbers. The calves won't be large enough to sell by spring, but we can sell the rest of the steers and some of the heifers."

"What about the new calves?" Lydia said, "They won't be ready to sell for two years at least, and if we sell the steers and heifers, then we won't be able to breed more."

"Not necessarily," Peter said. "We have an established reputation of good breeding stock now, and we can sell young calves as breeding stock. In fact, we may command a higher price for them because they'll have a greater breeding life the younger they're sold. Now that I think about it, we can keep the older cattle and sell the younger cattle."

"So we sell breeding stock, not beef," Lydia said. She didn't seem convinced.

"I think that's probably the best thing to do," Peter said. "We'll never have a large enough herd to sell beef cattle. Not unless we somehow expand to a thousand acres or more. Since we're in debt like we are, I don't see that happening, but I do see us maintaining a strong business with repeat clients in the market for breeding stock."

"Hmm," Lydia said, "Well. I'll think about it. Thank you, Peter."

She looked pointedly down at the ledger, indicating the conversation was over. Peter stood for a second and tried to think of a way to talk to her about the incident with the journal, but he couldn't think of anything that would help. He sighed and walked away.

"Take the rest of the day off, Peter," she called after him. "You've earned it."

He stopped, then turned and nodded before continuing on his way.

She was giving him the day off, but what she really meant was that she didn't want to see him for the rest of the day. Well, that was fine. It was hard enough for him to be around her anyway.

He tried to tell himself that her coldness didn't hurt, but it did. He had been on the ranch for nearly a month, which he supposed wasn't very long, but long enough that he hoped to feel more welcome.

No, that wasn't right of him to feel either. He was welcomed here. Greg considered him a friend. Mary had been nothing but kind to him. The ranch's only remaining customer considered him the face of the ranch, regardless of his last name. Even Lydia had made attempts at making him part of the family, inviting him to join them for dinner and leaving him a book.

It was just that he could never tell what Lydia's behavior around him would be on any given day. She might be friendly to him, insist that he was a part of the family and include him in the ranch's financial planning, or she might be coldly civil and make it clear that she did not welcome his help with the ranch beyond the most narrow scope of his job.

Then she had read his journal and for the first time in years, his calm had broken, and he had ruined whatever little chance existed that they could be friends.

He reached his cabin and sighed as he took his hat and boots off. He supposed he might as well admit that a part of him hoped that he and Lydia could be more than friends. He hadn't written those words about her for no reason at all.

He picked up his journal and turned to the entry. It was still the most recent entry. He hadn't felt like writing any more since the fight. As he read the words he wrote, longing swept slowly over him, a feeling he hadn't felt since before Penelope's death.

When I first met you, you seemed as beautiful as Venus, a goddess, an angel. You are soft and lovely, but you are also strong and proud. You carry the weight of the world on your shoulders, yet even faced with loss and the predation of wolves—he thought of John when he read that, as he had when he wrote it, and his jaw tightened. *You keep your head held high. Your eyes are as bright and clear as a summer sky and if I could live but one moment more, I would spend that moment with you, admiring your golden locks that burn bright as sunlight, shimmering with a radiance that outshines every star in the sky.*

He read those words again and sighed. They were foolish words, the words of a youth in the first blush of love, not the words of a man who had already loved and lost and had no business loving again, especially not a woman like Lydia.

That explained her behavior the past three days. He would have expected her to be either cold as ice to him, refusing even basic politeness, or to be mortified at her own behavior. Instead, she hadn't so much as mentioned the incident, and seemed unsure whether she wanted to be friendly with him or distant.

She must know it was about her. It was as plain as day. The weight of the world, the predation of wolves—he was clearly referring to Lydia's management of the ranch through her parents' ineptitude and her resistance to John's wedding proposal. Besides, who else could he have written about? It wasn't as though he was preparing to court Dorothy.

There was a knock at the door, and he quickly closed the journal and tossed it onto the bed. Could that be Lydia? He hoped and feared that in equal measure.

He opened the door to find not Lydia but Mary standing there, smiling, with a covered dish and a fork and knife. "Good evening, Peter," she said, "I brought you supper."

He felt a rush of warmth for the older woman. He realized now how much he valued the simple kindnesses she showed him. He smiled at her, and for the second time since they met, she said, "A smile looks good on you, Peter. I hope to see it more often."

"Thank you, Mary," he said, accepting the dish. "I surely do appreciate it."

"I appreciate you," she said. "May I come in?"

"Oh," he said, quickly stepping aside. "Of course. Come on in."

She laughed and said, "No need to look so chagrined, Peter. You aren't a terrible person for not thinking to invite me in the instant you saw me. I have yet to meet a man who could think clearly when face to face with one of my roasts."

Peter set the dish on his table, and when he lifted the cover off, his eyes widened appreciatively. "I can see why. This looks delicious."

"Wait until you taste it," Mary said.

He did and decided she was absolutely right. There was no chance of thinking clearly when in the presence of such a feast. Later, he would think of how ravenously he ate this meal and decide with some embarrassment that it was another sign of his inability to remember his manners in the moment.

While he ate, Mary said, "Lydia appreciates you too."

He nearly choked. He cleared his throat and said, "I...well...I'm sure she does."

"No you aren't," she said with a smile. "You think she's mad at you."

He chose his words carefully. "I think she's unsure of me. That's to be expected, all things considered."

Mary nodded. "I think both of you are unsure of your feelings for each other."

He nearly choked again, but this time could think of nothing to say in response to her assertion.

"That's all right," she continued. "It goes without saying that the timing is less than ideal for both of you. And," she sighed, "You've both had to deal with constant teasing. I'm responsible for part of that, and I'm sorry."

"You have no reason to apologize, Mary," he said.

"Yes I do," she replied. "And it's okay for you to accept that. I just wanted to tell you that I won't be teasing you or Lydia anymore. I can't speak for my husband. Greg is a decent man, but he's hopeless when it comes to understanding others."

Peter nodded but didn't voice his agreement aloud.

"Please stay," she said.

He blinked. "Well, of course I will."

She smiled again, but there was grief in this smile. "I know you mean that now," she said, "but there may come a time when you don't. Please stay anyway. It may be months or years before you and Lydia are in a place to explore your feelings for each other. You may never be in that place. But whether you two marry or remain apart for the rest of your lives, you are a part of this ranch and a part of this family. So please don't give up on us."

Peter felt a second rush of warmth for this lovely woman and at the same time felt a surge of determination. He met her eyes and said, "Mary, I promise you. I won't go anywhere."

She smiled once more, and this time, her smile shone with gratitude. "Thank you, Peter."

She stayed with him while he finished his meal. Their talk turned to other, less serious things, but once more, Mary's kind welcome made Peter feel that he truly had found his home.

Chapter Seventeen

Lydia looked out the window at the bright blue of the sky. The day was warm, but not so warm as a month ago. Summer would end soon, and winter would spell either the end of her ranch or its beginning.

The Homestead Act protection ended January 31st of next year. That gave them four months and nineteen days before John could expect regular payments on the debt they owed or force foreclosure. They had the money to postpone foreclosure for another season, but if the sale to Double Bar S didn't go through or if they were unable to replenish the herd, they were only delaying the inevitable.

Still, any time was better than no time at all. She might still have a noose wrapped around her neck, but for the moment at least it was comfortably loose.

Things with Peter were better too. He was no longer so awkward and closed off. He was far from open with her, but he was friendly when they talked, and he didn't seem upset with her over the journal incident. They still ate dinner together most nights and would talk at least briefly most days around lunchtime when Lydia sat on the porch and Peter would walk from the barn to his cabin or sometimes to meet Mary for the occasional lunches they shared.

The new stable was beautiful. It stood in clear contrast to the dilapidated barn and house. The barn would be ready by winter, Peter promised, and the house touched up at least enough to keep them warm. It was looking likely that they would be able to keep the calves and their mothers safe and warm as well. Things were looking up, or if not up, at least no further down, and Lydia decided that amounted to the same thing.

She heard hoofbeats and looked up to see the Flisters' wagon approaching. She smiled, excited to see her friend. They had seen little of each other since her brother's birthday celebration. Lydia feared that her conflict with Dorothy earlier had soured their relationship, but when Dorothy jumped from the wagon and rushed inside, throwing her arms around Lydia, she decided she was worried about nothing.

"Lydia, darling, it's been ages!" she cried.

Lydia chuckled. "I just saw you yesterday at church, Dorothy."

"Well, yes, but that doesn't count," Dorothy said, waving her hand dismissively.

"Don't tell Reverend Whittier that," Lydia said.

"Why? We're supposed to go to church to commune with God, not with friends."

"Good point," Lydia conceded. She smiled at Eugene who had just made his way up the porch. "Good morning, Eugene. Would you care for some coffee?"

"Oh that would be incredible, Miss Lydia, thank you," he said.

Lydia poured the coffee and Eugene drank it in one gulp, seemingly unconcerned by the heat of the near-boiling liquid.

"Another cup?" Lydia asked with a wry smile.

Eugene shook his head, "No thank you, Miss Lydia. I'm helping Greg and Peter with the barn today. Peter wants to have the beams for the frame cut today."

"Don't let him work you too ragged," Lydia admonished.

"Yes, Papa," Dorothy teased, "You don't have to be ashamed that he's so much younger and stronger than you."

Eugene laid a hand on her shoulder and smiled. "I'm much too old to take offense at that kind of teasing, *Dotty.*"

He left then, retaining his smug smile and leaving Dotty pouting and Lydia stifling laughter. When he was gone, Dorothy offered an overly exaggerated sigh. "Men!"

Lydia couldn't stifle her laughter anymore. Dorothy joined in, and Lydia felt her spirits soar. It was going to be a good day.

"All right," Dorothy said when her laughter subsided. "I don't know about you, but I ate a very small breakfast in anticipation of this huckleberry pie, so let's get right to it. You have the huckleberries, right?"

"Oh no," Lydia said, opening her eyes wide in shock. "Oh no, I forgot to gather them!"

Dorothy examined Lydia's face and after a moment, deadpanned, "Ha ha. Very funny."

Lydia giggled and said, "I almost fooled you."

"Did not," Dorothy retorted. "Come on, Lydia, let's make pie! I'm hungry!"

Lydia regarded her friend's trim figure and said, "How can you manage to stay so thin with such an obsession over food?"

Dorothy shrugged with the easy unconcern of youth and headed to the kitchen. Lydia followed her and they began to work on the pie.

The huckleberries were in the peak of their season, plump, juicy and a deep purple-red in color. Despite her teasing words to Dorothy, Lydia felt her stomach growl in anticipation as she mixed the ingredients for the crust while Dorothy prepared the filling.

They had just finished mixing when the door opened and Peter walked in. He walked toward the kitchen but stopped when he saw the two women. "Oh," he said, "I'm sorry to interrupt."

"Nonsense!" Dorothy said, "Come join us!" She considered and said, "Well, you can watch anyway. It would be good to have some conversation with a man."

She looked at Lydia and put a lilt in her voice when she said that. Lydia rolled her eyes and said, "You're welcome to stay if you'd like, Peter."

"Thank you kindly, Lydia," he said, fiddling with his hat in his hand. "I only came inside for the kitchen knife."

"The knife?" Lydia said.

"Yes. I guess Eugene wants it to show us how to sharpen tools by stropping."

"Ah," Lydia said, "Why the knife, though?"

"Well," he said, "I already sharpened the axe on the grinding wheel. My own knife too. He says he needs a dull blade so he can show us how it works."

"He's just showing off," Dorothy said, "He's like that. He thinks because he can sharpen a knife on his boot he's a genuine mountain man."

"Well, that's all right," Lydia said, retrieving the knife. "The knife could use some sharpening."

She handed the blade to Peter. His hand touched hers briefly as he accepted it, and Lydia felt as though she were struck by lightning. She gasped softly, and judging by the heat that spread across Peter's cheeks, he felt the same as her.

She blinked and realized she was still holding the knife. She released it, certain her face was as red as Peter's. They stood awkwardly a moment before Peter cleared his throat and said, "Thank you, Lydia."

"You're welcome, Peter," she said, her voice awkward and stilted in her ears.

He rushed off, and only after he left did Lydia turn and see the grin on Dorothy's face.

She rolled her eyes. "Don't start."

"Start what?" Dorothy asked innocently.

"Good," Lydia said.

Dorothy examined her fingernails and asked sweetly, "Have you thought about who you'll dance with at the anniversary festival?"

The anniversary festival to celebrate the date the town was first settled was next week. Lydia had forgotten all about it. After John had strong-armed her into dancing with him at the previous festival, she had resolved not to attend again.

"I don't believe I'll attend this year," Lydia said, "There's a lot of work to be done at the ranch."

"At night?" Dorothy asked.

"No," Lydia said, hiding the touch of irritation she felt at Dorothy's persistence, "but early that morning and early the next morning."

"Maybe Peter can work a little harder the next few days and get everything done early so you can take the night off."

"Peter's been working quite hard enough," Lydia retorted. "I'm not going to ask him to work even harder just so I can go to a dance."

"Have you asked him?" Dorothy asked. "Maybe he'd like to go with you."

"Why don't you ask him?" Lydia said, no longer hiding her irritation. "I'm sure he'd love to attend with you."

"I'm going with Colton Bowers," Dorothy said, "but I'll be absolutely lost without you. You must come with me, and you can't go alone."

"I'm not going alone," Lydia said, "if I must go, I'll be going with you."

Dorothy sighed with exasperation. "Just invite Peter," she said. "Why do you fight so hard to avoid him?"

"I don't fight to avoid him," Lydia said, "I just don't allow you and my parents to insist on a relationship between us that doesn't exist. I'm too old for these games, Dorothy, and frankly, I've been very patient with all three of you. Please let this go."

"Lydia, I—" Dorothy began. Seeing the look on Lydia's face, she sighed and said, "All right. If you insist."

"I do," Lydia said, "now let's talk about this Colton Bowers."

Dorothy's eyes lit up and Lydia patiently endured twenty minutes of gushing over the handsome, smart, strong Colton Bowers. She smiled wistfully at the beauty of young love, but try as she might to avoid it, she couldn't help but imagine her and Peter dancing and holding each other under the soft moonlight.

Chapter Eighteen

"All right," Peter said. "You two pull, and I'll push."

"Shouldn't it be the other way around?" Greg asked.

Eugene glanced at Peter but said nothing. It should be the other way around, but frankly, Greg wasn't going to be much help no matter where he was. Peter, being stronger than Eugene, should be the one pushing the wall up while Eugene pulled with the rope. It would be difficult, but Peter had separated the wall into nine separate sections, so they could accomplish the work.

"No, this is the right way to do it," Peter insisted. "I'm taller than you two, so I can push harder."

"Ah," Greg said, nodding understanding.

Eugene shared another look with Peter, then pulled on his rope. Greg pulled on his, and Peter pushed upward with the pole. The section of wall rose steadily and then leaned against the frame.

Greg pumped his arms and cheered. Eugene and Peter once more glanced at each other, but this time they smiled. It was an excessive reaction for the small victory, but neither of them begrudged him the joy.

The next sections of wall went up one after the other. It took an hour or so of work, and when they were finished, Greg was sweating heavily. "Oh goodness," he said, "I'm getting too old for this."

Eugene, who was only two years younger than Greg, just nodded. Peter didn't feel tired either, but he didn't want Greg to feel bad, and they had made great progress today. The barn would likely be finished late next month, just in time for

169

the harvest and a comfortable month before the winter storms would begin. There was no need to hurry.

So, he rested and talked with the men. A moment later, he wished he hadn't.

"So the anniversary festival is coming up," Greg said.

"The what?" Peter asked.

"It's the anniversary of the town's founding," Eugene explained. There's a potluck, a shooting contest, games for the kids, a pie contest..." he smiled at Peter, "and a dance."

Peter sighed inwardly and prepared himself.

"You know, Lydia loves to dance," Greg said offhandedly.

"You don't say?" Peter replied drily.

"Oh for sure," Greg said. "She and I used to dance all around the house when she was younger, back in Baltimore." His smile became wistful. "She was such a happy child. Always smiling and giggling. I miss that."

He paused a moment, then his smile became mischievous again. "I'm a little old to dance these days. Mary and I usually just sit and watch the younger ones dance. If only there was a strong young man to dance with Lydia."

Peter rolled his eyes. Eugene didn't bother pretending innocence. "Why, Greg," he said, smiling. "There's a strong young man standing right next to you."

"Well, look at that," Greg said, grinning at Peter. "Peter, would you mind taking Lydia to the dance? I know she'd be happy to go with you."

Peter sighed. "I'm not sure that would be appropriate, Greg. She's my employer after all."

"Nonsense," Greg said. "You're family."

"Family," Peter said. "Right."

"You know," Eugene said, "you could always order him to take Lydia to the dance."

Peter glared at Eugene, who returned an innocent stare.

"Hey," Peter said, "that's right!" His voice grew stern, and he said, "Peter, as your boss, I command you to take my daughter to the Anniversary festival and dance with her!"

Peter sighed again and forced a smile. "I would love to."

"Brilliant!" Greg said, "it's settled. I'll tell Lydia—"

"No need for that," Peter interrupted. "I'll ask her myself."

"Good idea," Eugene said, "we don't want her to think he's only doing this because you forced him to."

Even though that's exactly what you're doing, Peter thought to himself.

"You're right," Greg said, "Well, Peter, I think you'll enjoy yourself. It'll be good for you to get to know your neighbors."

Peter had to admit he had a point there. He preferred to keep to himself, but if he was going to represent the ranch, he needed people to know and trust him. "I look forward to it," he said.

Their victory won, Eugene and Greg left off teasing Peter and the conversation turned to other subjects. Peter discussed the sales to Double Bar S and the potential for a long-term relationship. Eugene suggested that he should try to invest money when he could to increase the size of the herd and find other customers so he wasn't completely reliant on Double Bar S. Greg pointed out that to do that, they would need more land, and that launched a conversation about strategies to raise more cattle on less land by supplementing pasture with grain feed and harvested hay.

Peter didn't say it out loud, but the real reason they couldn't expand the herd was financial. They couldn't afford to buy more cattle in the hope they might sell it, not with John lurking in the shadows waiting for the moment the ranch became insolvent so he could take it from them and take Lydia for his own.

Anger surged through him at that thought. His jaw clenched, and he promised himself that would never happen. He would not allow that snake anywhere near her.

"Well," Eugene said, "I should get back home. The sheep are in need of shearing, and I best get started or I won't finish before the festival."

"You want some help?" Greg said.

"Oh, that's all right," Eugene said, "you two have your work cut out for you with this barn."

"You've helped us a lot," Greg said, "let us return the favor."

Eugene glanced at Peter and Peter nodded. "He's right, Eugene. You've been a big help to us. We can spare a day to help you shear your sheep."

"All right," Eugene said, "Thank you, kindly."

***

Hours later, Greg and Peter headed home. Peter was far more sore and tired than he expected to be. Sheep were smaller and weaker than cattle but infinitely more stubborn, and they proved to be difficult to wrangle and hold still while Eugene sheared them, and Greg gathered the wool.

Greg was as exhausted as Peter, and they completed the drive home in uncharacteristic silence. When they reached the house, Greg said, "I'll let you wash up first. You worked harder than me wrestling those sheep."

"That's all right," Peter said, "I'll wash at the creek. It's only a few hundred yards past my cabin anyway."

"All right," Greg said gratefully. "Will I see you at dinner?"

Peter looked at the horizon. The sun had already dipped below the ground and the sky was rapidly darkening. "I reckon not," he said, "It'll be past dinner by the time we finish washing."

"You're probably right," Greg said. "Well, I'll see you in the morning then. Good work today."

It surprised Peter to find he was grateful for Greg's praise. He nodded and said, "Thank you, Greg. I appreciate that."

"We appreciate you," Greg said. "I know we say that a lot, but it's true. We'd be nowhere without you."

Peter nodded uncomfortably, but managed to repeat, "Thank you."

He left Greg at the house and headed to his cabin for a towel and a change of clothes. He didn't feel he was working any harder than he needed to, although he supposed his idea of hard work had changed after the war. Still, it made him a little uncomfortable that the Gutenbergs relied so heavily on him. He didn't like feeling that it was his responsibility to save the ranch, but he liked worse the idea that it—and Lydia—should pass into John's possession, so he would continue to do whatever he needed to keep that from happening.

He washed slowly, relishing the briskness of the late summer night. He didn't mind the cold. Columbus was only slightly warmer than Stevensville, at least at this time of year, and the air was much cleaner without coal-fired manufacturing plants spewing smoke.

When he was clean, he headed back to his cabin. He had started *Great Expectations* and found it, like other Dickens works he had read, to be depressing and heavy, but with just enough hope to keep him reading. In his experience, these stories ended relatively happily, but there was always pain with the joy.

He appreciated Dickens' perspective. It was like life. Things might work out in the end, but the scars of the past remained. He found it more believable than authors who insisted on everything working out wonderfully for everyone involved. Such stories might be gratifying on the surface, but it was hard for him to believe his own life could ever end so beautifully.

The longer he spent here, though, the more he thought that he might be able to find happiness in spite of his pain. The scars would always remain, but scars, though ugly and sometimes painful, were a sign of healing. It meant the wound had closed. The more time he spent here, the more he felt his wounds close. Maybe he could finally get rid of the revolver he kept hidden in his closet.

John's leering face crossed his mind and his mood soured. He would keep the revolver for now. He prayed he wouldn't have to use it, but it was good to have when wolves prowled.

He read a chapter of *Great Expectations* and started on a second when there was a knock at the door. Probably Mary bringing him supper. He stood and walked to the door. When he opened it, it wasn't Mary but Lydia who stood in front of him holding a covered dish.

She smiled tentatively at him. "I brought you some stew."

"Thank you," he said, taking the dish. "Would you like to come in a moment?"

She grinned. "I would love to, now that I've been invited in instead of just sneaking in."

He didn't reply, and her smile faded after a moment. "That was a poor joke," she said, "I'm sorry."

"No," he said, "it's all right. I guess I overreacted a little. Come on in."

His face burned, and he was grateful for the dimness of the light the lantern provided. His reaction wasn't so much caused by the fact that she had entered his cabin without permission but that she had read the words he'd written about her. He was keenly aware of the journal lying on the table.

Lydia glanced at the journal and reddened slightly. "I apologize for reading that," she said, "and I know I shouldn't say this, but I thought that what you wrote was beautiful."

Peter felt his face flame. "Really?"

"It was," Lydia repeated. "She's a lucky woman, whoever she is."

So she didn't know he wrote those words about her. He sighed inwardly with relief but was surprised to find that with his relief came disappointment.

"Did you leave her behind?" she asked. "In Columbus?"

He didn't answer right away. After a moment, she blushed and lowered her eyes., "I'm sorry. I shouldn't be prying like this. It's none of my business."

"It's all right," Peter said. "I didn't leave her in Columbus. I..."

He hesitated. Should he tell her that he was writing about her, or should he pretend those words had been about Penelope? His thoughts warred with each other, and they must have warred too long because after a moment, Lydia said, "Oh. I'm so sorry."

"It's all right," Peter said, choosing not to correct her. "It was a long time ago."

"The past leaves scars," Lydia said, smiling sadly at him. "I understand how that feels."

"It does leave scars," Peter said, "but scars are signs of healing."

Lydia beamed at him, and Peter felt warmth spread through him. "You have a beautiful way with words, Peter. Have you considered writing?"

"Oh," he said, shuffling his feet. "I suppose I haven't given it much thought other than that journal."

"You should," she said, "I think you'd enjoy it."

Peter nodded. "I reckon I might."

He smiled at her, and Lydia said, "You should do that more often too."

"Do what?"

"Smile. It looks good on you."

Peter met her eyes and marveled at the depth of their blue, as brilliant as the larkspurs that now bloomed in the fields surrounding the ranch. He felt a sudden longing for her, and wished he could bring himself to tell her how much he...

He couldn't, though. It wasn't right. She had a ranch to save, and his place was to help her save it. He had nothing to offer her other than his hard work, and a woman like Lydia deserved more than just hard work.

After a moment of heavy silence, Lydia stood. "Well," she said, "I should get back home. My mother tires early these days, and I need to help her with the chores or she'll work herself to death."

"All right," Peter said. "Thank you. For the supper."

"You're welcome," she said. Her smile widened a little. "For the supper."

Peter watched her walk home, the lantern casting a soft shadow over her figure as she made her way to the house. The longing he felt a moment ago remained, and his heart ached as he watched her leave.

If only they had met years ago. If only the ranch wasn't in such dire straits. If only love was enough to carry them through life and they could simply go on together without worrying about the wolves that prowled the edges of their lives.

He looked back at the journal. After a moment of consideration, he sat at the table, picked up his quill and began to write.

Chapter Nineteen

The shell exploded yards away from their position. Peter cursed and hit the ground just before the shrapnel from the shell sliced the air into shreds above him. Jacob wasn't so lucky. Peter watched in horror as his friend's body sprouted multiple spreading blooms of deep-red. The young man cast huge, confused eyes at Peter, then collapsed. Peter stared a moment longer as blood trickled from the corner of Jacob's mouth.

Peter left the body where it fell. If they were fortunate, they would win this skirmish and be able to retrieve him, along with the others who had fallen.

They were rarely fortunate. Bull Run had once more proved to be a disaster for the Union army, and Peter estimated they had a day left at best before they were routed.

He couldn't shake the image of blood trickling from Jacob's mouth. As he ran, keeping his head down to avoid the shelling, his fear transformed into anger. He changed direction, sprinting toward the emplacement. The officer manning the gun saw him approach and shouted commands to the rebels guarding the weapon. They raised their rifles.

Too late. Snarling, Peter raised his handgun and fired.

"Peter!"

Peter started awake. Instinctively, he grabbed the coat of the man who had woken him and with a grunt of effort, threw him violently down. He stood and reached for his knife, but it wasn't on his hip where it should be. He blinked and looked down into Greg's terrified face.

He shook himself and stumbled backward. "Greg," he said. "Greg, I'm so sorry."

"It's all right," the older man said, getting to his feet, "but I need you now. One of the cattle is giving birth, but there's something wrong with her."

Peter's chagrin receded instantly to the background as his responsibilities took over. He dressed quickly and said, "Is the calf all right?"

"I don't know," Greg said.

"Ride for Eugene," Peter instructed. "We'll need his help." He couldn't rely on Greg's inexperienced hands to assist him, especially since his own experience was limited.

Greg nodded and rushed off. Peter finished dressing and jogged over to the pens. He could already hear the distressed cow lowing.

As he drew closer, the acrid, metallic smell of blood assaulted his nose. His nostrils flared, and images of the battlefield flashed across his mind. He shook them off and forced himself to calm as he entered the pens.

Mary and Lydia were standing a few yards away from the cow. Mary wrung her hands helplessly, and Lydia's face appeared a sickly yellow in the moonlight.

The other cattle gave the injured cow a wide berth. Animals had a sixth sense when it came to disease. Peter didn't like the looks in their eyes. He liked less what he saw when he came to the cow.

Blood pooled on the ground underneath her, far too much blood. She was in labor far too early, months too early.

Her eyes were glazed, and her lips pulled back over her teeth. Foam speckled her nose and the ground around her head. Peter's heart froze when he saw blood in the foam.

"Peter, what do we do?" Mary asked.

"Go bring me some water," he said, "and linens. Boil some of the water and leave some cool."

Mary rushed off, and Lydia looked at him. Her expression told Peter that she, too, knew the water was pointless. Peter gave Mary that instruction to give her something to do, not because he thought it would actually help. It was too late for the mother, and the infant had never had a chance to begin with.

"She's in breech," he told Lydia. "The calf's coming out rump first instead of headfirst. If we don't act soon, we'll lose both of them."

Lydia's grim expression didn't change, but she nodded and said, "What can I do to help?"

"Get some rope from the barn," he said, "and a hook. Bring one of the horses too. We'll tie the rope around the cattle's feet and hook it to the pommel of one of the saddles. We need to get this calf out of her before—"

The cow cried loudly, a sound that was more a wail than a low. She stiffened, her legs and head lifting off the ground and shaking. Then she collapsed and lay still.

Peter and Lydia stared silently at the cow. A few minutes later, Peter said, "Go tell your mother not to worry about the water."

Lydia nodded silently and walked slowly back to the house. Peter continued to stare at the dead cow, the scent of blood invading his nostrils.

***

The five of them sat around the table, staring at their breakfast. No one felt like eating. As the food grew cold, Peter finally forced himself to speak.

"It looks like the cattle are infected," he said, "Worms. We can feed them some plantain and yarrow and switch the mothers to grain feed, but..."

"But?" Lydia asked tonelessly.

Peter sighed. "But I think we'll lose more calves. Probably most of them."

Lydia looked at Eugene, who nodded dejectedly.

They had seen worms leaving the cow's body after she died. The three men had quickly dragged the body—or rather bodies—away and burned them, but further inspection had revealed symptoms of infection in a dozen of the other cattle. They would finish inspecting the herd today and separate any that were ill, but in all likelihood, their hopes of future sales had vanished.

After another long moment of silence, Lydia stood. "I need to look at the books," she said. "I need to find out how much this will cost us."

No one else moved. Even Greg had lost his typical ebullience. Eugene sighed and said, "I should get back home and take a look at my sheep. I'll be by later to help with the cattle."

Greg nodded. Peter managed a thank-you.

After Eugene left, Mary burst into tears, burying her head in her hands. Greg put his arm around his wife, but there was little comfort to be had.

This was what Peter feared. The ranch was riding on a knife-edge and now it had fallen off. A larger ranch with more capital that wasn't in debt could weather storms like this, but they had no room for error.

They were in trouble. Real trouble.

After brooding for several more minutes, Peter finally stood. "I'm going to go check on Lydia," he said, "see if she needs help with the numbers."

Greg nodded. Mary continued to weep.

He headed to the porch, where Lydia sat with the ledger. Her shoulders were tense, and her lips were set in a thin line. Her eyes were red and puffy, and Peter knew she had been crying.

He cleared his throat. "Can I help with the books, Lydia?"

She chuckled bitterly. "Can you turn back time and bring that cow and her calf back to life? Better yet, go back five years ago and tell my father that quitting his job at the bank and moving thousands of miles away to try his hand at cattle ranching at the age of fifty-one with no experience at all is a foolish idea."

Peter didn't reply right away. Finally, he said, "We can separate the healthy cattle and sell them. The ones that are too old for beef will sell for leather. It won't bring as much money as meat, but it will be enough to keep us afloat for a few months longer."

"And after that?" Lydia asked.

Peter didn't answer.

"By my calculations, we have eight months at the outside. The money you earned from the sales to Double Bar S will pull us out of default and pay the minimum installment on our debt through February. If you do manage to sell the rest of the herd, that will carry us through May. So what happens then? We have no money to buy more cattle. If the cows are all suffering the way the one that died last night was, then they're going to be no help to us. They probably won't even survive to breed again. Even if by some miracle they did, the calves won't be grown in time for us to sell them."

"We can't lose hope, Lydia," Peter offered. "We have to keep fighting."

Lydia offered another bitter laugh. "Well, that's easy for you to say, Peter. You can find another job. You're an experienced ranch hand now. You'll have no trouble working your way South like you worked your way West and finding employment. I'm sure the Double Bar S will hire you."

"I'm with you until the end," Peter said, "I promised Mary—"

"You're with us until the end of the ranch, Peter," Lydia said, "what then? Will you marry John with me?"

"That snake will not touch you," Peter said vehemently.

"Or what?" Lydia fired back. "What will you do, Peter? Will you shoot him with that revolver you keep hidden in your closet?"

Her words cut Peter like a knife. He drew in a steadying breath as he said, "I understand that you're worried, Lydia. I promise you that I won't leave you to founder, and I promise you, John will never touch you. We have enough to last several months. We have time to think of a solution that will help us survive."

Lydia huffed in exasperation and turned narrowed eyes to him. "You know, if we didn't have your salary to pay, we could survive a lot longer. Have you thought about that?"

The knife in Peter's chest twisted. He stood back. "Very well, ma'am. I'll search for a new job right away."

He turned and left without waiting for a response from Lydia, and when he heard her call his name, he didn't answer. He headed straight for his cabin, and when he reached it, he began to gather his belongings, throwing them roughly into his bag.

She had no cause to talk like that to him! All he had ever done was try to help. He had worked himself to the bone every day to save their ranch, and as Lydia herself had pointed out, he could easily find another job. He could find one now. He could have found one months ago. He didn't need to stay. He could have arrived at their run-down, poorly managed disaster of a ranch, took one look at the sorry place and left without looking back. Instead, he stayed and worked every day to save them from their own mistakes.

Well, it was time for him to leave now. He wasn't wanted here. He would head to town in the morning and take the next train out of town. It didn't matter where. He'd figure out a destination once he was away.

There was a knock on the door, and Peter sighed heavily. He wasn't in the mood for an apology right now. He opened the door, prepared to tell Lydia to go away, but it wasn't Lydia. It was Mary, and she was crying.

"You promised!" she said accusingly. "You promised me you would stay!"

"I did stay, ma'am," he said.

"Don't call me ma'am!" she shouted at him.

Peter thought how much she looked like her daughter when she said that.

"You promised!" she repeated.

"I kept my promise, Mary," he said, much more gently than before. "I stayed until the end. The end came a little sooner than either of us wanted, but I stayed until my employer made it clear that I'm not wanted anymore."

"Lydia's not your only employer," Mary said. "I am. So is Greg. We both want you to stay. If you need to hear it from Greg, I'll march him over and have him tell you the same thing. Lydia wants you to stay too."

Her voice softened, and Peter could hear real anguish when she said, "She's just scared, Peter. She's scared and angry and humiliated and—"

"Humiliated?" Peter's eyes widened in surprise. "Why is she humiliated?"

"I told you, Peter, she thinks it's her responsibility to take care of me and Greg. She feels guilty over her brother's death, and she feels it's her fault that the ranch is failing."

"How could she think it's her fault?"

"She doesn't *think* it's her fault," Mary said, "but she *feels* it's her fault. Do you understand?"

"I honestly don't," Peter said softly.

"Well, you don't have to," Mary said, wiping tears from her eyes. "You just have to keep your promise. I feel that with you, we have a chance. Don't ask me how, this isn't what I *think*, it's how I *feel*. Right now, that's enough. Please don't go."

Peter didn't answer right away, but he knew what his answer would be even before he said it. It would hurt him terribly to have to hold his head up in front of Lydia every day, but it would hurt him worse to leave Mary desolate.

"All right," he said softly. "I'll stay."

"Oh, thank you!" Mary cried.

She rushed into his arms and wept against his chest, saying over and over, "Thank you. Thank you."

He held her while she wept and stared blankly ahead. Mary felt they had a chance with him. But Peter didn't have the luxury of clinging to hope. Without the cattle, they had no chance, no chance at all. They could survive at least eight months. With effort, they could possibly last a year.

Unless a miracle happened within that year, though, they would all lose their home.

He held Mary and his feelings were uncomfortably similar to those he had lying in the trenches at Bull Run. They had already lost. All they were waiting for was for the enemy to realize it.

Chapter Twenty

Lydia lay awake in bed, as she had every night for the past five days. She stared up at the ceiling and replayed her last conversation with Peter over and over. She could see as clear as the day it happened the hurt in his eyes when she had attacked him about his salary.

Over and over, she played that scene in her mind, and over and over, she wished she had said anything else, done anything else other than attack the one good thing that had happened to them—happened to *her*—in the years since they had arrived in Montana. Well, save for Eugene and Dorothy, but as kind as Eugene and Dorothy were, they wouldn't save the ranch. Peter might yet. He had already pulled them from the brink of destruction. Maybe he could do it again.

And she had attacked and insulted him. She covered her eyes with her hand, and as she had done every night for the past five nights, she wept bitterly, stifling the sound to keep from waking her parents.

She had seen little of Peter the past five days, which was understandable. He hadn't attended dinner, and if they saw each other out on the ranch, he limited his interactions to a cold, "morning, ma'am," or "evening, ma'am."

God, she hated that word so much more now.

Her parents, also understandably, were not happy with her. The day she had turned on Peter, she had received the worst tongue-lashing she could remember from her mother before she rushed to Peter's cabin to beg him to stay. Mary had succeeded in keeping Peter on the ranch, but she had been just as coldly civil to her daughter as Peter had been.

Her father's reaction was somehow worse. He wasn't angry. He simply looked at Lydia, his eyes filled with hurt, and asked, "Why would you say that? He's worked so hard to help us." He hadn't been cold to Lydia, but his downcast eyes and defeated expression didn't feel any better than her mother's cold stares and clipped tones.

Not that Lydia had made any attempt to heal that relationship. She was humiliated, but also angry that her mother so clearly saw Peter as their salvation and thought nothing of the years of work Lydia had done to keep them warm and safe and fed. True, the ranch was in dire straits when Peter arrived, and true, he had come close to saving them, but it hurt to be so taken for granted.

The worst part was that they were right. She was utterly wrong to attack Peter the way she had. She might feel insulted or taken for granted, but it didn't matter. Those feelings were used to justify her actions after the fact, but they weren't what prompted her to attack him.

The sad truth was that she was just angry and scared and had lashed out at the nearest thing she could. Why did that thing have to be the one person who stood a chance of helping them?

She couldn't take it anymore. She rolled out of bed and dressed. She needed to apologize to him. She needed to make this right, or she would spend the rest of her life with this thorn in her side.

She took the lantern from the porch and lit it before making her way across the courtyard toward his cabin. Only when she was halfway there did it occur to her that Peter would probably not appreciate being woken in the middle of the night. She could just as easily make this apology in the morning.

She nearly turned and headed back to the house when she heard the door to his cabin open and saw him step outside.

He walked slowly in her direction, face pointed up at the sky, which as always was lit by a beautiful canopy of stars.

She took a breath and walked toward him. "Peter?"

His eyes snapped down to her. He stared at her a moment, then his eyes narrowed. He turned and started to walk back to his cabin.

"Peter, wait!" she called out, rushing toward him. "Wait, please!"

He stopped but didn't turn. She rushed to him. "Peter, please! Please, can I talk to you?"

"I don't see that we have much to talk about, ma'am," he said coldly. "If you need something from me, you can ask me in the morning during working hours."

"Peter, I'm sorry," she said, coming around to face him. "I'm sorry. I shouldn't have said what I said."

"You said what you felt," he replied. "There's no harm in being honest."

"I'm being honest now," she said. "I shouldn't have said those things to you."

"But you did," he said, "and you meant them."

"No," she said, shaking her head. "No, I didn't. I promise you, I didn't."

"I hear that word an awful lot lately," he said irritably. "Still not sure what it's supposed to mean to you."

"Peter, will you please talk to me?" Lydia said, forcing back tears. "I...I don't know what else to do right now."

He took a breath and said, "All right. Why don't you come inside?"

"We don't have to," she said, "I know I interrupted your walk."

"Well, I'm going inside," he said, walking past her toward the cabin. "You can follow me or not."

It wasn't like him to speak so disrespectfully to her. She knew he was still hurting deeply from her earlier words, or he wouldn't talk to her like this. She followed him, wiping tears from her face as they headed inside.

Peter sat on the bed and gestured to the chair. She sat and they spent a moment saying nothing before Lydia said, "I'm scared, Peter. I'm terrified. I...I've known for a while that this ranch wasn't going to succeed. I guess I knew it the day we left Baltimore. I went along because I didn't feel I had a choice, and I stayed because without me, the ranch would have failed years ago, and my parents would be homeless debtors or... or worse.

"When you arrived, I felt hope for the first time. The more you helped us, the more you found solutions where there weren't any, the more I thought maybe we had a chance, and..." She took a breath. "I guess I was afraid to trust that hope. I didn't want to believe that we could be saved only to have that hope dashed from me again.

"Then we lost the cow and from what I've overheard, we'll lose most of the other cows and their calves as well."

Peter nodded. "Yes. That's true."

"I figured," Lydia said, her shoulders slumping. "When we lost that cow, I just saw all of my fears coming true, and I was scared and hurt and angry. I was so angry, Peter. I'm still angry. I took that anger out on you, and I'm sorry for it.

"But I'm not angry at you, Peter. I don't blame you for what happened. I just... I'm so scared. I don't know what to do, and I'm scared, and I don't want you to go. Please don't go."

She couldn't hold back anymore. She buried her face in her hands and began to weep. A moment later, she felt strong arms wrap around her and hold her close. She wept for what felt like hours, sobbing into Peter's shoulder as he held her and softly stroked her hair. Slowly but surely, her tears ebbed, his strength driving away her fear.

When her tears had dried, she sat up and looked down at her knees, redfaced. "Thank you," she said softly.

"That's all right, Lydia," he said, "It's all right."

Her name had never sounded so beautiful to her.

She looked at him and offered a trembling smile. "Will you stay?" she asked.

He nodded. "Yes, I'll stay. I already told Mary. I'm here until the end."

She sighed with relief. "Thank you."

They fell silent a moment. This time, it was Peter who broke the silence. "I've been thinking, ma'am, and I really think that selling the herd off is the way to go. I've contacted some leatherworkers in Denver and offered to sell the herd for twenty dollars a head. After we cull the sick animals, that will leave us forty head. That's eight hundred dollars. It's not everything we owe, but it's a substantial portion of the remaining debt."

He fell silent, and Lydia said, "How much time will that buy us?"

He took a breath. "It won't."

Her blood ran cold. "What do you mean?"

"Well," he said, "we can pay off about three-fourths of the debt with that money, but that leaves us no money to operate."

"But how will we..." her voice trailed off when she realized what he was suggesting.

"We need to sell," he said. "Eugene thinks we can make another hundred or so for the equipment and maybe another hundred for the horses and anything we don't need from the house. That should be enough to keep us alive until I can find a job. We can head west to San Francisco. Greg might be able to get a job as a clerk again. I can work any job that needs manual labor. You should be able to find work as a serving girl or cleaning woman. It isn't glamorous, but it's better than what awaits you with John."

Lydia thought of the rumors that still rumbled through town about John's last wife, the screams the neighbors reported and the silence after. She knew Peter was right, and if it were only the two of them, she could even bring herself to give up her home to survive. But her parents couldn't. They were already old. The move from Baltimore was hard enough, and they'd had a place to go that time. Living on nothing but a prayer was too much to ask of them.

"We can't, Peter," she said. "If it was just you and me, I would follow you, but I can't ask my parents to do that. This is their home. They sacrificed everything to be here. We have to save their home. I don't know how, but we have to. Somehow, we have to find a way."

Peter nodded. After a moment, he sighed and said, "Well, to tell you the truth, I was worried about them as well. I just...well, Lydia, I won't lie to you. We don't have a choice as far as the herd's concerned. There's no coming back from what we've lost. We have to sell the cattle, and then we have to sell the horses just to live. If we're frugal, we can survive off of the hundred we make from the horses for four months. I know the Flisters will help as much as they can. That will keep us alive until February. By then... well, by then we need to hope we've come upon a miracle or some other idea."

Lydia nodded and squared her shoulders. "Well, we're still alive, so it's not over yet."

Peter stared at her a moment. Then he chuckled. That chuckle turned into a laugh and Lydia stared at him incredulously. "What on Earth is so funny?"

"Well," Peter said, wiping tears from his eyes. "Nothing, I guess. It's just that's something my old lieutenant used to tell us during the war. We'd be running from the rebs, camping in the dark and the cold because we couldn't risk a fire being spotted, and he'd walk around and tell us, 'We're alive. That means it's not over yet.'"

Lydia grinned. She still didn't quite understand why that was funny, but this was the first time she had seen Peter laugh, and she found she liked the sound of it. "If you ever see this lieutenant again, make sure you thank him for me."

His smile faded slightly. "Well, he died. Gettysburg. Sharpshooter got him just under the right eye." He looked at Lydia's shocked expression and said, "Sorry. You didn't need to hear that."

She remained silent a moment. Then she said, "Well, is it absolutely horrible of me to say I hope we have better luck than your lieutenant?"

Peter stared at her a moment. Then he began to laugh again. This time, Lydia joined him. They laughed uproariously, tears streaming down their faces, and for the first time in years, she felt not a hint of fear or grief.

When their laughter subsided, Lydia stood. "Well, Peter. I'm glad we talked."

"Yes," Peter said, "Me too."

She headed for the door but stopped before leaving. She turned and said, "The town's anniversary festival is tomorrow. There will be a potluck and a dance. Will I see you there?"

He smiled at her. "I'll be there."

She returned his smile. "Good."

The air was cold as she walked back to the house, and a fresh breeze chilled it even further, but Lydia felt perfectly warm.

Chapter Twenty-One

Lydia stared at herself in the mirror. She looked... different.

She hadn't dressed like this since before leaving Baltimore. In fact, this was the same dress she wore the first time Timothy came to call. It was a dark green cotton gown with just a touch of lace on the collar, hem and sleeves. Over the dress, she wore a red wool coat that set off the green dress. Lydia was concerned that it clashed with the deep blue of her eyes, but Dorothy assured her that she looked beautiful.

Of course, she could wear a potato sack and her friend would tell her she looked beautiful, but Lydia herself thought she looked...she couldn't bring herself to say it, but...oh why not? She looked beautiful.

She was older than she was the last time she wore this dress. Her cheeks were not so round or soft as they were six and a half years ago, and the corners of her eyes showed hints of the lines that would soon deepen into crows' feet, but she was beautiful all the same.

It felt so strange to look at herself like this. When had she last cared how she looked? In the beginning with Timothy, it seemed like her appearance was the most important thing on Earth. She wasn't tall and she wasn't particularly slender. She recalled how much it worried her that Timothy might think her short or stumpy. Now, she felt no such concern. Peter was not the sort of man to judge a woman based on her appearance. Not that he didn't appreciate beauty. He had eyes, after all. Maybe it was more accurate to say that she was confident he would find her attractive no matter what she wore.

She saw a flush creep into her cheeks. Now why had she thought that?

There was a knock on her bedroom door. "Come in," she said, "I'm decent."

"Well, we'll let God be the judge of that," Dorothy said, opening the door and walking inside, "but you look absolutely beautiful."

Lydia smiled. She turned to show her profile to the mirror. "I do look rather fetching, don't I?"

She laughed at herself and shook her head in disbelief. "Look at me, tittering like a schoolgirl."

"It looks good on you," Dorothy said, "you should be kind to yourself like this all the time. And you *do* look fetching. Although–" Her smile grew mischievous. "We should let your escort be the judge of that."

"Dorothy, behave," Lydia said, "Peter's attending the festival with *us,* he's not escorting *me.*"

Dorothy sighed. "If you *must* deny the attraction between you two, that's your right, but you should know I'll insist on it anyway."

Lydia rolled her eyes but kept her smile. "I suppose I can't stop you."

"You can't," Dorothy said brightly. She grabbed Lydia's hand and half-dragged her from the room. "Come, milady. Your prince awaits."

"*Please* be gentle on the man," Lydia said, "he's been through a lot recently."

Dorothy grinned at her. "I'm sure all will be made well when he sees you."

"Well, I can only..." Lydia's eyes widened when she reached the parlor and saw Peter standing there with Eugene and her parents. "...hope."

Peter wore a new wool suit, with a well-fitted woolen jacket over it. His boots were polished to such a high shine that they appeared new. His hair was oiled and combed back, and he looked stunningly handsome. She stared at him in shock and didn't even try to stifle the flush that crept to her cheeks.

He looked at her with the same expression she felt on her own face, and when he spoke, it was with the same breathless awe. "You look beautiful, Lydia."

Her flush deepened, and she replied, "You look quite handsome yourself."

"Thank you," he said.

He shifted his feet awkwardly, and she lowered her eyes demurely. They stood silently a moment while the other four grinned at them. Perhaps not surprisingly, it was Dorothy who broke the silence.

"Oh, you two look so incredible! Come, stand next to each other."

She didn't offer them a choice but pushed Lydia forward until she was next to Peter and turned them so that they faced the other four. Eugene beamed proudly at Peter as though it were his son standing there. Mary wiped tears from her eyes and clasped her hands in front of her. Greg puffed his chest out and grinned broadly, looking between the two of them. "Well, you two will be the belles of this ball, that's for sure."

Lydia sighed, but couldn't quite cover the giggle that escaped. "All right, you've all had your look. Let's go get this over with."

They headed into town, Eugene and Dorothy ahead in their wagon with the pies they had baked for the potluck, Peter and the Gutenbergs following in their own. Mary and Greg talked up a storm during the drive, while Lydia and Peter responded whenever they could get a word in edgewise.

Somewhere along the way, Lydia realized that her parents were perfectly happy. Their herd was days away from being sold off, along with all the horses but their cart horse and a single riding horse. Their ranch was almost certainly doomed, and they would almost certainly spend the next year struggling for every meal, but today they were happy.

Almost without thinking, Lydia reached over and grasped Peter's hand. He took it and smiled down at her, and for a blissful moment, all was right in Lydia's world.

They reached the town just as the festival was swinging into full gear. Dorothy commandeered the five of them to help her carry the pies to the dessert table in the church, where she left it with Mrs. Haversham under strict instructions *not* to allow anyone to taste them until dessert was served. Mrs. Haversham listened to her with a tolerant smile and assured her that not a single finger would touch their pies before the appointed time.

So satisfied, Dorothy scampered off to find her sweetheart. Lydia thought Colton a rather clumsy, plain-looking fellow, but he had an earnest face and kind eyes, and he looked at Dorothy as though she were an angel of God. Lydia decided he was an improvement over Micah.

Peter stood awkwardly, fiddling with his hat while Eugene and the Gutenbergs mingled with the other homesteaders. Lydia watched him for a moment, covering her mouth to hide her mirthful smile. After a moment, she took pity on him and approached.

"Shall we watch the shooting contest, Peter?" she asked.

He nodded and said, "Sure."

She waited patiently, and after a moment, he said, "Oh," and offered her his arm. She laughed and took it, then led him to the firing line, where several of the townsfolk, including Eugene, stood to try their hand. The prize this year was a massive pig–three hundred pounds, the Mayor claimed, and raised on a diet of corn supplemented with acorns and hazelnuts.

Lydia thought it rather unlikely that the pig had been fed any substantial quantity of nuts, but she doubted anyone took that claim seriously. Embellishment was as much as part of these contests as the contest itself. It was all in good fun, and Heaven knew they needed it right now.

The first group of men lined up and aimed their rifles. The targets were set fifty yards away in a small hill just behind the sheriff's station. Eugene took a breath and sighted down the barrel. The Mayor dropped his hand and the men fired. Dorothy cheered loudly when Eugene was announced as the frontrunner.

"Good shot," Peter said. "Listed a quarter inch right and an inch high."

Lydia turned to him and raised her eyebrow. "Perhaps you should try your hand."

He quickly shook his head. "No, that's all right. I've done enough shooting in my life."

Lydia decided not to push him. They watched as group after group of men tried and failed to beat Eugene's mark.

Finally, there was only one group left. Lydia didn't recognize the men in this group. They looked rough and dangerous. One of them wore a handgun low and tied down on his hip. He turned to her and offered a leering grin as he tipped his cap, revealing a prematurely balding head. Her grip on Peter's arm tightened reflexively. The stranger laughed and turned to aim his rifle.

The mayor's hand dropped, and the strangers fired. The mayor examined the targets and announced that the balding stranger had beaten Eugene's mark.

"Are there any other challengers?" the mayor asked.

"Oh please!" Dorothy said, turning imploringly to Peter. "Please, Peter, you have to avenge my father!"

Peter hesitated, but Lydia, motivated a little by the strange disquiet she felt from the stranger, squeezed his hand and said, "Go on. For me."

He looked at her and sighed. Then he nodded. "I don't have a rifle, though."

"You can use mine," Eugene said.

Peter took the weapon. "Much obliged."

He broke the barrel and quickly inspected the weapon, his fingers moving with astonishing speed and assurance. A hush fell over the crowd as they watched him. After a moment, he nodded, satisfied and stepped to the line.

He took a breath, and when he exhaled, his face changed. All emotion disappeared, leaving only a quiet, cold confidence. Lydia felt a chill run through her and a voice in the back of her head screamed that she shouldn't have pushed him to shoot.

He lifted the rifle to his shoulder and took a breath. When he exhaled, he fired. The center of the target disappeared. The crowd watched in shock as he levered another round and fired, then another, then another. One by one, the centers of each target disappeared. When the final shot rang out, Peter lowered the rifle and calmly handed it back to Eugene.

The crowd watched in stunned silence for a moment. Then they erupted into cheers. Only the strange men, the last group to fire, didn't cheer. The balding man looked appraisingly at Peter, and Lydia felt another chill as she saw his hand stroke the butt of his handgun almost lovingly.

Peter returned to her, and she searched his face. For a moment, he retained his frightening expressionless look. Then he smiled, and Lydia sighed with a relief so palpable it nearly shocked her.

"Guess I won," he said.

She chuckled, "Yes, I think you did. And in so doing, you've brought us food for the next three months."

"Easiest hunt I've ever made," he said with a smile.

Lydia laughed, then saw Dorothy just in time to jump to the side before Dorothy knocked her over on the way to Peter.

Dorothy threw her arms around him, planting a big smack on his cheek. Peter's face flamed bright red, and Lydia couldn't help but laugh.

The mayor promised them the pig would be delivered to them the next morning, then announced that the Anniversary ball would begin in ten minutes. Peter and Lydia headed into the church house, which had hastily been converted into a dance floor.

The band began to play. Lydia realized that she was nervous almost to the point of fright. She turned to Peter and took a breath. "Um," she said, "I...um...it's been a long time."

"It's all right," he said. "Me too."

He took her hand and placed his other around her waist. Then he led her onto the floor and Lydia was swept away.

Peter moved with such grace and self-assurance. It was so unlike his normal awkward gait. His steps flowed with the music, and Lydia's anxiety melted away as he confidently led her around the floor. The noise of the band seemed to soften and expand until it filled the air around her. The crowd gathered in the church house faded away. Even Dorothy and her parents seemed to recede into the background and then disappear entirely.

There was only her and Peter. She looked into his soft brown eyes, so strong and so kind, and in that moment she believed that everything would be okay. Whatever happened to the ranch, whatever happened with John, everything would work out so long as Peter was here.

He smiled at her, and Lydia was in love. She knew that now as clearly as she knew her own name. She was in love, and it didn't matter that she was nearer thirty-one than thirty or that she stood on the verge of losing her home. All that mattered was being with the man she loved, the man who held her in his arms and in his eyes.

On a sudden impulse, she leaned forward and kissed him. When their lips touched, lightning coursed through her body from her toes all the way to her fingertips. She wrapped her arms around him and held him tightly, kissing him deeply, showing him with her kiss what she didn't say with her words.

The music stopped. Their lips parted. The world stopped spinning and came into focus. Peter looked at her with shock in his eyes, but behind the shock was the same joy Lydia felt.

She smiled at him, and when she heard Dorothy leading the cheers of the crowd, she blushed and looked away.

202

The music started again. Dorothy slipped in between the two of them and pulled Peter away, winking at Lydia. Lydia danced with Colton and found him just as clumsy as he looked, but just as earnest and adorable. He glanced at Dorothy almost constantly, and Lydia couldn't help but smile.

For her part, she glanced at Peter. He met her eyes several times, and each time, she blushed and looked away.

Lydia knew that she would have to deal with the consequences of their kiss later. She knew she would have to face the problem of the ranch and John's looming threat. For the moment, though, she was happy, and that was enough for her.

Chapter Twenty-Two

Peter stood outside of the barn and gazed out at the rising sun. He had gotten very little work done that morning. Normally, that would frustrate him immensely, but today, he didn't feel that frustration. He couldn't blame himself for his distraction. His lips still burned from his kiss with Lydia the night before.

He'd been so surprised when she leaned forward and pressed her lips to his. The last thing he expected was a kiss. They had repaired their working relationship, but Peter no longer felt Lydia had any sort of attraction to him. True, she had invited him to the dance, but he assumed that was only because she wanted to extend an olive branch.

Now...

Now what? In a perfect world, he and Lydia could be together. They could court, marry and raise a family on a small homestead like this one and be happy.

This wasn't a perfect world.

He recalled the men he beat in the rifle competition, hard-looking strangers who kept to themselves and had nothing but a cold stare for any of the townsfolk who attempted to introduce themselves.

They were gunfighters. He recognized the type. Sean O'Malley's gang was composed primarily of gunfighters, professional killers who lacked the talent or luck or work ethic to find a real job after the war and chose to do the only thing they knew how to do...shoot people.

These men were different. Other than O'Malley himself, the men in his gang didn't delight in violence. They had nothing against violence and showed little remorse when they perpetrated it, but they didn't revel in it.

These men did. Peter had seen other men like them in the war—men who enjoyed the chance to hurt and maim and kill others. They fought on both sides, and in the Union Army, at least, they were tolerated because they were generally very good at it. In a war, qualities that society would abhor and reject under ordinary circumstances were valued and even esteemed.

It wasn't a war anymore, and that was a problem. During the war, men like this were contained so they couldn't impact innocents. Now, there was nothing to keep them from harming others. In most western towns, Peter had seen a strong law enforcement presence, but in Stevensville, there seemed to be little law enforcement of any kind.

Men like that could cause serious destruction in a town like this.

That was why Peter had eventually agreed to compete in the rifle shoot. He wanted those men to know that he was more dangerous than they were. It made him almost nauseous to get into that mindset again, but the only reason men like that would waste time in a town of homesteaders like Stevensville was if a wealthy townsperson hired them.

John Smith was the only townsperson wealthy enough to hire men like that, and if he hired them, it was for one purpose. Peter wanted to make it clear that if they intended to complete their job, some or all of them would die.

He hated that he had to do that. He hated that he was capable of that violence. Losing everyone close to him was a terrible tragedy, but it wasn't the worst thing that had happened to him in the war.

And now he would be called upon to use those skills again. He was so tired of fighting. If it weren't Lydia and her parents' lives that were threatened, he would probably just take his out and leave for somewhere farther west where he could work a simple job and live a simple life, hidden in the crowd of others like him who wished to forget.

He didn't have that luxury anymore.

"Morning, Peter," Greg said.

Peter turned to see Greg approaching with a smile. He reddened slightly and looked away. He was acutely aware of the fact that he and Lydia had kissed almost directly in front of Lydia's parents.

Greg seemed to notice and understand Peter's embarrassment. His grin widened, and he said, "That was some dance last night, wasn't it?"

Peter nodded. "Yes. Sure was. Thank you for having me."

"Oh, it wasn't my choice," Greg said. "I don't think Lydia would ever have forgiven me if I had left you home."

Peter only nodded at that. He could feel his cheeks burning.

"You have my permission, by the way," Greg said.

Peter's brow furrowed. "For what?" he asked.

"To marry her," Greg said. "You have my permission."

A whirlwind of emotion coursed through Peter. His initial reaction was one of elation. An image of Lydia in a beautiful blue cotton gown, her hair braided and her collar adorned with lace, came to his mind. He imagined their kiss and felt his lips burn again.

But fear followed hard on the heels of his brief elation. Greg and Lydia remained unaware of the danger. Peter hadn't wanted to worry them the night before, and he wasn't sure how to tell them what they faced now. Greg was offering his daughter in marriage to Peter at the worst possible time for Peter to consider that offer, the worst possible time for Lydia to be offered.

"This is usually when you'd say something in response," Greg said with a smile.

"Sorry," Peter said, "I guess I was a little taken aback."

Greg chuckled. "Yeah, Mary warned me you'd be humble. Well, I understand that, but before you tell me why you're not good enough for her, let me tell you why you are."

Peter did feel he wasn't good enough for Lydia, but that wasn't his primary concern at the moment. Still, he didn't want to scare Greg right now, so he let him talk.

"Lydia has never, ever put herself first, Peter," Greg said. "I love her for it, but it hurts to watch her constantly give and never take." His smile faded slightly. "It hurts to be a father and know you can't provide for your daughter."

"You're doing the best you can, Greg," Peter said.

"I know," Greg said. "I also know that I'm woefully useless as a rancher."

Peter shook his head. "That's not true. You're learning. You're getting better every day."

"No," he said, "I'm not." He smiled again. "I appreciate your kindness, but I'm going to be serious right now, and I need you to be the same. Can you let go of your admirable urge to be polite and be honest with me, no matter how hard it is?"

Peter nodded slowly.

"Good," Greg said, "I'm useless as a rancher. To be perfectly honest, if I could do it all over again, I wouldn't leave Baltimore. That was the biggest mistake of my life."

Peter didn't answer. Greg fell silent a moment, and Peter could see in his expression that he felt the weight of that mistake. It was the same look Peter saw in his own reflection. The weight he carried was different from Peter's, but it crushed him just the same.

After a moment, Greg took a deep breath and looked Peter squarely in the eye. "You can help me fix that mistake."

Peter shuffled his feet. "Greg, I'll do my best, but...well, you wanted me to be honest, so I will be. Honestly, Greg, there's no hope for the ranch. The money we'll make from liquidating the herd, horses and equipment will give us enough to survive until we find another place to live, but even if John forgives the debt, and I know for a fact he won't, we won't be able to replenish the herd."

"I know that," Greg said, "and I know that Lydia will sacrifice her life once more to care for me and Mary. You won't let her do that."

Peter stared at him. "Sir?"

"You heard me," Greg repeated. "You will not let her waste her life on me and Mary. You will marry her before we lose the ranch, and I don't care how much she cries and begs, you will make sure that she puts herself first for once."

Peter had no idea what to say, so he said the first thing that came to his mind. "What about you and Mary?"

"Mary and I will be fine," Greg said, "I can still find work as a clerk. We'll have to move, of course, probably either back to Baltimore or maybe west to San Francisco. It won't be easy, but we can handle a lot more hardship than Lydia thinks we can. As for you two, you're welcome to go wherever you'd like. You can even follow us as long as you make sure that Lydia doesn't waste her life on us. I mean it, Peter. Her needs are to come first."

For the first time since he'd known Greg, the older man spoke to him with strength and authority. Maybe for that reason or maybe because of the desperate nature of his request, Peter couldn't bring himself to refuse. "Okay," he said, "I will."

Greg beamed. "Wonderful. In that case, let me be the first to congratulate you on your engagement."

He threw his arms around Peter and hugged him tightly. Peter returned the embrace, but his emotions still whirled around uncontrollably.

Greg released him and said, "You should probably get around to proposing to her soon before she recovers from the kiss and starts telling herself all of the reasons why this can't work. She's still swooning over you. Don't tell her I said that."

Peter returned a half-hearted smile. Greg clapped him on the shoulder and said, "Well, I'll let you get back to work. Thank you, Peter. I mean that."

He clapped Peter on the shoulder once more and left.

Peter continued to gaze out at the eastern horizon. The sun had climbed completely over the horizon now, and slowly warmed the chill away. Peter knew that in a few weeks, the chill would grow strong enough that the sun would no longer be enough to drive it away.

Winter would come, and with it, hardship.

Peter sighed and began to work. Today, he was cutting beams for the hayloft he would install in the ranch. The beams needed to be short and sturdy, but light enough that they could be moved by the three men.

He tried to immerse himself in his work and drown his thoughts like he always did, but today he couldn't.

He should be happy. He was falling in love with Lydia. It would be very easy for him to spend the rest of his life with her under ordinary circumstances. With Greg's blessing and encouragement, he should be on cloud nine.

Of course, these weren't ordinary circumstances.

His thoughts returned to those men, those gunfighters. John hired them for a reason. Peter had intimidated him when he threatened Lydia the last time. Men like John couldn't handle the knowledge that someone could face them down. Really they couldn't handle the knowledge that someone could intimidate them in front of others and prove to those others that they were cowards.

He had exposed John as a coward, and he knew that John would focus on that until Peter was dead. Peter could accept that risk for himself, but he couldn't accept it for Lydia. If John didn't have an interest in Lydia, Peter could easily spare the Gutenbergs the danger by simply leaving and making sure John or his employees saw him go.

But then, John did have an interest in Lydia. He desired her. He wanted Lydia for his own, and just like he would fixate on his humiliation at Peter's hands, he would fixate on Lydia's continued denials of his attentions. He wouldn't rest until he had Lydia, and Peter couldn't let that happen. He had promised Mary he wouldn't. He had promised Lydia he wouldn't. He had promised Greg he wouldn't, and he had promised himself he wouldn't.

He had made those promises before the gunfighters showed up. Now he needed to decide whether his presence increased the danger the Gutenbergs faced.

A thought came to his head. He tried to suppress it, but the thought coalesced into an idea before he could push it away.

In the war, he and a select few soldiers had ambushed enemy artillery emplacements. They would sneak in under cover of darkness and use their knives and pistols to wipe the enemy out before they could respond. Peter was one of the best at that job.

If he could learn where the outlaws were staying, he could do the same job again.

Images flashed in his mind, of men torn apart, blown apart, shrieking while they stared at stumps where their arms and legs used to be. Worse were the memories of men he had fought, men he had killed, up close and personal, their blood spraying on his clothes as he took their lives and left them where they fell.

His breathing quickened. He set his saw down and staggered over to a stool, collapsing onto it and putting his head in between his knees. Gradually, his breathing calmed, and he was able to think clearly again.

He couldn't attack these men. He couldn't become that person again. He needed to find another way.

He sighed and sat up straight. He needed to tell the Gutenbergs about the danger. There was precious little they could do about it, but they deserved to know anyway.

But if he did that, then Lydia might be cowed into agreeing to marry John, and that was something Peter couldn't handle.

He needed to talk to Lydia first.

He stood, and took another deep breath, then picked up his saw. He wasn't confident about the situation at all, but now that he had some sort of plan to approach it, he could push the worry into the background of his mind.

But he knew he couldn't keep it there for long or his worry would once more become a terrifying reality.

Chapter Twenty-Three

Lydia looked up from her seat on the porch to see Peter approaching. Her breath caught in her throat. Her heart began to pound, and she felt heat creep up her cheeks. She tried to shake the emotions away, but she couldn't stop fantasizing about the kiss they shared at the dance.

The kiss they shared? Oh, who was she kidding? The kiss she had given him. She, for some reason, had kissed him. She couldn't believe herself. For heaven's sake, what was she thinking? Sure, it would be nice if the two of them could be together, but they lived in the real world, not a dream world. The real world, where John waited in the shadows to take advantage of her plight and force her into a marriage that would certainly be violent and could possibly be fatal. The real world, where her ranch was failing and the best hope they had was to fail in a way that allowed them to survive long enough to find a new home.

It didn't matter how she felt about Peter. They weren't meant to be. She could focus on the unfairness of that fact, or she could accept it and do what was right for her family.

"Good morning, Peter," she said, her tone even and professional in spite of her flaming face and pounding heart.

"Mornin', Lydia," he replied.

She was somewhat comforted to see that his cheeks were also flushed, and he was as uncomfortable as she was. She smiled and said, "I assume you're here to tell me about the sale?"

"Yes, ma—Lydia," he said.

She nearly giggled at that. When he was particularly nervous, he would slip into calling her ma'am again and catch himself. It was the most adorable thing she had ever seen. She forced herself not to dwell on that thought. "Well?" she asked.

"Good news," he says, "Hampton Leather will buy the rest of the herd and the postal service will take the horses."

"That's wonderful!" Lydia said. "So we have money to pay the debt?"

"Three-fourths of it, just like we expected," he said,

"That's good," Lydia replied. "Do you think John will accept that?"

Peter shook his head. "As paid in full? No. He'll want his full amount. He won't have a choice but to refrain from foreclosing, though, and that will give us time to make other arrangements."

He looked away from Lydia when he said that, and she could tell he was hiding something. "You're worried," she said, "Why?"

He shrugged. "Well, if something unexpected happens between now and delivery of these cattle, then we don't have another option."

"That's not it, is it?" Lydia said.

He was silent for a moment. Then he said, "I think we should talk about what happened between us at the dance."

She blinked, surprised. She expected him to raise a concern about John's reaction to learning he no longer had leverage to force Lydia to marry him. She didn't expect him to broach a subject she was certain neither of them wanted to address.

But he had, and now she had to address it.

"Yes," she said reluctantly, "yes, I suppose we should." She sighed. "Well, Peter... I... I'm not sure what to say. I don't regret our kiss, and I don't want you to regret it either. That being said... it just isn't the right time for me right now."

Peter's eyes fell, and Lydia felt a pang. She wished desperately that she could have had a future with him. She forced herself to remain calm and not burst into tears in front of him. "I'm so sorry I kissed you, Peter. No, I don't mean that. I'm not sorry. I'm just sorry that...That we can't..."

"It's all right," he said. "I understand."

He smiled, but there was something strange in his smile. Lydia assumed it was regret that they couldn't have more than that single kiss. She understood that.

"I really do wish things could be different," she said. "I'm sorry."

"No need to apologize." He cleared his throat. "So I'll deliver the herd and the horses tomorrow. Eugene's going to help me, and Greg drives them into town. We should have the money upon delivery. I asked them to pay us in cash since John could intercept anything sent to the bank."

"Thank you, Peter," she said. "That was smart."

He smiled at her, but his smile faded almost immediately. "Well, I'll see you at dinner. I have to go get the herd ready for delivery."

"Of course," she said. "Thank you."

He smiled briefly again, then tipped his cap and headed away. Lydia watched him go. He looked so strong and tall and handsome. Her eyes welled with tears. She wished so much that they could have a life together! It wasn't fair. It just wasn't fair.

Then again, life was never fair.

***

The next day, the three men returned to the Gutenberg ranch, beaming. Well, Greg was beaming. Eugene was smiling slightly, and Peter simply looked pleased.

Lydia watched them approach and couldn't help but smile herself. Greg surprised her with an embrace, causing her to stagger and nearly lose her balance.

"Okay, Pa, okay," she said with a laugh. "I'm guessing the sale went well?"

"Very well," he said, "Peter tells me we have enough now to avoid foreclosure!"

"We do," she confirmed. "After we pay John today, we will have as much time as we need to find somewhere to go."

"Wonderful!" he said, "I'll miss the ranch, but I'll miss it a lot less knowing we won't be homeless when it's gone."

The cavalier way he threw that out bothered Lydia, but she let it pass. He was encouraged, and she knew this might be the last encouraging moment they had for a while. Better to let him enjoy himself now. They had a long, rough road ahead of them.

Mary came to the porch then. "What's all the excitement— Oh!"

She cried out when Greg literally swept her off of her feet and spun her around, kissing her passionately.

"Gregory Gutenberg!" Mary cried out when he pulled away. "What on Earth has gotten into you?"

"Good news, my love!" Greg said gallantly. "I am just about to leave for John's office to pay him enough money to avoid foreclosure! We shall have more than enough time to find a nice, quiet place to retire in. Well, not retire. I'll probably end up working for a bank again. Maybe John will hire me!"

He laughed at that. The others didn't find it funny.

"Greg, why don't you let me go pay John?" Peter said. "You should stay here and celebrate with your wife and daughter."

"Yes," Lydia agreed. "That's a good idea."

"Nonsense!" Greg said, "Peter, I appreciate everything you've done for us, but this is my debt, not yours. I should be the one to pay it."

Peter frowned. Lydia's lips thinned. Leave it to her father to put his pride ahead of his common sense. "I really think you should let Peter go," she said.

"Why?" Greg asked, "what's John going to do? Shoot me?"

Once more, his family found his attempt at humor unsuccessful.

"Look," Greg said with a sigh. "I want to do this. I know that John's been pressuring you into marrying him, Lydia. Don't look so surprised. There's no other reason for him to always want to talk to you specifically. Well, this is my chance to protect you."

"You don't need to protect me," Lydia said.

"Well not anymore."

"Greg," Mary began.

"Mary, let me do this," Greg said forcefully.

The rest of them fell silent. Eugene looked at his feet. Peter looked at Lydia. Lydia looked at Peter. Mary looked at Greg, but after a moment, her eyes fell.

"I'll be okay," Greg said. "John's a mean old cur, but he's not going to risk his freedom and wealth to hurt me. I'll be all right."

"I hope you're right, Greg," Mary said.

Lydia considered his words. She was absolutely convinced that John was capable of great violence, but she agreed with her father that he wasn't likely to do anything that could get him in trouble.

She recalled the strange, hard-faced men she saw at that Anniversary festival three days ago. She didn't know that they were working for John, but it wouldn't surprise her to find out they were. Still, Greg was handing him money. She couldn't imagine John was so foolish that he would punish someone for bringing him money.

"Just be safe," she said to her father.

"I will," he answered. "You all worry too much."

He left, and a few minutes later, Eugene left to work on his own ranch, leaving Peter alone with Mary and Lydia. Mary lingered, and Lydia knew her mother was worried about her father. She shared that worry.

"Well," Lydia said, "you've had a long ride, Peter. Mother, would you help me with lunch and coffee?"

Mary brightened visibly, happy to have something to take her mind off of her fear. "Of course, dear. Peter, come inside and make yourself at home."

Lydia felt a pang at that. This wouldn't be her home for much longer.

Still, overall, she was in good spirits. She wouldn't have to marry John. She could finally admit to herself that if things had become dire enough, she would have made that sacrifice rather than leave her parents to suffer. Now she wouldn't have to. That alone was enough to bring a genuine smile to her face, and she, Mary and Peter enjoyed a nice lunch.

Their good mood was dashed as soon as Greg returned home. Lydia could tell right away by his haggard expression and lined face that his conversation with John hadn't gone well.

Her mother could as well. "Greg, what happened?" she asked softly.

Greg sighed. "Well, he took the money."

"That's good!" Mary said hopefully. "Isn't it?"

Greg met her eyes. For the first time in Lydia's memory, he seemed at a loss for words. He only shook his head and looked down at the floor again.

"Lydia," Peter said, "will you please get your father some coffee?"

His voice was calm and kind but also strong and commanding. She nodded and headed to the kitchen to comply. While she poured the coffee, she heard Peter direct Greg to sit in front of the fireplace and take his boots off while Mary stoked the fire and added a log.

When Lydia returned to the parlor, she saw Greg sitting on the couch, his head in his hands. Mary sat next to him with her hand over his shoulders. Peter stood, his arms folded across his chest.

Lydia handed Greg the coffee. "Father, what is it? Tell us what happened."

Greg slowly sat straight. His drawn face made him appear ten years older. Lydia realized for the first time how far from youth her father was. She hated that he had to suffer like this now.

"Well," Greg said, "like I said, he took the money. When I mentioned that this should prevent foreclosure, he..." He chuckled bitterly. "He laughed at me. He told me that he wanted the balance of his debt by the end of this month, or he would have us evicted."

"What?" Mary cried.

"He can't do that!" Lydia said, "That's illegal!"

"I told him that," Greg said. "He laughed at me again and said I was absolutely right. He told me to go tell the sheriff and see what happened. Then he told me that we owe him another two hundred fifty dollars by the end of this month or he would have us evicted."

"He can't evict us," Lydia said. "Not without legal authority."

"I told him that too," Greg said, "and he told me that he would have us forcibly removed. He made it clear that he meant forcibly. He introduced me to a gentleman named Isaac Slade. He used the word gentleman. I wouldn't. This Slade...I don't know who he is, but he wears a handgun tied low on his hip."

Peter swore under his breath. Lydia looked sharply at him, and he said, "I saw him at the rifle shoot where I won that pig."

The image of the stranger with his gun tied low flashed through Lydia's mind. She gasped. "Did they hurt you?" she asked her father.

"No," Greg said, "Isaac actually held the door for me to leave." He chuckled hollowly. "I thought he was going to take a shot on the way out, but he didn't. I guess he thought he didn't need to."

"So John told you that you needed to pay the balance of your debt or he'd sic Isaac Slade and his dogs on you."

Greg nodded.

Peter's face set in a hard line. "I won't let that happen. You don't need to worry about them."

Mary relaxed visibly at Peter's assurance. Lydia felt some comfort knowing Peter would help. But what was one man, however dangerous, against an entire gang of armed gunfighters?

"Let's not act too hastily, Peter," she said, "he's given us until the end of the month. That's seventeen days. We should wait and see if we can find another option. Maybe we can arrange to be moved out before then."

Peter didn't look confident about that, but he nodded. Mary and Greg did as well. Lydia saw the anxiety on all three faces and decided it fell to her to help soften their fear somehow.

"Let's have dinner," she said, "I'll make a pork roast. There's nothing we can do about things now, so let's not worry about it. In the morning, we'll approach the situation with fresh eyes and fresh minds."

The other three nodded, and Lydia headed to the kitchen. She managed to keep herself moving as she prepared dinner, but despite her strong outward demeanor, her palms felt clammy and her mouth dry.

If ever they needed a miracle, they needed one now.

Chapter Twenty-Four

Dinner was as somber an affair as Peter could recall. There had been bleak times during the war, particularly during the winters, where he and his comrades had spent long nights awake, huddling together for body heat. The expressions on his fellow soldiers' faces then matched the expressions on everyone's face now.

The worst part was that Peter should have seen this coming. He should have known the money wasn't important to John. John didn't want money, he wanted to win. That mattered more than anything. Besides, the ranch was done for no matter what. John was no fool. He knew they didn't have the ability to recoup their losses. Now, the only barrier between John and everything he wanted was the law, and the law was evidently no help here.

He hadn't mentioned Lydia. That was the one comfort Peter had, but even that was slim comfort. For all he knew, John *had* mentioned Lydia and Greg simply had chosen not to repeat that.

He needed to figure out their next steps. They wouldn't be able to come up with the money. That was for sure. Their only chance was to get out before John could force them out. The law was weak here, but it was strong elsewhere. John was strong here, but he was only strong here. They needed to find a way out.

After dinner, Lydia was preoccupied caring for her parents. She didn't exactly tell him to leave them alone, but he could sense that his presence caused her tension, so he stepped outside. That was all right with him. He needed space to clear his head and think of what to do.

He was surprised to look up and see that Eugene had returned. The older man dismounted and walked over to Peter, lifting a hand in greeting.

"I'm glad to see you still up," Eugene said. "I was hoping to talk to you alone."

"What about?" Peter asked.

Eugene smiled sadly. "What do you think?"

Peter nodded. "Yeah, I figured."

"What are you planning to do?" Eugene asked.

Peter shook his head. "I don't know," he said. "I would say we should talk to the sheriff, but I get the sense that would be a waste of time."

"Worse than a waste of time," Eugene said. "He'd only tell John and John would pay you back—meaning pay the Gutenbergs back—with violence."

"How does this man get so much power?" Peter wondered. "Why hasn't anyone put a stop to it?"

Eugene sighed. "I don't mean this with any judgment at all. Even if I did, I'd be judging myself. People here aren't fighters, Peter. Most of us came here to get away from fighting, and those that came after came to flee the memories of fighting. Things are good enough for most of us, and when things are good enough for people who aren't fighters, they'll look the other way to avoid great many troubles."

Peter's jaw tightened. He could understand the desire to avoid a fight, but to carry it so far that they would allow this tyrant to bully people was just too much.

Eugene saw his face and said, "I know what you're thinking, and I understand it. I even agree with it, to a point.

223

But don't blame the sheep for the ravages of the wolf. It would be nice if everyone had teeth, but it would be nicer if no one did."

"It would be," Peter said, "but some people do, whether we like it or not. It's fine to be a sheep, but only if you have a good sheepdog to protect you. That's where sheriffs and marshals come in. What I don't understand is why this town hasn't reached out to find someone who can handle the violence that no one else can."

Eugene smiled. "Well, we did. Lydia did, at least. She just didn't know that's who she was hiring."

Peter felt the weight of Eugene's words lay heavily on him. He turned away and said, "I can't stop John on my own, Eugene. Anyway, I didn't come here to be the sheepdog. I came here to be...I guess an ox or a mule."

"'Some have greatness thrust upon them,'" Eugene quoted.

Peter's eyes widened. "You've read Shakespeare?"

Eugene smiled. "Barbara read everything he ever wrote. She had a great big illuminated manuscript of Macbeth. Used to read it aloud to us. I thought it was dark and terrible stuff, but she ate it up. When she passed, I...well, I read Shakespeare, and it reminded me of her. Helped the grief pass. I still read it sometimes. Can't get Dotty to read anything other than *Romeo and Juliet*, but that's all right."

"What if I fail?" Peter asked.

He blinked in shock at his own words. He didn't expect to tell anyone that fear, especially not Eugene.

The older man's reaction surprised him even more. "Then you fail," he said simply. "You fail, and it will hurt terribly.

Believe me, though, it will feel better to fail than it will not to try. I tell Greg that all the time."

"I can't imagine he feels better about failing than not trying," Peter said.

"No," Eugene said, "probably not. So, what are you going to do?"

"I don't know," Peter said. He didn't want to tell Eugene about his thought of taking the fight to John. If things didn't go well, he didn't want it to come back to the Flisters or the Gutenbergs.

"Well," Eugene said, "I hope you stay to the end. I know you have no obligation to. This isn't your fight, and while Lydia never meant harm by it, it wasn't right of her to hire you knowing how desperate their situation was. Still, I hope you stay. The Gutenbergs will suffer terribly without you. With you, they might suffer, but they won't be destroyed."

"They have you," Peter said.

"And I will do whatever I can to help them," Eugene said, "but—and please forgive me for being blunt—I have a daughter to care for. I'll help as much as I can, but eventually John's going to threaten me, and when he does, I won't be able to stand against him even if I want to."

"You won't stand alone," Peter promised. "None of you will."

Eugene smiled. "Good. I'm glad to hear it. I'm sure you're tired of hearing this, but I think with you on our side, we really do have a chance."

Peter couldn't bring himself to return Eugene's smile.

The door opened and Greg came outside. "Eugene," he said, "I didn't expect to see you back tonight."

"Thought I'd come by and offer my company," Eugene said. "I know it ain't much, but it's what I got right now."

Peter didn't blame Eugene for choosing not to include Greg in their conversation, but it made the weight on his shoulders feel that much heavier.

"How are Mary and Lydia?" Eugene asked.

"They're asleep," Greg said, "so as good as they can be, I suppose."

"I take it you couldn't sleep," Eugene said.

"No," Greg replied, shaking his head. "No, sleep isn't in the cards for me tonight. I don't know about you two, but I could use a drink."

Peter opened his mouth to decline, but Eugene spoke first. "That sounds wonderful. We'll join you."

Peter cast a slightly irritated glance at Eugene but nodded assent.

"Wonderful," Greg said, "We'll take my wagon."

"You two take the wagon," Peter said. "I'll ride Moonlight."

"Can't handle two old men jawing at each other for an hour?" Greg asked with a smile.

"No, I just want to make sure there's room for someone to lay down in the wagon if one of us gets too drunk to ride."

Peter hadn't meant it as a joke, but Eugene and Greg burst into laughter anyway. Peter smiled, more at their mirth than anything else, then went to get the horses.

The three men headed into town. Greg and Eugene made small talk on the way. Peter remained silent, chewing over their situation. It was a puzzle that offered no solution other than simply leaving. If it weren't for Mary, Peter would have left that night, but the older woman likely wouldn't do well drifting until they could find work and a place to live.

He sighed. The only option seemed to be to fight John. That meant learning where his gunfighters were, hoping he could sneak up on them and killing them, all without getting shot himself, or alerting John, or running afoul of John's puppet sheriff.

That wasn't a guarantee. He was more dangerous than any one of those men, but there were at least a half dozen of them, and that Isaac Slade character was dangerous in his own right. Peter would beat him in a fight, but he wasn't confident he could keep the element of surprise with him. Some wolves were cunning.

They reached the saloon, and Peter decided to leave the problem behind for the moment. He wasn't solving anything wrestling with it fruitlessly as he was.

They sat at the bar and Greg loudly called for three whiskeys. The bartender shared a glance with Eugene, then calmly filled their orders. Peter tossed a coin on the counter to pay for the drinks, and Greg said, "Well, thank you kindly, Peter. I sure do appreciate that."

Peter nodded and smiled, happy to see a little joy in his friend's face.

Eugene bought the second round, and Peter the third. He tried to refuse a fourth, but Greg and Eugene, already somewhat tipsy, cajoled him into taking it anyway. Peter hadn't had a drink since arriving in Stevensville, and the alcohol began to affect him. He was relieved when Greg and Eugene launched into a very detailed discussion of raising sheep for wool compared to raising them for meat and didn't call for more drinks.

While they talked, his mind drifted to Lydia. He thought of her graceful figure, her full lips and bright eyes. He could feel the cool softness of her lips on his and the curves of her body in his arms.

Greg and Eugene ordered another drink, and once more, Peter tried to refuse before allowing himself to be coaxed into drinking it. They roped him into their conversation on sheep, and Peter smiled and nodded and interjected every now and then, but his thoughts remained on Lydia.

She was so beautiful. She was so strong. She was so kind. She was everything he had ever wanted in a woman.

He thought suddenly of Penelope. He recalled being deeply in love with her, but try as he might to recall those feelings, he couldn't. He could remember her face, her smile, her figure, slender and lithe where Lydia's was strong and full. He could remember her laugh as though from a dream, but he couldn't recall the emotions he felt. He knew that at one point he believed he would never love another. He even knew that he had believed that when he arrived at Lydia's ranch. When had that changed?

He supposed it had changed slowly, then all at once. In Peter's experience, most changes came suddenly. And the ones that didn't weren't recognized as changes until the change was so far along that it appeared to be sudden whether it was or not.

Whether sudden or only appearing that way, there could be no doubt now that he was in love with Lydia. Their kiss had erased every doubt in his mind.

"We'll let Peter break the tie," Greg said.

Peter blinked, his thoughts pulled suddenly away from Lydia and Penelope. "Tie for what?"

Eugene and Greg laughed. "I guess you weren't paying attention," Eugene said.

"What's the matter boy?" Greg asked. "Can't hold your liquor?"

Peter decided not to point out that Greg slurred his words when he said that.

"We were talking about eating," Eugene said, "beef or lamb, which is best?"

Peter considered. "Well, I don't rightly know that I've ever had lamb."

Eugene's eyes widened. "You've never had lamb? How have you been my neighbor for two months and have never had lamb? I'm going to make you some lamb for dinner tomorrow. You'll never eat a beefsteak again."

Two months? Had it only been two months? It seemed so much longer to Peter, but it wasn't. He had been here just less than twice as long as it took him to travel here, and already his life had changed so much.

He had a family now. A new family. He realized he hadn't thought of biting down on his revolver since arriving here. He had filled his days with work, but lately he could stand not to work every waking minute and not fall into a spiral of depression.

He had a family now.

And John Smith was threatening his family.

Greg and Eugene were arguing over something else now, and neither of them noticed the look that came to Peter's face.

He had lost one family already. He would not lose another.

He had left his revolver at home, but tomorrow night, he would bring it with him.

Count your days, John, he thought to himself. *I warned you to back off. Now you'll pay the price for your evil.*

Chapter Twenty-Five

Greg set his glass on the counter. "That's it. I can't drink anymore."

Wise choice, Peter thought wryly, glancing at the half-dozen empty glasses in front of Greg. He himself was drunk, but Greg was barely upright.

Eugene didn't look much better, but he was able to stand without falling over. Peter couldn't say the same for Greg, who would have collapsed to the floor if he and Eugene hadn't caught him.

Greg mumbled an old drinking song as Eugene and Peter carried him to the wagon and helped him up. Eugene got into the driver's seat, then looked at Peter.

"I think I'll stay a while," Peter said, "do a little more thinking."

Eugene smiled knowingly and tapped his head. "Thinking. Sure."

Peter offered a tolerant smile of his own.

"Wish I was young," Greg mumbled. "I'd drink both of you under the table."

"Sure you would," Eugene said. "All right, Peter. Have fun. I'll see you tomorrow."

"See you tomorrow."

When he returned to the bar, the saloon girl—she could hardly be called a girl; she was closer in age to Mary than to Lydia—smiled and said, "Hey there, handsome."

Peter smiled politely and lifted a hand in greeting.

"Do you feel lucky, big man?" she crooned.

Peter kept his smile despite the slight disgust he felt at her advances. "Lucky as anyone, I guess," he said noncommittally.

"Well," she said, batting her eyelashes at him. "There's some folks here need another for their poker table. I thought maybe a handsome, lucky fellow like yourself might want to join."

Peter had never been much of a gambler. The last time he'd played cards was during the war, betting things like socks and spare buttons for his jacket. He was about to refuse when a thought struck him.

He supposed it could be the whiskey that made him feel this way, but he considered that if he actually did win, he might be able to contribute some to the Gutenbergs' upkeep. He didn't imagine he'd win enough to pay the debt, but maybe he could ease their minds a little more about the future. If he lost—well, he only had a few dollars to lose anyway.

He nodded and said, "All right. Who are these men?"

The saloon girl—he couldn't remember her name—pointed at a table a few yards from the bar. Five men wearing ill-fitting silk suits sat and watched him. They smiled genially when he looked in their direction and one lifted an ostentatious top hat, revealing thinning hair.

They looked like traveling card sharks. Peter decided his chances of winning were pretty much nonexistent, but anyway, he had only a few dollars to lose, and sometimes people got lucky.

He stood and headed over to the table. The man with the top hat extended his hand. "Chester Montgomery."

"Peter Kerouac," Peter said, taking the offered hand.

The others introduced themselves, and Chester said, "Kerouac? That's French, right?"

"French Canadian," Peter confirmed. "My great-grandfather was a fur trapper in Ontario. He fell in love with a woman from Ohio and when the War of Independence was fought, he stayed with the Americans."

"Did he fight?" one of the younger of the men asked.

"Well, I don't know," Peter said, "He might have. He was of that age. I don't know much about him to tell the truth. Just that he came from Ontario and settled in Ohio. He was dead before I was born."

"Great-grandparents have a bad habit of dying on you," one of the men commented.

He burst into laughter at his own joke, and Peter smiled in spite of himself. He didn't consider himself much of a conversationalist, and he found he actually enjoyed being a part of a group. It was another sign that he was healing. Actually, it was probably just the drink, but he didn't begrudge himself the drink. He was in for hard times soon enough. Might as well enjoy one night of freedom and fun.

Chester dealt the cards, and Peter was grateful to see a full house in his hand. He didn't think he'd manage to bluff them well enough to keep them from knowing, but the alcohol must have affected them too, because the pot held nearly twenty dollars when he called and came up with the winning hand.

"Beginner's luck," one of the older gamblers said sourly.

"Probably is," Peter said.

As the game wore on, though, Peter's luck continued. He watched in disbelief as his pile of money grew and grew. He couldn't allow himself to believe he could actually earn real money, but when his earnings climbed over a hundred dollars, he began entertaining hopes he considered foolish only an hour ago.

The evening continued and the saloon slowly started emptying. Peter spent a few dollars of his winnings on rounds for the table and earned them back and then some.

Chester finally sighed and said, "Well, gents. I'm cleaned out. I suspect Mr. Kerouac here has beaten us at his own game."

The other gamblers grumbled, and Chester lifted a hand. "Now, now. We've won more than our fair share in life. It's only natural that one of these days someone would come along and give us a taste of our own medicine. Let's be civilized about this and congratulate Mr. Kerouac."

The five gamblers grudgingly shook Peter's hand and bid him goodnight. They filed out, leaving Peter alone in the saloon.

He counted his money, heart beating fast. He didn't dare believe that he might have won as much as he had, but the proof was right in front of him.

Three hundred forty-two dollars. Enough to pay off the remainder of the ranch's debt with almost a hundred dollars besides.

They could rebuild. With their original loan satisfied and with a recommendation from the Double Bar S and Hampton Leather, they could purchase more cattle and rebuild the herd. It would mean another loan, but Peter would make sure that loan was with a bank other than John's. He was confident that he could continue to earn money for the ranch.

He could manage to grow the business into something that could sustain them. They didn't have to lose the ranch after all.

With a trembling hand, he began to smooth out the crumpled bills. He would bring them home and tell Lydia in the morning. He smiled as he imagined her tears of gratitude. He imagined she would embrace him. Maybe she would even kiss him again. Maybe his promise to marry her could be kept after all.

He hadn't told her of that yet. She had enough on her mind without knowing that Greg had assumed their one kiss constituted a proposal.

He would give her a proper proposal. He would court her the way a gentleman should—take her on picnics, accompany her on outings into town, write her poetry. He grinned. He had already written poetry about her. She just didn't know it was about her. He could tell her. He could write more. They could fall in love the way men and women were supposed to fall in love, without the specter of ruin hanging over their heads.

He was so preoccupied with his drunken fantasy that he didn't hear the others enter the saloon.

Just as he smoothed out the last of the bills and prepared to fold them and put them in his pocket, he heard a venomous, lilting voice say, "Well, well, well. If it isn't the crack shot."

The hair on the back of Peter's neck stood straight up and his smile faded. He looked up to see a half dozen hard-faced men standing in a semicircle around him, smiling everywhere but their eyes.

The man directly in front of him was tall, nearly as tall as Peter himself, and at the edges of his hat's brim, Peter could see the telltale signs of thinning hair.

"Hello, Isaac," he said evenly.

Isaac Slade's eyes widened in exaggerated surprise. "Did you hear that, boys? He called me by my first name. Like we was friends. Are we friends, Levi?"

"No sir, Mr. Slade," a mangy-looking runt of a man to Peter's left answered. "No, we ain't friends at all."

"Well, there's no reason why we can't be," Slade said. "After all, we came here to extend an olive branch, didn't we?"

Peter's happy haze had vanished completely. He was keenly aware of the emptiness on his hip where his handgun would have been had he worn it.

"I don't reckon there's much call for peace between us, Isaac," he said, keeping his tone calm.

"No?" Slade replied. "Well, that's funny. See, I would think that a man in your position would want to be friends with a man in my position."

"How do you figure that?" Peter asked.

"Well, simple," Slade replied. "See, we all have guns. You don't. We work for the most powerful man in town. You work for the least powerful man in town."

"I heard tell he don't work for no man at all," one of the other outlaws said with a vicious grin. "I heard he follows a woman's coattails, just like a beatdown old cur."

"Makes sense," said another. "He is a beatdown old cur. Just look at him. Long in the tooth and he ain't even forty."

"Now, now," Slade said, lifting his hands for quiet. "There ain't no need to rush to conclusions. I'm sure Mr. Kerouac here is a reasonable man. He's a soldier after all, just like we are. He survived the war just like we did. He must have some sense in his head."

To Peter, he said, "Now Mr. Kerouac—oh, I'm sorry. I almost forgot. We're friends."

He grinned evilly and Peter noticed how his hand hovered over the butt of his pistol. "Now Peter," he said, "I'll do you the respect of treating you like you have sense. You do me the respect of treating me like I have sense. Sound all right to you?"

Peter didn't answer. After a moment, Slade continued. "See, Mr. Smith, our employer, is the kind of man who takes what he wants, and he's not the kind of man who asks permission. Say what you want about him, hate him if you must, but he takes what he wants. Now you have something he wants."

Peter bristled at the suggestion that he could own Lydia or her ranch, but he kept silent as Slade continued. "All we're asking is that you move on. We won't hurt you. We won't look for you. Hell, we'll wish you the best, and if we run into you sometime in the future, I hope you'll let us buy you a drink. But you need to move on and leave what belongs to Mr. Smith to Mr. Smith. You understand what I'm saying?"

Peter made to stand and one of the outlaws reached forward to shove him back into his seat. Peter caught the man's arm and yanked backward, pulling him off balance. He stumbled forward and Peter drove his knee into his gut.

The outlaw collapsed to the ground, gasping. The others looked at him in amazement, and Peter took advantage of the confusion to send a crashing right hand into the jaw of another of the men. He dropped instantly.

The other outlaws sprang into action. Peter dodged and blocked a flurry of blows, but there were four of them and only one of him, and he was slowly forced back. When he felt the bar press into his back, he dropped to his knees.

One of the outlaws, the beanpole Slade had called Levi, drew back to kick him. Peter launched himself upright, driving his fist into Levi's chin so hard he lifted the man bodily off the ground. Levi flew through the air and fell in a heap, eyes rolling backwards in his head.

Peter went on the offensive then. He drove a fist into one man's stomach and when he doubled over brought his fist crashing down behind the man's head. He sank to his knees as though he were praying and remained there.

Slade and one man were all that was left. Peter waited calmly for one of them to make the first move. Slade's eyes filled with hate. Then the hate vanished. The outlaw smiled and chuckled. "Well," he said, "better a coward then dead."

With a blur of motion, he drew his handgun. Peter felt two hard blows to his midsection. He looked down to see spreading blooms of red in his gut.

He threw himself at Slade, but the bullet wounds were already robbing him of his strength. Slade sidestepped and brought the butt of his pistol down on Peter's head. Peter dropped and rolled to his back, gasping as pain reverberated through his body.

"Boy howdy," Slade said, "you sure can brawl, Peter. It really is too bad you and I couldn't be friends, but..." He shrugged. Then his smile vanished. "You get home quick enough and get your woman to tend to those wounds and you'll pull through. They're gutshots, and they're gonna hurt something fierce, but they won't kill you if you move quick. You listen to me, though. The next time I pull this pistol on you, I will aim straight between your eyes, you understand me? You might be hell on wheels with a rifle, but I can outdraw any man in the territory and I will make sure it only takes one shot to end you." He grinned again. "The rest I save for your woman."

He walked out then, stopping only to take the money on the table, leaving Peter on the floor, gasping and clutching his stomach. His companions slowly got up, groggy and moaning. All except Levi, who had to be carried out, his eyes still rolling sightlessly in his head.

Peter collapsed onto his back and stared up at the ceiling. His breath came in shallow gasps, but it wasn't his own health he worried about.

He knew now that John didn't care about the money. He wanted to hurt Lydia. He wanted to punish her for refusing him.

Peter had to get home.

He slowly got to his feet and stumbled outside. He walked a quarter mile before he collapsed. His vision swam. He was losing blood too fast.

He just managed to reach Moonlight without collapsing. With a cry of effort, he pulled himself into the saddle and turned the mare around.

"Take me home, girl," he said.

Then he faded into blackness.

Chapter Twenty-Six

Lydia heard her father before she saw him. She felt a flash of anger at him for arriving home so late. What was he doing going out drinking like that anyway? Wasting what little money they had on alcohol?

Well, probably Eugene bought his drinks. Lydia sighed in exasperation. She supposed she couldn't blame her father for indulging in a moment of happiness. Heaven knew they would have little enough of that for a while.

Still, she intended to give him a piece of her mind and stood on the porch, arms crossed, a stern expression on her face. When her father arrived, she could see that he was in no state to be scolded. He probably wouldn't even remember talking to her in the morning.

So she turned her attention to Eugene. "What on Earth did you boys do?" she asked.

He grinned sheepishly at her. "Got a drink."

"More than one, by the looks of it."

He shrugged and chuckled. "Yeah, I guess so."

She rolled her eyes and looked around. "Where's Peter?"

"Peter is a young man!" Greg declared groggily. "He's...drinking."

She looked at Eugene, who said, "He wanted to stay and have a few more. Greg here was done, so I brought him home."

"You're both done," Lydia said. Then a thought occurred to her. "Eugene, you left Dorothy all by herself?"

Eugene shuffled his feet guiltily. "She's a good shot with that Henry rifle," he said.

Lydia sighed in exasperation. "I'm not worried for her safety, Eugene, I'm worried that she'll worry for yours. For Heaven's sake you two. At your age." She shook her head. "All right. Help me get him outside." To her father, she said, "You can sleep on the couch. The last thing Mother needs to see is you coming home smelling like a whiskey barrel."

"I...I love you, Liddie," Greg said. He reached up and tried to caress Lydia's cheek, but only succeeded in poking her eye.

She pulled away irritably and rubbed her wounded orb. "For heaven's sake, you better not throw up in the house. I'll make you clean it up."

Greg mumbled something about cleaning and whistles while Lydia and Eugene half-carried him to the couch. He fell backwards heavily and in an instant was fast asleep.

Lydia turned to Eugene, frowning.

"I'm sorry, Miss Lydia," Eugene said contritely. "I only felt bad. I wanted him to have one good night before...well, you know."

Lydia took a deep breath and sighed. "Well, all right. Can you make it home?"

"Sure, sure," he said, "I'll be all right."

"Well," Lydia said, "all right then. Good night, Eugene."

She watched Eugene until his horse disappeared from view down the road. She shook her head and walked back inside to fetch her father a blanket.

She covered him up, wondering how many other daughters had to tuck their fathers in instead of the other way around. Seriously, drinking himself into a stupor like this? At his age?

Well, he had reason enough to drink, didn't he? He had put everything of himself into this ranch, and he had failed.

Lydia looked down at her father and for the first time saw how truly old he looked. His face was lined with wrinkles and even though he slept, exhaustion showed in the dark circles under his eyes and the turned-down corners of his mouth.

She caressed his cheek softly. He stirred but didn't wake. Lydia remained there, stroking his cheeks until the lines smoothed somewhat and his sleep came more easily. She shook her head and gently tucked the blanket around him.

She left her father and went to the porch to sit and wait for Peter. He would receive a tongue-lashing of his own when he returned to the house, but she wouldn't be too hard on him. He too faced failure and loss.

She glanced up at the moon, wondering if she should go to town and see if Peter had passed out drunk at the saloon and was now sleeping it off in a jail cell. She shook her head and chuckled to herself, but her laughter felt forced.

She worried for him. She thought suddenly of the hard-faced man with the handgun at the shooting contest, the man who now worked as John's enforcer. She couldn't believe Ben Roberts would allow John to do anything to Peter in town, but on the road, accidents could happen, and the good sheriff could wash his hands of any responsibility.

When she saw the shadow of a horse and rider approaching, she breathed a sigh of relief. She walked to the front of the porch and waited, arms crossed. Peter swayed unsteadily on the saddle and she shook her head. "Well, what a fine sight to see," she scolded. "First my father and now you, coming home drunk as sin. Did you get your fill?"

He didn't answer her. She sighed irritably and shook her head. "What's the matter?" she asked. "Too drunk to talk?"

He still didn't answer, not even to mumble. She peered at him as he approached and saw his eyes were closed and he was covered in dirt. She flung her arms up in exasperation. "Let me guess. You fell asleep and fell out of the saddle. And now you're sleeping again." She shook her head. "Well, let's get you inside before you..."

Moonlight walked into the light of the lantern, and Lydia's voice trailed off. Her eyes widened in shock as she saw that what she first thought was mud was in fact blood, not all of it dry.

"Oh no," she whispered.

Moonlight stopped just in front of her, and when he stopped, Peter pitched to one side and fell. She shrieked and leapt forward to catch him, but only succeeded in slowing his fall before he knocked her sprawling.

"Help!" she cried out. "Mother! Help!"

She stood and tried to help Peter stand, but he remained where he fell. His breathing was shallow and labored, and his skin was pale and papery.

"Help!" she cried again.

The front door opened, and Mary rushed outside, followed by a Greg who was now shocked into sobriety.

"What happened?" Mary shrieked when she saw him. "Is he dead? Please say he isn't dead!"

"Not yet," Lydia said before she could stop herself.

Hearing those words pass her lips chilled her veins, but also drove away her paralysis. "Help me get him inside," she said to Greg. "Mother, start boiling some water."

Mary rushed to do as Lydia asked and Greg helped Lydia carry Peter into the house. Blood trickled from a wound in Peter's stomach and more from a larger, more ragged wound in his back.

Greg and Lydia set Peter on the couch and began to cut away his shirt. Mary wept softly as she busied herself with the kettle.

Peter stirred and mumbled, "Gotta leave town afore O'Malley comes back."

"Who?" Lydia asked. "Is O'Malley the man that shot you?"

"Horses are no good," Peter mumbled. "We go in on foot."

"He's delirious," Greg said, "we need something to stop the blood. Mary!"

Mary, who had finished with the kettle and now stood wringing her hands waiting for it to boil, rushed for the linens.

Lydia looked down at Peter, her lips pinched tightly closed. They might be too late to stop the bleeding. She pushed that thought from her mind and said, "I'm going to make a poultice for the wound. Call me if…"

She let the sentence lie unfinished. Greg nodded and said, "I'll watch him."

She went to the pantry and gathered the herbs she would need. She kept plantain and yarrow root on hand in case of an injury, but she never imagined using it for anything worse than a cut finger.

She took a deep breath and forced herself to focus as she ground the leaves and roots and mixed them with linseed oil. She worked the mixture until it was a paste, then returned to the parlor.

Mary had already returned with the linens and Greg was now pressing one to Peter's wound. Peter's breathing came in short, rapid gasps and Mary stood over him, weeping and wringing her hands.

"Mother, help me with this," Lydia commanded.

Mary grabbed another linen and soaked it in the warm water from the kettle while Lydia rubbed some of the poultice into another linen.

Blood continued to trickle from Peter's wound, the skin around it puffy and hotter than the warm poultice could have caused. This was bad. If the blood loss didn't kill him, infection could.

Mary dabbed at the wound with the cloth, wiping away the dirt and dried blood that surrounded it. When the wound was clean and dried, Lydia applied the poultice, tying the cloth underneath him.

"Help me turn him," she said.

The wound where the bullet had exited took longer to clean than the wound in the front, but eventually, Lydia was able to apply the poultice to the other side and tie the wound closed.

"That's all we can do for him right now," Greg said, "We'll have to hope it's enough."

Lydia nodded, trembling with fear and exhaustion. "I'll stay up with him," she said. "You two should get some rest. It won't help anyone if we all spend a sleepless night."

Greg shook his head. "I'm running for Doctor Anderson."

Lydia nodded assent.

"Oh, Lydia!" Mary cried, "I'm so sorry!"

"Hush, Mother," Lydia said, more sternly than she intended. In a gentler tone, she said, "Let's not give up hope."

Greg led the weeping Mary to the bedroom, then headed for the doctor. Lydia sat and faced Peter. His breathing was calmer now, but his face remained pale and drawn, and blood still trickled from his wound, staining the bandage with a slowly expanding bloom of red.

"Oh, Peter," she said, "what happened to you?"

"Got shot," he whispered.

She jumped, startled. "Peter?" she asked. "Peter, can you hear me?"

"I have to leave town," he mumbled. "We all do. We have to leave."

"Peter, who did this to you?" she asked. "Was it Slade? Was it John"

"Have to leave," he mumbled again before falling unconscious once more.

Lydia checked his bandages and saw that the bleeding seemed to have stopped. That could mean that the blood had finally started to clot, or it could mean that he had no more blood left to lose. She hoped desperately for the former.

She felt a sudden and intense surge of anger at Peter. What was he thinking, staying in town by himself and drinking like that? In all his time at the ranch, Lydia had never seen him touch a drop! Now, when they needed him most, when *she* needed him most, he had gone and gotten drunk and maybe killed.

She stood and crossed her arms over her chest, staring out the window, at the fire, at the floor, anywhere but at Peter. Tears came to her eyes, and eventually, she turned to look at him. He slept softly now, but his breathing was still so harsh and labored. "Please, Peter," she whispered. "Please don't leave me."

The doctor arrived just as the gray of pre-dawn began to light the sky. He examined Peter's wound and sighed heavily.

"He's hurt gravely," he said to Lydia–a rather unhelpful observation, she thought. "You've cared well for him. There's nothing left to do but wait. If he survives the next day, he'll probably pull through. I'll be by to check on him tomorrow evening. In the meantime if he wakes, don't let him move. The wound didn't pierce his gut, thank God. He should be able to eat, but he should be limited to broth and thin porridge for now. Have him drink plenty of water as well, but only if he's awake. If he's asleep, let him sleep."

Greg and Lydia thanked him, and he nodded and left, once more promising to be by in the afternoon to check on Peter. Greg went to bed and Lydia remained where she was.

She intended to watch him through the night. But she must have slept at some point, because she dreamed of herself weeping at the foot of Peter's grave while John laughed in the background.

Chapter Twenty-Seven

Lydia woke to the smell of coffee. She stirred and slowly straightened, her body aching from sleeping in the chair.

Peter still slept, and Lydia was comforted somewhat to see his breathing was less labored and some color had returned to his cheeks. She stood and headed to retrieve more linens to replace his bandages.

When she returned, Mary was in the parlor. She set two cups of coffee down on the occasional table and smiled tenderly at Lydia. Her panic of the night before had eased but tears still filled her eyes.

"I would say good morning, but that seems a foolish sentiment at the moment," she said to Lydia.

"It could be worse," Lydia said, hating the truth of that statement.

"Yes," Mary said softly. "I suppose it could be."

Neither of them brought up the very real possibility that it would be worse very soon.

Mary helped Lydia replace Peter's bandages. Peter stirred softly but didn't wake.

His wound no longer seeped blood, but the skin around it was angry and purple. If the infection spread, it would mean a slow, debilitating death preceded by several days of fever and pain and anguish. It would be kinder to—

She didn't allow herself to finish that thought. He wasn't dead yet. He could still recover.

"Do you think John did this?" her mother asked softly.

"I think he paid someone to do this," Lydia said, "I don't think he did it himself."

"The coward!" Mary hissed.

"Yes," Lydia said, "he is a coward." *For all the good that will do us*, she didn't say out loud.

"What are we going to do, Lydia?" Mary asked.

"How should I know, Mother?" Lydia asked softly.

She didn't intend for her words to be cruel, but they sounded that way in her ears. Mary began to weep softly, but Lydia found she didn't have the energy to comfort her. She was too exhausted and frightened.

She heard footfalls behind her and turned to see her father walk into the parlor. He laid a hand on Mary's shoulder, and Mary grasped it and turned to him, weeping and clinging tightly to him.

Lydia felt tears come to her own eyes and looked away, not wanting to add her grief to their own. Peter continued to sleep.

Eventually, Greg left to work on the ranch and Mary started her chores. Lydia watched while Peter slept. After an hour or two, she went to her room to get a book, and tried to read, but after another hour, she put the book down, unable to focus on it.

The morning came and went. Mary and Lydia ate lunch silently. After they finished, Mary took food out to Greg and Lydia went to sit with Peter again.

Five minutes after Mary left the house, Peter finally stirred. He opened his eyes and muttered something.

Lydia went instantly to his side, grasping his hand. "Yes, Peter," she said, "I'm here."

Peter turned and gazed at her. "Lydia," he said softly.

"Yes, Peter," she said once more. "I'm here."

"We have to leave, Lydia."

"What happened?" Lydia asked.

Peter sighed and turned his head to stare at the ceiling. "John hired those men."

"The gunfighters we saw at the festival," Lydia said.

"Yes. He hired them. I think he hired the gamblers too."

"Gamblers?"

Peter nodded. "I won money, Lydia. A lot of money. Enough to pay the rest of the ranch's debt."

Fresh tears filled Lydia's eyes when he said that. "And they stole it?"

He nodded. "There were some gamblers sitting at a table at the saloon. After Greg and Eugene left, they invited me to play with them. Said they needed someone else at their table. I won a lot of money. Over three hundred dollars."

Lydia gasped. That wouldn't only have paid off the ranch, it would have given them enough to support themselves until they found work again. Her tears began to slide down her cheeks as anger joined her grief.

It was so unfair. Every time they were close to safety, John robbed them of it in the most vicious way possible.

"They set me up," Peter said. "Left me alone at the saloon and next thing I knew, Slade was there with his men. Got me drunk so I wouldn't notice them...wouldn't be aware. I fought back. Nearly got them all, but Slade pulled a gun on me. Shot me in the gut."

"Coward," Lydia hissed, echoing her mother's sentiment of the night before. "That *coward*."

"Yes," Peter agreed. "He is a coward. A cunning coward."

"John or Slade?" she asked bitterly.

"Both of them," he said, "I took out four of his men before he shot me. He can claim I attacked them in a drunken rage, and he only shot me in self-defense. If I survive, they can have me arrested for assault. Or Slade can lie in wait and finish the job."

"Don't talk like that!" Lydia said, "we can think of something. We can find something, some way to make it out of this."

"There's no way," he said. "We have to leave. John has a team of gunfighters on his side and the sheriff in his pocket, or at least under his thumb. We have no one."

"That's not true," Lydia said, "we have Eugene."

The excuse sounded thin even to Lydia's own ears. Peter shook his head. "We can't ask him to endanger himself for us. I'm sorry, Lydia. I truly am."

"Hush now," Lydia said, "You just rest. We'll worry about tomorrow when tomorrow comes."

Peter nodded softly. "I was in love once," he said.

Lydia's brow furrowed. "What?"

"I was in love. Penelope. Girl from my neighborhood growing up. Sweet, soft green eyes, beautiful laugh, long blonde hair. Used to write poems for her."

Lydia's lips thinned. She recalled the poem she had read in his diary. "Yes, I know," she said, more unkindly than she intended.

If Peter noticed her tone, he didn't let on. His eyes remained turned up to the ceiling, but his gaze was unfocused. Lydia wasn't sure if he was aware or delirious.

"She died during the war. Stray bullet. Don't know if it was a rebel bullet or a Union bullet that did it. It was quick. The bullet passed through her left eye and exited through the brainstem."

Lydia gasped at the graphic description but stopped herself from asking him to stop talking. He needed to say this, and horrifying as it was, Lydia was surprised to find she wanted to know. He was so closed off, so withdrawn. This might be the only chance she had to know who he was and what he had gone through. As horrible as it was to hear, it must have been far worse to experience.

"Didn't see the body," he continued. "That was a mercy, I guess. They buried her with full military honors and gave her family a pension. Of everything I lost, I carried her loss hardest, I think."

Lydia lowered her eyes.

"Losing my parents and sisters was hard, but losing Penelope...I guess I saw it as my job to protect her. To keep her safe. When she died, I felt like it was my fault, like I had let her down. I hated myself for it. Still do sometimes, I guess."

Lydia didn't know if Peter could hear her or not, but she tried anyway. "It wasn't your fault, Peter."

If he did hear her, he didn't react. "I can't lose you like that. Love you too much."

Lydia gasped softly. Her eyes flew to his, which still stared vacantly up at the ceiling. "Love?" she whispered. "You love me?"

"You're so strong," Peter said, "and so kind. You give of yourself and ask so little in return. I don't agree with you about marrying John to save your family, but I admire you for being brave enough to do it."

"Well, that's out of the question now," Lydia said as much to herself as to him. "We know for sure now that he's a murderer."

"I thought I was just going to work myself to death," Peter continued. "I thought I would just work until I couldn't take my mind off the memories anymore. Then I planned to use my handgun one last time."

Lydia gasped again. She grabbed Peter's hand and held it in both of hers. "Don't," she said softly. "Don't."

"I don't need to do that now," he said. "I have something else to live for. Someone else to live for. We need to leave, Lydia."

He turned to look at her, and this time his eyes were sharply focused. "We can't stay here. John wants you, but he has no influence outside of the territory. He'll content himself with taking the ranch and running us out of town. Let him have it. His day will come. We don't need to risk death to save a piece of land."

Lydia's lips thinned. She recalled the words he'd spoken moments ago and knew in her heart that she felt the same, though she didn't say the words aloud. "He will not hurt you again," she said.

"Not me I'm worried about," Peter said. "You and your parents. Slade won't stop at hurting a woman, not even an old one. John, neither. I've seen men like them before. They'll hurt you and your mother just for the fun of it. If we stay, I'll have to kill them, and if I kill them..."

His eyes turned away from hers again. "If I kill them, I lose the last part of myself."

He lowered his eyes, and his grip softened. "I could do it. I've killed many men," he said. "I killed more with my knife and my pistol than I did with my rifle. Slade said he could outdraw any man in the territory, but he wouldn't have time to draw, wouldn't even know I was there to shoot at if I didn't want him to. I could kill him and his gang and bury them in the river like I did at Bull Run."

His voice changed as he said this, growing flat and emotionless. His eyes hardened and though his hand hung loosely in Lydia's grasp, he felt tense, like a coiled snake ready to strike.

"Kill all those sons of bitches," he said. "John too."

Lydia felt a chill run through her veins. She had never heard him swear before. She gripped his hand tightly and said, "Listen to me. You're not a murderer."

He blinked and said, "No." His face softened, and the killing stare left his eyes. "No," he repeated. "I'm not a murderer."

He looked at Lydia and once more, his gaze was sharp and his voice clear. "If we stay here, Lydia, I'll have to be. There's no stopping men like John and Slade any other way."

Lydia didn't respond. She knew in her deepest heart that Peter was right. John wouldn't stop unless they stopped him, and the only way to do that was to kill him.

Could she kill John? She had daydreamed about his death often enough, but fantasizing about the man's heart stopping or imagining him falling from his horse and breaking his neck was a different thing from putting a gun in his face and pulling the trigger.

That thought conjured up a terrifying image, and she breathed in sharply and sat back, pulling her hand away.

Peter's eyes closed and he turned away from her. Guilt flooded Lydia, and she quickly took his hand back, but Peter was already asleep.

Lydia held onto his hand while tears streamed silently down her cheeks. It wasn't fair. They had already suffered so much. Peter more than any of them. She had been so preoccupied with her own tragedies that she never considered what Peter had to go through. She had seen only brief glimpses of the war, and those glimpses were enough to tell her that she wanted no part of it. Peter had been in the middle of it. He was so kind and gentle and sweet, and he had been forced to become something monstrous.

She couldn't do that to him again. He was right. They needed to leave.

She lifted his hand and kissed it softly. Then she finally said the words she had felt for months already but only just now realized were true.

"I love you, Peter."

Chapter Twenty-Eight

Peter twisted carefully from side to side. His wound ached, but there were no sharp stabs of fresh pain.

He told this to Doctor Anderson, and the doctor smiled. "Good. Can you lift your left leg as high as you can?"

Peter complied. He lifted his leg to his waist but could go no further without causing a jolt of pain to shoot through his body.

"That's all right," the doctor said, "now the other leg."

He was able to lift his right leg slightly higher than his left, but not much.

"Okay," the doctor said, "well, I have to say your recovery is progressing nicely. Based on my earlier examination, there is no more infection, and your muscles are healing quickly."

"Can I work?"

The doctor blinked. "You can't seriously be asking me that."

"I am," Peter said. "I'm no use to anyone sitting here like an invalid."

"You're no use to anyone tearing your wound open again and risking infection and more serious scarring, not to mention the far longer recovery you'll experience. Peter, you were shot in the abdomen. You're lucky the ball didn't puncture any vital organs. You're beyond lucky that the wound was a through-and-through. Pardon the analogy, but you could fire a thousand rounds into a thousand bellies and not one of those wounds would be as minor—so to speak—as yours. Still, your injury is serious, and it will require more than this one week of recovery before you can perform manual labor."

"How long?"

"Three weeks at least before you can perform light labor. Another four to six before you can move on to sturdier tasks."

Peter sighed and ran his hands through his hair. "Doc, I can't wait that long."

"You have to," the doctor said, gently but firmly. "I'm sorry, Peter. I understand that your ranch is in a dire situation, but there's no way around it."

Peter stewed at the news. True the ranch wasn't so much a ranch anymore as a near-derelict homestead, but that didn't mean there wasn't work to be done, and Greg simply wasn't up to the task. "What if I supervise?" he asked. "Can I direct others to work?"

The Doctor hesitated a moment before asking, "Is Greg really that hopeless?"

Peter searched the doctor's face before answering and found only compassion. "Yes," he admitted, "I'm afraid so."

Anderson sighed. He tapped his spectacles on his knee a moment. Finally, he said, "Have you given any more thought to going to the sheriff about your injury?"

Peter sighed. "I appreciate it, Doctor, but the men who injured me are almost certainly far from the jurisdiction by now."

That was almost certainly untrue, but Peter didn't think it wise or helpful to tell the doctor that those men were almost certainly drinking and laughing at the saloon every night, telling everyone who would listen how they shot and left Peter for dead. He didn't want to take even the slight chance that

Doctor Anderson would feel a need to go to their weakling sheriff himself and possibly put himself in John Smith's crosshairs.

The doctor beat Peter to the punch, though. "These were John Smith's men," he said. Noticing Peter's shocked expression, he said, "It's an open secret in town that Sheriff Roberts is intimidated by the man. It's not a secret at all that he hired a gang of toughs to enforce his position as lord of his petty fiefdom. Were these men responsible?"

Peter didn't answer. He didn't need to. After a moment, Doctor Anderson sighed and said, "I think you should send someone to Virginia City to fetch the Marshals."

Peter had considered that himself. "I can't," he said. "It could be weeks before the Marshals even send someone over here, and then no one witnessed the shooting. There's no way to prove these men shot me, and I don't want to think about what John would do to Lydia and her parents if he learned that I went to the law."

The doctor sighed. "Yes. I suppose you're right." He tapped his spectacles on his knee again. "Something has to be done about that man."

"Something will be done," Peter said. "Men like him never last. One day, the town will be fed up with him. If he's lucky, they'll find a real sheriff to bring him to justice. If he isn't, well..." He left that part unsaid.

The doctor remained silent a long while. Finally, he said, "You may supervise work if you must, but you are not to ride, do you understand? I want you off horseback for another month, at least."

"Fine," Peter said. "I'll make do."

Anderson nodded, then stood. "All right, Peter. I'll be back in a week's time to check on you. In the meantime, I'll charge Miss Lydia with making sure you follow my instructions and don't overexert yourself. I understand that she, at least, can get you to behave."

Peter nodded assent and walked the doctor to the door. As the doctor pulled on his boots and coat, he said, "Good woman, Miss Lydia. When you find a safe place, you should make an honest woman of her."

"She is honest," Peter said,

"You know what I mean," Anderson said with a smile.

Peter couldn't resist a smile of his own. "Well, let me work on that safe place part first." A snug home, food on the table, Lydia greeting each day with a smile instead of that pinched, worried expression...the sudden wave of longing stabbed as hard as the pain in his gut.

"You do that," Anderson said, "I'll see you later, Peter."

After the doctor left, Peter headed toward the barn where Greg worked on polishing the tack. Peter expected almost nothing to be done, and he wasn't disappointed. Greg stood with his hands on his hips, staring dejectedly at a jumbled pile of tack, oils, and cleaning cloths. His eyes widened in alarm when he saw Peter. "What are you doing here? You should be resting."

"Doc cleared me to supervise," Peter explained. "I won't do any of the work, but I'll help you know what to do."

"Oh," Greg said with obvious relief. "That would help a lot actually, thank you." He chuckled. "You'd think with only two horses I could figure this out without needing to be babysat. Guess that was asking too much."

"That's all right," Peter said. "What have you done so far?"

"Well," Greg said, squatting down and poking at the jumbled mixture of saddles, bits, reins and stirrups. "I started to polish this doohickey right here." He picked up one of the bits. "But the oil tarnished it something fierce."

"That's mink oil," Peter said, "That's for leather. You want to use vinegar and flour paste to polish brass."

"Oh," Greg said, "I see."

He stared at his boots dejectedly.

"That's all right," Peter said patiently. "We'll get this done. Let's start by oiling the leather since we have the mink oil right here."

After a few more minutes of patient explanation, Greg managed to get a good rhythm going on the tack. When Peter was confident he had a handle on it, he decided now was as good a time as any to talk to Greg about leaving.

"I've been thinking," he said. "I think it would be wise for you, Mary and Lydia to move on somewhere."

Greg stopped and stared at Peter. "Without you?"

"Temporarily," Peter said. "I was thinking you three could go stay in Virginia City for a while. You have enough money to keep yourselves for a month, two if you…" He almost said, "if you're thrifty," but decided that wasn't enough. "…if you let Lydia manage the money."

"Not a chance," Greg said.

Peter took a breath and explained patiently, "Greg, I don't mean that as an insult to you. I'm sure you're capable of handling money, but Lydia has been managing the ranch's finances since you arrived here. She's become very good at

261

managing money, and I think she would be best suited to handle that for the three of you, at least until you find work."

"I don't care about the money," Greg said, "I mean there's not a chance we're leaving you behind."

Peter was surprised for a moment, but decided he shouldn't be. "Greg, that's mighty kind of you, but things are becoming dangerous around here. John started with me, but he won't stop with me."

"You're right," Greg said, "but it doesn't matter. You're family, and where one goes, we all go. When you're well, we'll figure out our next move. Until then, we stay here."

"Greg, Lydia is your family. She's in more danger than any of us. You need to think about her, first."

"Have you talked to Lydia about this?" Greg asked.

"No," Peter admitted. "I wanted to talk to you first."

"Why?"

"What?"

"Why did you want to talk to me first?" This time, it was Greg's turn to talk with parental patience.

Peter looked away. The truth was he wanted to talk to Greg first because he knew Lydia wouldn't agree. He hoped that with Greg on his side, Mary and Lydia would follow.

Greg evidently saw straight through that plan. "You came to me because you knew Lydia wouldn't agree, and you thought I would be the easiest to convince."

Peter sighed but still didn't answer.

"It was a good effort, Peter," Greg said, "but the answer's no. I am fully aware of the danger to Lydia. What you surprisingly are still not aware of is that Lydia's future is bound up in yours. You two will likely be the last to accept that fact, but Mary and I knew it the day you arrived. We're old folks, Peter, and far out of our depth here, but we know our daughter, and the day you walked into our lives, Lydia gained hers back. We love you, and we want you two to marry for your happiness as well as hers, but make no mistake, her happiness was and is first in our minds. There's a chance that I could convince Lydia to leave before you, but I doubt it. And if I did and something were to happen to you, then she would never recover. Forget the fact she'd never forgive Mary or me. She'd die a brokenhearted widow without even the ring to comfort her."

Peter knew Greg was right, but Lydia's safety was more important. Better she live brokenhearted than live as a slave to the desires of a man like John Smith. If he even allowed her to live.

He tried again. "Nothing will happen to me, Greg. It means a lot to me to know that you and Mary see me the way you do. You should know that I see the two of you as a father and mother as well."

As the words left his mouth, Peter realized they were true. He had lost his parents and his beloved in Columbus. He had found them again here in Stevensville. A lump formed in his throat and he looked away from Greg so the older man wouldn't see the tears that came to his eyes, "That's why you need to leave first. John's already beaten me. If he sees the three of you leaving and me nursing my wounds and preparing to leave as well, then he'll know he's won, and he'll leave me be. I can join the three of you in Virginia City where there's real law and John Smith has no influence. We can build a life for ourselves either there or wherever we end up."

"Look at me, Peter."

Peter turned to Greg, shocked by the sudden command in the man's voice. Greg met his eyes evenly. "Don't lie to me. You know as well as I do that John won't stop until you're in the ground. You're only alive now because you haven't left town. Slade's not trying to run you off, he's trying to get you alone somewhere he can dry-gulch you, or more likely just shoot you and leave your body on the side of the road. You've been doing a lot of thinking Peter, and so have I. I gave John more than enough money for him to settle our debt. The money Slade stole from you more than covers the remainder. The debt is paid. The ranch is worthless. It'll be a year or two at least before it's worth anything, and that's only if he wants to invest the time and energy into rebuilding. I strongly doubt he'll do that for a one-hundred-sixty-acre homestead that'll never do much more than pay for itself. He wants to beat you, Peter. I don't even know if he still wants Lydia for himself or if he only wants her to spite you. You intimidated him and ran him off. A man like John Smith can't bear a humiliation like that. He's patient, but he's patient like a snake, only waiting for the right moment to strike. We're not leaving you to die. As far as I'm concerned, you're my son, and I will not leave my son to die."

Peter opened his mouth to protest, but Greg's expression made it clear that the matter was closed. Peter wasn't happy with the decision, but he felt a rush of pride and admiration for the older man anyway. He sounded strong.

Despite his fear, Peter couldn't resist a smile. "Well then... Pa. We should talk about what to do about John."

"Well," Greg said, "I'm glad you brought that up. Eugene invited us to dinner tonight to discuss just that."

Peter's eyes widened in surprise.

Greg smiled. "Old men can keep secrets too."

Greg finished cleaning the tack, with Peter's help. Then the two of them went to the house to tell Mary and Lydia they would be eating with Eugene tonight.

After a great deal of argument, Lydia finally agreed to allow Peter to go, under strict orders to eat only broth and drink only water.

Eugene arrived a few minutes later. Dorothy immediately flew to Lydia and pulled her away, chatting her ear off about her latest outing with Colton. Eugene shared a nod with Greg and Peter and the three men left to eat and plan.

Chapter Twenty-Nine

"You sure they won't be here?" Greg asked.

"They aren't here," Eugene said, "I overheard Slade tell Jackson the other night over at the saloon that John was sending them out to Bannack to take care of some business of his over there. They won't be back until the day after tomorrow at the earliest."

"You better be right about that," Greg said, shaking his head. "Last thing we need is to bring trouble down on our heads because Slade or John catches us talking to the sheriff."

The evening before, Greg had been enthusiastic about their plan, but the morning had brought with it the realization of the danger they could be in. Still, while the plan carried some risk, it was the best shot they had. Well, aside from leaving town altogether, but Greg had been clear that he wouldn't leave without Peter, and if the wagon ride into town was any indication, it really would be weeks before Peter was well enough to travel. As it was, Greg and Eugene had to help Peter down from the wagon and half-carry him inside the jail.

Ben Roberts looked up from his desk and Peter got his first good look at the man. He was not at all what Peter had expected. Based on what he had been told about the sheriff, he expected Roberts to be a smallish weakling of a man clearly out of his depth. The massive ox sitting in front of him looked nearly capable of outwrestling an actual ox. Even sitting down, it was clear to Peter that Ben was much taller than his own six-foot-three and built like a tree trunk. His hands were massive and strong, his arms thickly muscled, and his chest as powerful as a steam locomotive. Why on Earth would a man like this be afraid of John Smith?

The sheriff sighed heavily when he saw them and leaned back in his chair. "You're here about the shooting at the saloon a few days ago. Look, I'm sorry, but I can't prosecute without evidence, and at the moment, it's Mr. Kerouac's word against Mr. Slade's. Mr. Slade has the backing of John Smith, the most respected member of our community. I can't press charges against Slade without incontrovertible evidence that he pulled the trigger, and you don't have that. I'm sorry to say there's nothing I can do. You might be best off following Mr. Slade's advice and leaving town."

"So you know that Mr. Slade warned Peter to leave town, but you don't believe that he shot him?" Eugene asked, looking the sheriff squarely in the eye.

Roberts wilted under Eugene's gaze, and Peter was once more amazed that a man so strong and powerful could be so timid. "Well, I... I suppose that's also Mr. Slade's word against Mr. Kerouac's. I only mean..."

Greg interrupted. "You only mean that you're afraid of John and because you're afraid of him, you won't do anything but bury your head in the sand like you always do."

Roberts reddened and stood his full height, which Peter guessed about six-foot-eight. He pointed a sausage-sized finger at Greg and said, "Now you listen here, Mr. Gutenberg. I ain't never buried my head in the sand for anyone. You may resent Mr. Smith for his designs on your ranch and your daughter, and I don't blame you, but that doesn't give you the right to demand I act outside of the law."

"Is that what you told Chester Porterfield when John blackmailed Corinne into marrying him?" Eugene asked, his gaze still firmly on the sheriff.

The blood drained from Roberts' face. "That's not what happened!" he thundered. Or tried to thunder, at least. To

267

Peter, it sounded like the plaintive whine of a child caught with his hand inside the taffy jar at the general store.

This wasn't going well. Coward or not, they needed the sheriff on their side if they were going to act. "May I speak?" Peter asked softly.

All three men turned to Peter. Roberts stammered a moment, then nodded and said, "All right. What do you have to say?"

"Thank you, Sheriff," Peter said. "Now I know that as an officer of the law, you can't say certain things out loud even if you know them to be true. So I'm going to talk, and if you don't want to reply, that's all right."

Roberts regarded Peter warily. The other two just looked confused. Peter's soft tone and contrite demeanor were far different from their own accusatory stares, and they deviated from the original plan to browbeat Roberts into helping.

Well, browbeating hadn't worked. It was time to put the vinegar away and try honey.

"John Smith has terrorized this town for years, Sheriff. Now I'm new here, so if I'm wrong, feel free to tell me. If I'm right, you don't have to say anything at all."

Roberts seemed to debate replying, but in the end, he remained silent.

After a moment, Peter nodded. "He has, from what I've heard, been responsible for the deaths of three of his wives so far, to say nothing of the ruin he's brought to their families and the families of many others. The homesteaders that remain live, like you, in abject fear of the man and refuse to act against him."

Roberts reddened at the insinuation that he was afraid of John but remained silent.

"That ain't no way to live," Peter said. "These people, yourself included, have fought hard to carve out a life for themselves hundreds of miles away—no, thousands—from the wealth and comfort of the East. Even the growing metropolises of the West don't turn their eyes to Stevensville."

Greg and Eugene exchanged a glance. They hadn't expected Peter to be so eloquent. Peter realized this was the most he'd spoken in their presence since arriving here.

"The folks here don't seem to mind being left alone, but without an effective shepherd, the wolves have free reign, as John has had free reign in Stevensville."

Roberts reddened again, but Peter lifted his hand and continued. "I know you've done your best, Sheriff—" Greg scoffed at that, and Eugene placed a hand on his shoulder to calm him. "—but you're only one man. John has a dozen armed men at his side. What can you possibly do in the face of that?"

"Yes," Roberts said, nodding eagerly. "Exactly. I won't do anyone any good as a dead man."

"You're not doing much good as a living man," Greg interjected, earning another squeeze on his shoulder from Eugene.

"Greg's right, Sheriff," Peter said gently.

It was a risk, he knew, to attack the sheriff like that, but if he set the hook just right, he could use the sheriff's own insecurity to spur him to action. He wasn't particularly happy to manipulate a man into doing his job, but they were past the point where niceties mattered.

Roberts reddened, then sighed and hung his head. "Don't mean to be no good," he mumbled. "I try. Honest I do."

"Of course you do," Peter agreed, "but it's not enough. You know that."

Roberts nodded, the barest of movements.

"There's a simple and easy way to put an end to John's scourge for good," Peter said. "See, John has us all convinced that he outnumbers us, but that's not true. There's a dozen on his side, give or take a few. There's fifty or more able-bodied men on our side."

"Mr. Kerouac, you're not suggesting a firefight, are you?" Roberts asked.

"There won't be a firefight," Peter said, "Slade's no fool. I've seen his type. John might be a wolf, but Slade and his ilk are more like coyotes. They'll only prey on folks much smaller and weaker than themselves. Slade and his men jumped me in the saloon, and when it became clear I was gonna win that fight, Slade shot me, an unarmed man, in the gut. If four dozen men come to him armed, he'll move on."

"What if he comes back?" Roberts asked with real fear. "What if he comes back with more men? I've heard tell of rustler gangs fifty strong out Kansas way that take over entire towns when things don't go their way."

"He won't come back," Peter said, "Coyotes don't have pride. When a bear or cougar comes along, the coyote doesn't stick around to fight for what's his. He just moves on to where there are no bears or cougars."

"You seem real confident of this, Mr. Kerouac," Roberts said.

"I'm absolutely confident that John intends to kill me," Peter replied, "and I'm absolutely confident he intends to kill Miss Lydia too, but not before he's broken and humiliated her. He'll probably kill Greg and Miss Mary as well."

"Okay," Roberts said, lifting his hand. "Okay, I get your point."

Peter pressed his advantage. "I know this isn't comfortable to hear, Sheriff, but overwhelmed or not, you *are* responsible for the safety of the people in this town. How many more people have to die for you to accept that responsibility? How much more does your town need to suffer before you lose so much sleep at night you start looking for other ways to find peace?"

Greg and Eugene shifted uncomfortably at Peter's insinuation. Roberts lifted tormented eyes to Peter's own and Peter said, "I've been there, Sheriff. Cold steel starts feeling a lot warmer when there's nothing ahead but regret. This is your chance to stop that. This might be your only chance."

Eugene spoke then. "John's going to meet his end one day, Sheriff. You know that as well as I do. The Territory's growing and sooner or later, the law—the real law—is going to make its way to Stevensville. When it does, they won't tolerate John's behavior. He'll lose his freedom and maybe his life. You got to decide if you want them to walk in here and see you with your head buried in the sand or if you want them to see you've already handled the problem. What's your legacy gonna be, Sheriff?"

Peter could see the struggle behind Robert's eyes. He stared glumly at his hands for a long while wrestling with his conscience. When he looked up, Peter could tell he had failed.

"I can't." he said, his voice barely a whisper. "I'm sorry."

Greg laughed bitterly and shook his head. Eugene curled his lip in contempt. Peter nodded. "All right. Then stay out of my way."

All three men turned to him in shock. "W—what?" Roberts stammered.

"If you won't deal with John, Sheriff, then I will," Peter said, "If you want to hide, that's fine. Hide. I don't hide. So stay out of my way."

Roberts blinked, trying to summon some authority in his voice when he said, "Now, I can't abide you taking the law in your own hands, Mr. Kerouac. If you're thinking—"

"I'm done thinking, Sheriff," Peter said.

He stood with an effort and looked down at Roberts. "I'll ask you not to tell John what I just told you, but I doubt you'll be man enough to keep your mouth shut, and that's fine. I already warned John not to hurt us. He's chosen not to listen, and he'll suffer the consequences. As long as you stay out of my way, you won't have to join him."

ROberts' eyes widened, but he said nothing. Peter turned and left the jail. Greg and Eugene followed him. They offered to help him into the wagon, but he refused, climbing up under his own strength, though the effort left him weak and trembling.

They were silent as they rode through town. Greg sat with his arms folded and chin jutted outward. Eugene wore a grim expression. Peter imagined his own expression was similar.

When they were past the town limits, Eugene spoke. "If it comes to a firefight, you let me know," he told Peter. "I'll be there."

"Me too," Greg said, "I might be useless, but at least I'm more of a man than our stalwart sheriff."

Considering the conversation the three of them had just had with the sheriff in question, Peter had to agree.

They were silent once more the rest of the way home. When they reached the Gutenberg ranch, Dorothy and Lydia came down from the porch to greet them. Dorothy started to run to them, but stopped running when she saw the grim looks on the men's faces. Mary covered her face with her hands and started to weep softly. Lydia only looked pale, and when she saw Peter's expression, she grew even more pale.

"What did you do?" she asked him softly.

"Nothing yet," he said.

"Peter!" she hissed, grabbing his hand. "Don't be foolish."

He looked at her and said nothing. The determination in his mind must have shown because her lip started to tremble, and after a moment she released his arm. "Supper's ready," she said tersely, fear making her tone sharp. "Coffee's cold. You'll need to reheat it if you want some."

They headed inside and enjoyed a somber meal. Even Dorothy, normally unflappable in her good cheer, was subdued.

Later that evening, Peter sat awake in his cabin. He stared at the shelf in his closet for a long while before standing and taking out his handgun, carefully wrapped in its oilcloth. He opened the cloth and caressed the weapon almost lovingly. It was cold and hard, but then, war always was.

Chapter Thirty

Three weeks came and went. October arrived and with it, the first hints of autumn's chill. The days shortened and the trees began to trade their green for gold and red. Larkspurs covered the meadows and grew unchecked on the pastures of the Gutenberg Ranch, fallow for weeks now with no cattle to feed.

Lydia sat on her front porch one morning and gazed across the expanse of blue and green and white, wondering as she did every day if this would be the last morning she would sit here. She had learned from her father that Peter had intended for them to leave a month ago, but Greg had refused, saying that Peter was family, and they would leave together. Lydia, of course, had agreed.

She and Peter had never said again the words they had said out of the other's hearing. A strange superstition had convinced Lydia that if she confessed her feelings now, then Peter would surely die, and she would lose the only man she had ever truly loved. Perhaps Peter felt the same as she did. Either way, though they had spent considerable time together the past three weeks, they had talked only of the ranch and of their plans for after, when Peter was well.

And he was nearly well, she believed. He had begun riding and working again, though he kept to a light workload. His face no longer appeared pale and drawn when he returned home after work, and his breathing was no longer so labored.

Nothing had come yet of his not-so-veiled promise to take matters into his own hands concerning John, but he and Greg met almost daily with Eugene and the three of them never shared the details of their conversations. A few times, Lydia had tried to convince Peter to let go of his plan to fight, but each time, his face had shown her that he wouldn't be shaken from his course.

She had seen John yesterday in town. She was at the general store purchasing linens to replace the bloodstained ones she'd used for Peter's wound. She felt the hair on the back of her neck stand up and when she turned, he was there.

He smiled at her, but the smile ended long before his glittering obsidian eyes. He offered to pay for her linens, and when she refused, he said, "No please. I insist."

He dropped a bag of coins on the counter that could have bought half of the items in the store. Mr. Hafferty had taken the coins and disappeared, as good folk always seemed to do when John was threatening a woman.

"See?" John said, "isn't it so much easier to just let me have what I want?"

He offered her another edged smile, then left without waiting for her to respond.

She hadn't told Peter, and she wouldn't. The last thing she needed was for him to go get himself killed.

A chill breeze blew across the porch, but it was only a coincidence that she shivered at the same time. She stood and headed inside to dress. Dorothy had invited the Gutenbergs over for dinner, believing in her childlike innocence that a night of fun with friends and neighbors would dispel the black mood that hung over everyone. Lydia was determined to behave joyfully for her friend's sake regardless of how she really felt. Dorothy would discover soon enough that life was not a fairy tale. Or if it was, it was like one of the old fairy tales, the ones that mentioned the children who wandered to their deaths in hushed whispers if at all. The ones where monsters killed and ate, and good people huddled in their houses. Especially if she remained in Stevensville.

An ugly thought came to Lydia then. What if when she left, John turned his attention to Dorothy? Would Eugene also pick up and move? Would John allow him to?

She tried to put the thought from her mind. There was nothing she could do about it. If she had learned nothing else from the last five and a half years, it was that some things truly were out of her control.

She finished dressing and met Peter and her parents in the parlor. Mary cried out and rushed to her, beaming. "Oh, Lydia, you look wonderful! Doesn't she look wonderful, Peter?"

Peter smiled. "Pretty as a picture, Miss Mary."

Lydia offered a smile of her own and thanked Peter. Neither she nor Peter cared much what she looked like right now, but Mary needed to fill her head with romance just as Dorothy needed to fill hers with laughter, and neither Lydia nor Peter felt inclined to take that away from her.

They rode to the Gutenberg's house, Lydia driving so that Peter wouldn't strain himself unnecessarily. Dorothy was waiting when they arrived. She rushed over, arms outstretched, and practically pulled Lydia from the wagon before Eugene managed to reach her. He settled for helping Mary down instead.

"Oh, Lydia, I'm so glad you could make it!" she said.

Lydia smiled. "Dorothy, we see each other all the time. I live a mile away from you."

"So? I can't be grateful for my friend's presence?"

Lydia chuckled. "Of course you can. I'm sorry to be ungrateful."

Dorothy giggled. "Why so formal, Lydia? We've been friends since we were girls."

"Since you were a girl," Lydia corrected.

Dorothy crossed her arms in mock indignation and said, "Well, if you're going to be pedantic, you can lend your exacting mind to the queen cake recipe I'm trying."

So saying, she grabbed Lydia's arm and half-dragged her into the kitchen. When they reached it, she turned and held out both of her arms as though the excitement was almost too great to bear. Probably it was.

"Now," she said, "I tried molasses already, and you and I both know that didn't work out."

Lydia nodded. The resulting cakes had been sticky and mushy and so cloyingly sweet that they were inedible. Lydia suspected that had more to do with the amount of molasses added than the ingredient itself, but she kept that thought to herself. Part of the fun of baking for Dorothy was trying and failing.

"So *I* decided to try something new!"

"You don't say?" Lydia said, trying to keep the sarcasm from her voice.

"I decided to use..." She paused for dramatic effect. "Corn syrup!"

Lydia stared blankly at her. "Corn syrup?"

"Yes!" Dorothy bounced up and down, clapping her hands excitedly. "Oh, it's *so* sweet, Lydia. Have you ever had it before?"

"I can't say that I have," Lydia said.

In fact, she had never heard of corn syrup before. When Dorothy produced a dark brown liquid, Lydia rather suspected that Mr. Hemsworth had either played a trick on poor Dorothy and sold her slightly more refined and filtered molasses. More likely he himself had been fooled by some peddler.

Dorothy took a spoonful of the dark liquid and pressed it to Lydia's mouth as though feeding an infant. Lydia gently took the spoon from her friend and took the bite herself. Instantly, her senses were overwhelmed with a cloying sensation so powerful her face screwed up in a grimace.

"See?" Dorothy said, once more bouncing and clapping her hands giddily. Evidently this was the reaction she'd hoped for. "Oh, it's *decadent*, isn't it? I should probably only use two cups instead of four like I did with the molasses."

"Perhaps two tablespoons will suffice," Lydia suggested.

Dorothy looked at her as though she had just said the most foolish thing Dorothy had ever heard. "Well, I'll use half a cup, at least," she said. "It's for queen cakes, Lydia, not for dinner rolls."

Lydia stared at her friend. "What sort of dinner rolls are you eating?"

"Fire!" Mary shrieked.

The sound was so jarring and unexpected that Lydia didn't believe she had actually heard it at first. She and Dorothy stared blankly at each other for several seconds. It wasn't until Mary again shrieked, "Fire!" and Lydia heard the commotion from the men rushing outside that she understood that this was no nightmare but very, very real.

Time seemed to move slowly for Lydia as she made her way to the porch. She sprinted as fast as she could, but it felt as though ages passed between each footfall. Her senses dulled, her mother's shrieking a faraway wail. She thought with clinical detachment that her mind must already have sent her into shock to protect her from what she would see next.

When she stood on the porch, however, all of her senses returned in crystal clarity. She could hear her mother's shrieking, smell the sweet-char odor of burning pine and see the plume of black smoke rising from her house.

Mary stared at the smoke, shrieking over and over, hands raised in terror. Dorothy and Greg stared open-mouthed at the smoke while Peter and Eugene wore grim looks.

Peter was the first to act. "Greg, get the horses," he said.

Greg remained rooted to the spot, staring in disbelief.

"Greg!" Peter shouted.

As though struck by lightning, Greg sprinted toward the wagon. He heaved himself up onto the bench and Peter called, "Forget the wagon, just get the horses!"

Greg jumped from the wagon and struggled to unhitch the horses while Peter issued instructions to the others.

"Eugene, see if you can gather the neighbors. We need to put that blaze out before it spreads to the other homesteads."

"Town's faster," Eugene said, "We'll get more people quicker that way."

He rushed off to his stable to get his own horse and Peter turned to Lydia. "In that case, Lydia, you ride to the neighbors. Dorothy, you stay here with Mary."

"No!" Mary shrieked. "That's my house! That's my *home!*"

"Mary, you stay here," Peter said commandingly.

"No!" Mary cried. "They're burning down my *home!*"

"Your family is your home," Peter began.

"Peter, just take her," Lydia said.

"It's not safe," Peter argued.

"Nowhere's safe right now, Peter!" Lydia said. Choosing her words carefully, Lydia said, "I don't think it's a good idea for us to be alone right now. Not me, Dorothy or my mother, at least."

Peter regarded her a moment. Then he understood. John could still be nearby, and if he was, then leaving the women alone was the last thing they wanted to do.

He nodded and called, "Greg! Forget about it. We're taking the wagon after all."

Greg, who had made absolutely no progress with the horses, nodded at Peter and struggled into the seat again. Peter helped Lydia, Mary and Dorothy into the wagon, then told Greg to drive to the ranch.

"What about you?" Greg asked.

"I'll catch up," he said, starting toward the stable to get a horse.

Lydia stared ahead at the growing plume of smoke as her father drove them toward the ranch. Dorothy looked utterly shocked, continuing to stare open-mouthed at the blaze. Mary alternated between weeping and shrieking.

Peter caught up to them just as they crested the short rise before the ranch. Lydia gasped when she saw the destruction. The barn, stable and house were all burning, their smoke rising and meeting to form the vast plume that she saw from the Flister's porch.

The moment she saw the flames, she knew the ranch was gone.

"We can still save the animals," Peter said. "Lydia, take Dorothy and Mary to the barn. The cow and the chickens could still be alive. Greg, you're with me. We're going to try to put out the fire at the house."

Lydia and Greg nodded, and as soon as Greg dismounted, Lydia started the wagon toward the barn.

"Oh no," Mary keened. "Oh, why? How can he be so cruel?"

Lydia didn't know how to answer that. She didn't know if there was an answer.

"What do we do, Lydia?" Dorothy asked in a thin voice.

"We save the chickens," Lydia said. "It's too late for the cow."

"No!" Mary cried. "We can't leave her!"

"Mother, the barn is completely engulfed," Lydia said. "The coop is attached to the barn from the outside. There's a chance to save the chickens, but if we go inside that barn, we could be hurt."

Just then, their dairy cow bawled, a high-pitched squeal that sounded more like a shriek than a moo. Mary cried, "No!" and leapt from the wagon, rushing toward the barn.

"Mother!" Lydia cried. "Stop!"

Mary reached the doorway just as a loud crack sounded. The crossbeam of the door fell, landing on top of Mary in a shower of sparks. Mary unleashed an ear-splitting scream and fell to the ground, crushed by the weight of the beam.

Lydia and Dorothy rushed to Mary's side. The beam was almost completely charred through and the flames had extinguished when the beam fell, a silver lining since even burnt nearly to ash the beam was so heavy that Dorothy and Lydia struggled to move it.

They managed to free Mary just as another crack sounded. Lydia looked up to see the barn begin to list.

It was seconds from collapse.

"Help me get her on the wagon," Lydia told Dorothy.

Mary shrieked and wept as they moved her. She clutched her chest, and Lydia suspected she had broken some of her ribs.

They reached the wagon. "Mother, you have to help me."

"The chickens," Mary sobbed.

"Forget the chickens," Lydia said. "Let's save you."

Mary continued to weep but allowed Lydia and Dorothy to help her onto the wagon. They mounted after her and Lydia turned the wagon around and snapped the reins. Behind her, she heard another, much louder, crack, then an ear-splitting roar as the barn collapsed.

Greg and Peter were running buckets of water from the well to the house. The house was burning fiercely but in better shape than the barn. There was a chance to save the structure, although they would lose the roof for sure.

"Dorothy, stay with my mother, please," Lydia commanded.

"No," Mary said. "Help them. I'll be fine."

Lydia nodded and jumped from the wagon, Dorothy on her heels. They lined up behind Peter and Greg and passed buckets back and forth. It slowed the fire but wasn't enough to stop it.

They fought the fire for perhaps twenty minutes before Eugene arrived with twenty men from town. They made two separate lines, and with the extra buckets and extra hands, they were able to gain some ground on the fire.

It took hours to put the blaze out. Night fell, and they worked by the light of the fires behind them. At some point, the stable collapsed, and they worked by the light of the embers and the moon.

Finally, they won the battle. As they extinguished the last of the blaze, weariness overcame Lydia. She dropped the bucket in her hand and collapsed to her knees, staring at the charred remains of her home while her mother continued to weep in the wagon behind her.

Chapter Thirty-One

Lydia held her mother's hand, softly stroking her hair while Doctor Anderson examined her arm. Mary stared up from the couch at the charred ruin of their ceiling and through to the sky beyond. The fire had traveled across the ceiling miraculously sparing the furniture, which, save for a few char marks and the loss of the cushion on one of the upholstered chairs, was unharmed.

Peter and Eugene were outside saying their farewells to the people who had come to help them. Greg and Dorothy stood a few feet away. Dorothy cried softly and dabbed at her eyes while Greg stared dejectedly at his injured wife.

The doctor finished his examination and said, "Well, there are definitely some broken ribs. You'll need to rest a while—two months at least. No travel and no work. You should be in bed as much as possible."

Lydia's heart sank when she heard the news. With her mother unable to travel, they couldn't escape before John decided to do something worse to them.

Then again, there wasn't much worse he could do. He had already burned down their ranch, a rather pointless act considering the ranch had already failed.

Except the point was no longer to ruin them. The point was to hurt them. Lydia's lips thinned, and her breath came in hot, shallow gasps.

Why? Why them? Was it really just because of Lydia? He wanted her so badly that he was willing to hurt and kill the people she cared about until he had her?

"Miss Lydia?"

Lydia looked up, pulled from her thoughts by Anderson's call.

"Do you have a place you can stay?"

Lydia took a breath. "Um..."

Before she could answer, Dorothy interrupted. "They can stay with us. Mary and Lydia can stay in my room and I can sleep on the couch in the parlor. I'm sure Pa won't mind if Greg and Peter stay too."

"We'll talk about that later," Lydia said softly.

"It's important that your mother rest, Miss Lydia," Anderson said. "Miss Mary, you need to accept that. I know it's difficult to stay still, but it's crucial that you not reinjure yourself. If you'll pardon me for saying so, an injury like this at your age is far more serious than in someone younger. You need to take care of yourself."

Mary nodded, tears still streaming silently down her cheeks.

The doctor stood. "If you need anything else, Miss Lydia, send for me at any time."

He looked at Greg and motioned for them to leave to join the men. Lydia bristled a little at being excluded from the conversation, but she knew Peter would tell her whatever it was they discussed later, and she needed to stay with her mother.

Dorothy stood and said, "I'll make coffee. Do you think it's safe to use the stove?"

Lydia nodded. "The stove isn't damaged."

Dorothy nodded and headed to make the coffee. Lydia turned to Mary, but her mother was already asleep. Her face was drawn and pale and dark circles surrounded her eyes. She looked so old.

Lydia brushed a lock of hair back from Mary's face and released her hand. She stood and joined the men outside. When they saw her, Peter whispered briefly to Doctor Anderson. The doctor nodded and said to Greg, "Help me with your wife."

"She's asleep," Lydia said. "Can you wait to bind her arm until she wakes?"

Anderson shook his head and sighed softly. "I'm afraid not. The longer we leave the arm unbound, the greater the risk that it won't set properly. I'm sorry, Miss Lydia."

"I'll help," Lydia said.

"I think you should stay outside and talk to us," Peter said.

Lydia looked at him, then at Eugene, then her father. All three of them wore the same grim expression. She took a breath and nodded.

"She'll be all right," Greg said to her, forcing a brief smile that disappeared as soon as it arrived. "She's a tough woman, your mother."

Lydia thought of the dark circles under her mother's eyes and said nothing. Greg followed Doctor Anderson inside, leaving Lydia with Peter and Eugene.

Peter spoke first. He handed Lydia a scrap of paper and said, "Eugene found this on the pasture fence."

Lydia opened the note. The handwriting was cultured, almost effeminate. She knew who its author was even before she read it.

I warned Peter to leave town. He didn't listen. I warned you to give me what belongs to me. You didn't listen. Now you know I'm capable of taking what I want.

The note wasn't signed. It didn't need a signature. Lydia read it again, her lips tightening in anger.

She handed the note back to Peter, who folded it and put it in his pocket. "Well," she said, "I suppose that isn't a surprise."

Peter shook his head. "It's time to take matters into our own hands."

Eugene nodded.

"No," Lydia said.

The two men looked at her in surprise. "Lydia, he's not going to stop," Peter said, "He's shot me, he's burned your house down and even if he didn't beat her or shoot her, he's responsible for your mother's injury all the same. The sheriff won't do anything to help, and that note makes it clear that he's still after you."

"I know," Lydia said, "but what happens if you don't beat him, Peter? What happens if Slade and his men really are too much for you?"

"I've dealt with worse," Peter said.

"That doesn't mean you're invincible, Peter," Lydia said. "You should know that by now. John could kill you."

"John could kill *you*," Peter countered. "He could kill your family."

"He could, but he won't," Lydia said. "Not if I give him what he wants."

287

Peter's eyes narrowed. "That's out of the question."

"Peter, if you don't get past Slade and his men, then John will come back for us, and this time it won't be our ranch he's after. We can't flee, not with my mother in this condition, so if he does come for us, then he'll find us and he'll kill us. You're the only thing that's kept him acting in the shadows. You need to stay here to protect us."

"I've done that," Peter argued. "Look where it's gotten us." He gestured at the still-smoldering barn and stable behind them.

"Lydia's right, Peter," Eugene said, "they can't leave, and John *will* come for them if you're out of the picture."

"John *can't* come for them if *he's* out of the picture," Peter retorted.

"I think he's counting on that," Eugene said.

Peter lifted an eyebrow.

"I think he's hoping you'll come for Slade," Eugene explained. "I think Slade and his men expect you to come for him too. I think they're lying in wait."

"Better men than him have lain in wait," Peter said, "and I've beaten them too."

"The risk is too great, Peter," Lydia said. "We can't lose you. *I* can't lose you."

"So what do we do then?" Peter asked.

Just then, they heard Mary shriek as the doctor set her arm. Lydia and Peter flinched. Eugene laid a comforting hand on both of their shoulders.

"To hell with this," Peter growled suddenly. "I'm putting that whoreson in the ground."

Lydia recoiled in shock at the intensity of Peter's reaction. His eyes seemed to flash in the low light and his lips were pulled back in a snarl.

"Peter!" Eugene barked. "Calm down."

Peter blinked, and his eyes came back into focus. He took a breath and then slumped forward slightly. "Sorry," he said, "I just...he can't be allowed to get away with this."

"I agree," Eugene said, "but we're playing at a disadvantage right now. We need to be cautious or we'll put ourselves in even more danger."

"I've been thinking about that," Lydia said slowly, "and I don't think there's a need for you and Dorothy to put yourself in danger any further."

Seeing the point Lydia was leading to, Eugene shook his head, "Miss Lydia, we're not even considering that. You and your parents are friends of ours, and we're more than willing to help in any way possible."

"You're not John's focus right now," Lydia said, "but the more help you give us, the more you will be."

Eugene shook his head again and said firmly, "Lydia, we're not giving you to him. That's non-negotiable."

"How long before he decides to go after Dorothy?" Lydia said. "What if he doesn't come for me? What if he decides that he's finished with me, and he wants Dorothy instead? He might decide that he's wasted enough time on me and seek out someone younger and more fragile. No offense, Eugene, but Dorothy won't survive someone like John."

"No offense, Miss Lydia, but *you* might not surviv someone like John," Eugene said, "and if he kills you, he car still come after Dorothy. Peter's right, we need to put a sto to him."

Peter nodded, but before he could speak, Eugene said, "bu not the way you want to, Peter."

"So what?" Peter said. "What do we do?"

"We do what we should have done months ago. Years ago really. We go to the Marshals."

"That could take weeks!"

"Weeks that would have passed already if we had gone fo them in the first place. Weeks we have now since fleeing tow1 isn't an option anymore."

"And if John finds out?" Peter asked. "What happen: then?"

"Nothing that isn't already going to happen sooner o later," Eugene said. "This is what I suggest. You take the women home to my place. I have friends who can stay witl you to help watch out for Slade and his men. I'll ride for the Marshals in Virginia City."

"No," Lydia said, "it's too risky. Listen..."

Tears began to stream down her cheeks. She took i shuddering breath and laid a hand on Peter's arm.

"Peter, you are the most wonderful man I've ever met. I things were different, I could build a real life with you." Shi reached up and caressed his cheek. "But things aren' different. This is the hand we've been dealt. Some people are just fated to suffer in life."

"No!" Peter shouted. "I don't accept that."

"It doesn't matter," Lydia said softly. "I'm sorry, but this is for the best."

"He won't stop," Peter said, "not with you. Not with Dorothy either. He won't stop until he is stopped."

"So we'll stop him," Greg's voice said.

Lydia turned to see her father standing on the porch with the doctor. "Eugene, you ride to the Marshals, like you planned to. I'll ride to Sheriff Roberts. We'll give him one more chance to do the right thing. Peter, take the women back to the Flisters' ranch."

"Father–" Lydia began.

"I speak for Peter and myself when I tell you that we'd rather die than see you get hurt."

Peter nodded and Lydia protested, "You don't have the right to make that choice for me!"

"We're making it for ourselves," Greg said. "For you too, but for ourselves as well. Honey, we need to end this. I don't agree with Peter running out on his own, but I do agree that we need to take active steps to stop John. And I won't see you marry a snake like John Smith. You're my daughter, and while I might not be the best man to ever live, I will die before he hurts my daughter."

"I don't want you to die!" Lydia shouted. The tears fell from her eyes in streams now. "I don't want either of you to die! I can't watch anyone else I love die, don't you understand?"

"We do," Greg said softly. "That's why we're riding for help. Sun will rise in about two hours. When it does, Peter will take the three of you to Eugene's ranch. I'll ride for the sheriff and Eugene will ride for Virginia City. This will end soon, Lydia, but it will *not* end with you wearing John Smith's ring."

"Please," Lydia said, wiping tears from her eyes. "I can't feel like this anymore. I can't let anyone else get hurt because of me."

"No one's getting hurt because of you," Greg said. "Your brother didn't die because of you."

"Yes, he did!" Lydia said. "He died because of me, and if I don't give John what he wants now, you'll die because of me too!"

"Lydia," Greg said sternly. "This conversation is over." In a softer voice, he added, "I'm sorry, Lydia."

He headed inside, but stopped in the doorway and said, "You're wrong, Lydia. It's not your fault that your brother died. That was out of your control. So is this."

He walked inside and Lydia sank to her knees, defeated and angry and scared and sad and utterly overwhelmed.

Peter stooped next to her and wrapped her in his arms, pulling her close. She wept against his shoulder, too spent emotionally and physically to argue anymore. She wept and Peter held her and repeated a promise Lydia wanted desperately to believe but no longer could.

"It'll be all right, Lydia."

Chapter Thirty-Two

"Would you men like some coffee?" Dorothy asked.

Peter shook his head. The others at the table followed suit save for the sheriff and the doctor, who both nodded gratefully and thanked her. The doctor had spent the past week visiting Mary nearly every day and was understandably exhausted. The sheriff was simply terrified.

But he was here. That was a gift horse Peter wouldn't look in the mouth.

Dorothy left to make the coffee, and Peter said, "We really should have Lydia join us before we begin."

Greg nodded. "I'll get her. She's sitting with Mary right now."

"Well, there's no need to rush," Eugene said, "I'll send Dorothy to sit with Mary after she makes the coffee."

Greg looked at Peter, who nodded assent. Greg sat back down, and Peter said, "While we wait, I want to thank you for agreeing to help us, Sheriff. I know that it's asking a lot of you."

Greg and Eugene shared a glance at that. The two of them didn't see the need to thank the sheriff, who in their mind was partly responsible for John's behavior by allowing him to operate with impunity for so long. Peter understood their position, but he needed the sheriff to be as relaxed as possible.

A few minutes later, Dorothy arrived with coffee and then left to take over for Lydia. Lydia arrived a moment later and Peter stood so she could sit.

"All right," Eugene said, "I'll start. As you all know, I spoke to the Marshals in Virginia City. It turns out they've had suspicions about John Smith for a while now because of some shady financial dealings he's made throughout the territory, but they never chose to investigate. They assumed the sheriff would alert them to anything untoward he couldn't handle himself."

Roberts looked glumly at his coffee while Greg, Peter, Doctor Anderson and Lydia avoided looking at him.

"In any case," Eugene continued, "They've agreed to help. They'll be here tomorrow."

"They're coming to town?" Lydia asked.

"No," Eugene said, "they're going to camp on the other side of the foothills east of town."

"Why?" Lydia asked. "Wouldn't it make more sense for them to just come get him?"

"They're concerned he'll try to escape," Eugene said, "or that Slade and his men will react violently. They're hoping to catch him unawares and take him without a gunfight."

"How do they plan to do that?" Peter asked.

"That's where the sheriff comes in," Greg answered.

He looked expectantly at Roberts and the sheriff sighed. He took a deep sip of his coffee, then said, "I'm going to ride to John and tell him that Eugene went for the marshals."

"You can't do that!" Lydia said. "John will kill him!"

"Well, I'll tell John that the best thing to do is talk to the Marshals in Virginia City. I'll back him up. We can tell the Marshals that Peter instigated the fight at the saloon and Slade only acted in self-defense. He can explain that the

Gutenbergs are debtors protected by the homestead act and that after the failure of their business, they engaged in a campaign to slander Mr. Smith in an attempt to escape their financial obligations."

"So we're going to lie to him," Peter said, "and hope that he'll fall for it. And then what? Meet with the Marshals and they'll arrest him?"

"Yes," the sheriff said, "in the meantime, I'll form a posse. The Marshals and the posse will intercept and surround John, and then Slade and his men will be woefully outnumbered. They arrest John, and it's over."

"How do we know it's over after they arrest him?" Lydia asked.

"I have a friend in Virginia City," Doctor Anderson said. "He's a very accomplished litigator. We have more than enough evidence to convict John, especially with the note he left for you when he burned your house down. I can convince him to help us in front of the judge."

"What if he doesn't agree to talk to the Marshals?" Lydia asked. "He could demand that they come speak to him if they want to arrest him."

"They'll be watching for him to try to flee," Roberts said, "and so will the posse. He won't get away."

"Pardon me for my rudeness, Sheriff," Lydia said brittlely, "but why should we trust you?"

Roberts stared at his coffee a moment without saying anything. Then he sighed deeply. "When Greg told me about what happened to Miss Mary, I decided that was the final straw. I convinced myself for the longest time that leaving things alone was the best way to keep everyone safe. I'm not making excuses. I know I'm a coward. I'm just telling you that's how I justified it to myself. When Greg told me that Miss Mary broke her arm after John burned your ranch down, I...well, I can't anymore. I can't live like this."

"Can't say I blame you," Eugene said with only the barest hint of contempt.

"So essentially," Peter said, "what the Marshals want is to lure John outside of town so there's no collateral damage when they take him. Basically the same thing we believe John was planning to do to me."

"That's right," Eugene said, "and the sheriff will help by cutting off his means of escape."

"Again, though," Lydia said, "what if he doesn't come to talk to them?"

"Then it's business as usual," Eugene said. "They go to his home and get him. They expect a firefight if they do that, though, and frankly, so do I. They're hoping to avoid that if they can."

"Fair enough," Lydia said. "But John's cunning, and he has lawyers too. What if they arrest him and then he beats us in court?"

"My friend is a good lawyer," the sheriff assured her, "and John hasn't been as careful as he thinks he has. I have a lot of evidence of his wrongdoing going back years. I...I just never had the courage to do anything with it."

He looked up to meet Lydia's eyes and for the first time since he'd met him, Peter saw a hint of strength. "I have the courage now. Just enough to put John away then leave the sheriff job for someone better than me."

Lydia pursed her lips, clearly still not convinced, but she nodded.

After a moment, Peter said, "Well, unless someone has a better plan, then this is what we're going with."

No one offered an objection, and Peter nodded. "All right, then. Eugene, thank you. Sheriff, thank you as well. If you're willing, I'll lead the posse. I have experience leading men into combat. Hopefully it won't go that way, but if it does, I can make sure that we put an end to the fighting quickly."

Roberts nodded. "All right." He chuckled bitterly. "You'll do a better job than me."

"I'm joining the posse too," Greg said.

"No," the others said unanimously.

"Greg, you need to stay behind to protect the women in case something goes wrong and John sends people to the ranch," Eugene explained.

"Don't talk to me like I'm a child, Eugene," Greg rebuked gently. "We're all friends here. I'm less helpful in a firefight than Mary is. If Slade comes after us here, there won't be anything I can do to stop him."

"Greg, if you're not helpful in a firefight, than a firefight is the last place we should take you," Peter said. "It's all the more reason you should stay home."

Greg met Peter's eyes. "I don't have a home, Peter," he said, "John Smith burned it down. Let's be honest, though. If it weren't for you, I would have lost my home anyway. If the home was what John wanted, he could have just waited for the Homestead Act protection to expire and then taken the ranch legally and cleanly. He wants my daughter, and useless or not, I will stand and face the man who wants my daughter. I'll make whatever sacrifice I need to make."

Lydia chimed in, "Absolutely not. Mother needs you, father. You can't leave her."

"I'm going, Lydia," Greg said, "I've been less than a man for too long. I'm going to make up for it now."

"Father—"

"I'm going," Greg insisted. "Unless Peter here wants to tie me to the hitching post outside, I'm going."

Lydia looked at Peter as though she were seriously considering asking him to do just that. Then she turned back to Greg. "I'm coming too."

"No," the group again said in unison.

"Oh, don't even start," Lydia said, "if my father is too stubborn to stay, then I'm far too stubborn to stay. I have as much a right to look John in the eye as anyone here, if not more."

"We can't leave Dorothy and Miss Mary alone," Eugene said.

"I'll stay with them," Anderson said. "Miss Mary still needs medical attention. I'll need to be here anyway." Noticing Peter and Greg's irritated looks, he said, "I can't imagine you'll convince Miss Lydia to stay, so there's no point in trying."

Peter looked at Lydia, who returned his gaze with chin lifted and eyes blazing. She never looked so beautiful as she did in that moment.

"All right then," he said, "you'll ride with us. But you'll stay out of the way, and if there's fighting, you are to remember your mother and leave before you get hurt. Is that understood?"

Lydia nodded. "I understand."

Her expression told Peter that her understanding didn't translate into obedience, but he knew better than to argue further. He nodded to her, then turned to the sheriff. "Okay, then. Go talk to John. You'll have to find a way to get word of his answer to us. Try to make sure he doesn't see you."

"Mr. Sorley is supposed to see me to reshoe my horses this evening," Eugene said. "You can send word back with him."

"Perfect," the sheriff said, his courage growing now that they had come to a decision. He stood, the floorboards creaking under his weight. "I'll ride now, so I can talk to John before Sorley leaves town."

He said his goodbyes, then left. Eugene went to tend to his sheep, left alone in the pasture for the past week while he rode for the Marshals. Greg and Doctor Anderson returned to Mary, leaving Lydia alone with Peter.

"Do you think this will work?" she asked him.

He nodded. "John's days are numbered no matter what. If he stays in town, the fight will be a little bloodier than it needs to be, but either way, he's done."

"The only question is how many of us he takes with him," Lydia said.

Peter didn't respond to that.

After a moment, Lydia asked, "Why do you think he hasn't come for us? I mean, we were here for a week."

"Same reason he didn't come for you for the past several months," Peter said, "he's a coward. He knows how dangerous I am, and Slade probably told him that Eugene's a more than fair shot with the rifle. We're on guard already, and even though Slade outnumbers us, I think they both know that attacking us would be very risky. John isn't the sort of man who takes risks."

"He's not the sort of man who accepts defeat, either," Lydia countered.

"No, but surprisingly, he has the virtue of patience," Peter said. "He thinks he's won already. He's only waiting us out. We have to hope his caution works against him."

Lydia nodded. They fell silent again for a moment. Then she said, "What will you do? Once this is over, I mean. I know you've offered to help us get on our feet, but what happens after that?"

Peter looked at her. She was as breathtaking as the day he met her, more so now that he knew her and had seen firsthand the strength of her will and her character. He took her hand in his and met her eyes.

"After," he said, "I will court you the way you deserve to be courted."

Lydia smiled slightly. "Go on."

"I'll take you on outings," Peter said. "I'll write you some more terrible poems."

Lydia laughed. "They're not terrible, they're sweet!"

Peter chuckled. "Well, thank you," he said. "I'm glad you like them."

Lydia met his eyes and said, "Tell me more."

He smiled. "We'll sit on the porch and watch the stars."

"If we have a porch," Lydia reminded him.

"If we have a porch," Peter agreed. "I'll tell you about the home we'll have one day and the children we'll fill it with."

"Hold on," Lydia said with a giggle. "Let's not get *that* far ahead."

"And then I'll ask your father for your hand," Peter finished, "and I'll spend the rest of my life being the best husband I can possibly be to you."

Lydia's smile faded as she looked at him. "Do you promise?" he said.

He leaned forward and pulled her to him. She gasped, but that gasp ended when his lips pressed against hers. After a moment, she melted and her arm snaked behind his head.

They kissed longingly and passionately, and when Peter finally released her, Lydia's face was flushed, and her breathing came in short gasps.

"I promise," Peter said.

"Promise me again," she said.

He smiled and pulled her to him once more.

The next twenty-four hours would determine their future, but for the moment, Peter allowed himself to live in the present.

Chapter Thirty-Three

Lydia woke early, as she always did. She headed to the kitchen to make coffee. As usual, Peter was already up. He sat at the table and nodded at her.

"Morning, Lydia."

"Good morning, Peter."

She stopped and hesitated only a moment before walking to him. He looked up just in time for her to cup his face in her hands and kiss him softly. When she pulled away, he looked at her with a love that was almost frightening in its intensity. She smiled softly at him, then returned to the coffee.

"How's your wound?" she asked.

"Fair," he said, "I can ride, and I can shoot."

"Well," Lydia said, "let's hope it doesn't come to that."

Sorley had brought the good news the night before. The sheriff would lead John and Slade's men to the road to Virginia City. The posse would wait for the group to get out of sight over the ridge to the east of town, then follow after. The Marshals would accost John and arrest him. If all went well, there would be no violence and the posse would simply watch the whole thing. If not, then they would ride to cut off John's escape and provide support to the marshals.

Greg arrived in the kitchen just as the coffee finished brewing. He nodded seriously to Peter, then smiled at Lydia. "You ready?" he asked.

Lydia didn't answer that right away. She was terrified for her father's safety and for Peter's. She wasn't so terrified for her own, but she supposed that both Peter and Greg were more worried for her than for themselves. That was the nature of love. One would suffer any amount of pain they needed to suffer as long as their loved ones were safe.

Finally, she turned to her father and said, "I'm as ready as can be expected. I'm happy that this will finally end."

"Yeah," Greg said, "Me too."

They finished their coffee while Lydia made breakfast. Peter ate heartily, and when he saw the two of them picking at their food, he said, "Eat. You need your strength for what's to come."

With Peter's encouragement, the two of them finished their breakfast. Eugene and the doctor joined them a moment later.

Just as Lydia, Peter, Greg and Eugene started to lace up their boots to leave, Dorothy and Mary came downstairs, Dorothy's arm around Mary's shoulder.

Mary regarded the four of them, tears streaming from her cheeks. Greg stood and crossed the room to his wife. He pulled her close and kissed her as passionately as Peter had kissed Lydia the night before.

"Come home to me, my love," Mary whispered, looking up into Greg's eyes. "Please come home."

"I will," he said softly.

A lump formed in Lydia's throat and when Mary said goodbye to her, she held tightly to her mother. "I'll be safe," she whispered, "I promise."

"I know you will," Mary said, "you're a good girl."

Lydia chuckled in spite of her tears. "I haven't been a girl in over a decade, mother," she said.

Mary smiled and lifted her good hand to stroke Lydia's cheek. "You'll always be my baby girl."

Lydia couldn't hold back the tears any more. She wrapped her arms as tightly around Mary as she dared without risking hurting her arm and held her until she felt Peter's hand on her shoulder.

She released Mary and turned to Dorothy, who for the first time in the five years she'd known her was crying. "Take care of my mother, Dorothy," she said.

"I will," Dorothy promised. "For this afternoon only, you understand? After that, we'll *all* take care of her."

"We will," Eugene said, wrapping his daughter in her arms. "We will."

They said their goodbyes to Doctor Anderson, then the four of them left. They rode silently to town. There was nothing more to be said. Now, at last, was the time to act.

The posse waited for them at the saloon. There were thirteen men in all, including Sorley. All wore the grim expressions of men who knew they were about to risk their lives but risked it for something worth the cost.

Peter nodded to the gathered men. "I haven't been among you for long, but I've been here long enough to know that you've all suffered in one way or another at the hands of John Smith."

The men all nodded.

"Today, we put an end to that suffering."

The men didn't cheer. This wasn't really the time or place for cheers. Still, their low mutters of assent gave Peter all the encouragement he needed. Peter waited a moment, then said, "Now you all have a reason to want to hurt John, I at least as much as any of you, but the goal today is no fighting. You're all armed, and if the situation calls for it, I'll expect all of you to use your weapons effectively. I'll expect that you use your weapon *only* if the situation calls for it. Are we in agreement?"

The men once more voiced their understanding, and Peter waited for them to finish. Then he said, "You're all familiar with the plan: we'll wait for John to crest the rise west of town, then we'll follow quickly but as stealthily as possible. Miss Lydia–" He looked at Lydia. "--has agreed that she will remain at the rear of the group. If there's a firefight, she'll wait out of harm's way."

The men nodded agreement again, although several of them cast looks at Lydia that indicated their disapproval of a woman's presence. Lydia met their gazes until they looked away. She had as much cause to see John brought to justice as any of them. Like Peter, she had more cause than most.

"Does anyone have any questions?" Peter asked.

When he was met with silence, he nodded and said, "All right, then. Go about your day like normal. Mr. Sorley, you keep an eye out, and when you see the sheriff and John and his men leave town, you ride around and let us know. Miss Lydia and I will stay here and wait for your word. We'll meet next to the church house."

Mr. Sorley nodded and the men dispersed. Peter took a seat at a table near the door. Lydia joined him, and they settled down to wait.

The early morning crowd arrived a few minutes later. Crowd was a rather generous term. There were maybe a dozen or so individuals scattered across the saloon, which, like most saloons, did the majority of its business at night. The patrons paid no attention to Peter and Lydia. The sort of people who breakfasted at a saloon were not the sort to involve themselves in other people's business.

They sat in silence for a while, but finally, the quiet became too oppressive for Lydia. She said, "So once this is over, do you still think Virginia City is the best choice for us?"

Peter nodded. "Or Bannack. Temporarily, at least. Eventually, we'll probably need to head west to California. San Francisco is growing fast. It will be easy for you and me to find work there."

"And my parents?"

"Greg has experience as a clerk," Peter said. "He might be able to find work. Your mother shouldn't have to work. Frankly, I don't think she could handle it."

"No," Lydia said, "I don't think so either."

They lapsed into silence again, until once more Lydia broke it. "Do you think we'll be okay, Peter? Honestly."

"Honestly?" he sighed and leaned back in his chair. "You and I will be. We're still young. We have a lot of time to bounce back and we can handle living with little to nothing for a while if we have to. Your parents will have a harder time. The key will be to keep Mary's spirits up. If she's happy, Greg will be happy. We'll need to focus our attention on making her as comfortable as possible."

"Are you worried about her?" she asked.

He sighed and nodded. "Yes, I'm worried. She'll have the hardest time with the changes."

Lydia nodded. "Yes, I think so." A thought occurred to her. "Oh," she just said, fresh tears coming to her eyes. "I'd forgotten that I'll have to leave Dorothy behind."

She realized then how much the younger woman's friendship meant to her. For five years, she had felt alone in a strange place, carrying the weight of her family's survival on her shoulders. Dorothy's constant happiness and optimism had made that loneliness bearable long before Peter had arrived to sweep it all away. Knowing that the day rapidly approached when she would never see Dorothy again pierced her like a knife, and she dabbed at her eyes with her handkerchief as she thought of the day of their parting.

Peter took her hand in his and said, "I'm sorry. I truly am."

She looked into his eyes, dark and strong and earnest, and said, "Don't be. You did the best you could. That's all anyone can ask of themselves or anyone else."

He lowered his eyes. "Still doesn't mean I don't wish it was better."

She reached forward with her other hand and lifted his chin up. "It's good enough for me."

He smiled at her. "Thank you, Lydia. It means a lot."

Lydia looked into Peter's eyes and needed to say it. She took a breath and said, "Peter. I—"

The door opened then, and Sorley walked in. He looked somberly at the two of them and nodded.

Peter turned back to Lydia, his face set in grim determination. Lydia forced a smile and nodded to him. He pulled her to him suddenly and kissed her hard. She wrapped her arms around him and kissed him back, pouring into the kiss the emotion behind the words she couldn't say.

When they separated, Peter said, "I love you too."

Warmth filled Lydia from head to toe, and for a beautifu moment, she was perfectly happy.

Then he pulled away from her and turned to Sorley. H nodded and then stood. Lydia stood with him, and the two o them followed Sorley outside. They mounted their horses anc rode toward the church house to join the rest of them.

Lydia's jaw set in determination as she rode.

It's over now, John, she thought. *We're coming for you.*

Chapter Thirty-Four

The posse rode swiftly, but not at all quietly. Peter would just have to hope the marshals reached John before the sound of his pursuers did.

Not that it would matter much in the long run. The noose had tightened around John's neck. The best he could hope for was escape and life as a fugitive.

Still, a fugitive with nothing to lose was a dangerous fugitive. Sean O'Malley had spent his last heartbeats driving a knife into the chest of one of the constables arresting him. If John escaped long enough to realize his life was gone, he might choose to spend his last moments killing the Gutenbergs and Peter.

Peter decided to set that worry aside for the moment. The marshals knew what they were doing. Their ranks had swelled after the war as many former soldiers found employment with the agency. They had sent two dozen agents to apprehend John, and in all likelihood, Slade would avoid risking his life or his men's lives and leave John to his fate.

Peter wasn't worried about Slade. As he'd said before, Slade didn't have pride. He wouldn't mind fleeing the town and its environs and finding a place for himself and his men where his face wasn't known. In fact, he'd probably find the whole thing funny.

"Have to get to that point, first," he muttered under his breath.

They reached the hill behind town and Peter lifted his hand for the posse to stop. They did, and Peter dismounted and crouched low, creeping up to the summit of the rise. Just before the summit, he dropped to all fours and crawled the rest of the way to the edge.

He peered over and the situation that greeted him caused him to swear softly.

So Slade had fight in him after all.

The gang was dismounted, taking cover behind their horses and leveling their rifles at the marshals, who though outnumbered, were caught unprepared. Half of them didn't even have weapons drawn and those that did shifted nervously on their feet, knowing that the gang had the drop on them.

The leader of the troop wore a frown, more angry than frightened. His intent to accomplish John's arrest without bloodshed wasn't going according to plan.

"How do you think this ends for you, Mr. Smith?" he shouted. "You might kill a few federal agents. Then what? I'll tell you what. You become the most wanted man not only in the territory but in the country. You can go nowhere without someone recognizing your face and turning you in for a substantial reward. Is that really what you want?"

"Marshal, I assure you, this is all a complete misunderstanding," John said, venom behind his calm tone. "Sheriff Roberts can easily clear this matter up."

"Tell your men to lower their weapons and we can talk," the marshal said.

"I can't do that," John said, "I'm afraid your men attacked me and now I feel as though my life is in danger."

"No one attacked you, Mr. Smith," the marshal said, "You're under arrest, but not under threat of death."

"Well, that's an interesting story," John said with a smile. His smile disappeared and he said, "Here's another one. My men and I were ambushed on the road to Virginia City to discuss fraudulent claims levied against me by my debtors. Not knowing who the men were, my bodyguards quite understandably chose to protect me, returning violence with violence. Regrettably, none of the assailants were left alive."

The marshals quickly looked to their leader, who for the first time seemed worried. Peter lifted his arm and waved to the marshal. The man's eyes flickered to Peter, remained for a moment, then returned to John. His anxiety relaxed and he tapped his holster twice.

The other marshals relaxed as well, and Peter realized that was the signal that the posse had arrived. The sheriff sighed, and Peter could only hope that the outlaws would interpret his relief as dejection or fear.

The captain of the troop squared his stance and said in an authoritative voice, "John Smith, you are under arrest. Surrender quietly, or we will have no choice but to apprehend you forcefully."

"So be it," John hissed.

"Now!" Peter cried.

The posse charged over the hill, yelling and brandishing their weapons. John jumped and turned in shock as the sheriff's men rushed toward them. Sheriff Roberts sprinted toward a stand of trees at the side of the road, intending to hide behind them until the fighting was over. *Probably the best place for him,* Peter thought.

John's face set in a grimace of hate, and he shouted. "Kill him! Kill Peter Kerouac!"

Slade looked at his men and then dropped his rifle, lifting his hands and backing away.

The other gangsters followed suit, and Peter relaxed. The Marshal would get his wish after all.

"No!" John shrieked, his face beet red in fury. "No, no, no!"

"It's over, John," Peter said, stopping ten yards or so from the man. "Come quietly, and remember you've just threatened to kill the men coming to arrest you. It would be in your best interests to walk softly."

Half of the marshals busied themselves patting down Slade and his men while the other half approached John. John looked quickly around, lips pulled back in a snarl. He turned back to Peter, then grinned.

"Very well, Peter," he said. "But if I can't have what's mine, then neither can you!"

Peter frowned, wondering what John was talking about. Then his heart dropped to his feet. He turned to see Lydia standing a few yards behind him.

Just out of reach.

"Lydia!" he cried. "No!"

He turned to John, drawing his handgun as he turned, but John's weapon was already drawn.

Time slowed to a crawl. Peter saw John's crazed smile as he fired. He heard Lydia's shriek. He heard his own cry of rage and grief as he fired his own weapon. The bullet impacted John just below the breastbone and the man stumbled backwards then fell, dropping his own weapon in the process.

The marshals surrounded John, one of them kicking the gun away while another jerked the man's hands behind his back.

Peter spun, eyes wide with terror. "Lydia! Lydia!" he cried, rushing to her.

She stood stock still, face pale and mouth open in shock. She stared at the ground in front of her, her hands raised in fright. Peter reached her and patted her everywhere, checking for wounds. "Where are you hit?" he said hoarsely. "Where did he get you?"

In his shock and horror, he didn't realize what Lydia was staring at until he heard Greg's voice. "Didn't get her. Won't get her."

He looked down to see Greg lying at Lydia's feet, blood pouring from his chest as the bullet meant for Lydia emptied his life from his veins.

"Pa!" Lydia shouted, dropping to her knees and cradling her father's head in her arms. "Oh no. Pa!"

Peter looked down at his friend—his father—as tears blurred his vision. "Pa," he whispered.

Greg smiled up at him. He opened his mouth to speak, then coughed. Blood poured from the corners of his mouth as he did.

"Don't speak now," Peter said. "Save your strength."

"No point," Greg choked out. "Done for."

"Pa, don't say that," Lydia said, clutching his arm to her chest. "Don't leave me, please."

Greg turned his smile to her. "You haven't called me Pa since you were a girl."

"I'll call you Pa every day for the rest of my life," Lydia sobbed, "just please don't go."

Greg lifted his other hand and softly caressed her cheek "You're a good daughter, Liddie. Best a man could ever have."

"Pa," Lydia said, "no. Please!"

Greg turned his attention to Eugene, who stood behind Peter with his hat in his hands and tears streaming down his cheeks.

"You were a good friend, Eugene," he said. "You helped me and my family when no one else would. I could never repay you even if I wanted to."

"Don't matter," Eugene said, his voice thick. "I was happy to know you. You're a better man than most I met."

Greg nodded. "You take care of your little girl. You let her live her life the way she wants to live it. Don't make my mistakes."

"I won't," Eugene said. "I'll take care of Mary and Lydia too They'll stay with me, Greg. I ain't letting them struggle. promise you."

Greg reached up and Eugene stepped forward and clasped his friend's hand. Greg turned to Peter and said, "You take care of them too, you hear? You may not think you're a good man, Peter, but you're wrong. You're a good man, a great man, and any man worth his salt would be proud to have you as his son."

He burst into a coughing fit then, and Peter quickly knelt at his side. "I will, Greg. I'll take care of them. I won't let anything happen to them, I promise."

Greg smiled, his face gray and lined. He turned once more to Lydia and said, "I love you, Liddie."

"I love you too, Pa," she wept.

Greg smiled once more. Then his smile faded. He took a deep breath and released it.

Then he was gone.

Lydia wailed and clutched her father's hand to her chest, rocking back and forth.. Eugene reached forward with trembling hands and closed Greg's eyes.

Peter remained kneeling in front of his friend's body for a moment longer, grieving for the second time in his life the loss of a father. His grief cut him like a knife, then like a knife, it sharpened into anger.

He rose and stalked to where John lay on the ground. He drew his handgun again and thumbed back the hammer.

The captain of the marshals lifted his head from John. When he saw Peter's weapon drawn, he met Peter's eyes and said, "No need for that. The first one got him."

Peter met the marshal's eyes, then looked down at John's still body. He lay in a pool of blood, face frozen in a hideous grin, eyes staring lifelessly at the clear sky above. Peter regarded the corpse in front of him. At the end of it all, John was only a man. No less, no more. It was an idle thought, and brought him no happiness.

Behind him, Peter could hear Lydia's wails of grief. How much pain one man could cause when he cared only for himself. How terrible the ending of such a man, and how awful the destruction left in his wake.

He looked over at Slade, who stood handcuffed with his men. "What happens with them?" he asked the captain.

The captain sighed. "Well, they didn't actually fire on us, and we did have our weapons drawn when we accosted them. Once we announced Mr. Smith's arrest, they dropped their weapons and surrendered. I'm afraid we don't have cause to hold them. We can detain them until Mr. Smith's body is remanded to the custody of the Marshal's Office in Virginia City. After that, I'm afraid they'll be allowed to leave on their own recognizance."

His expression and tone of voice indicated that he wasn't happy with that fact. Peter wasn't exactly overjoyed either, but he had expected this, so he wasn't surprised.

He started toward Slade, but the marshal placed a hand on his chest, stopping him. "You mind holstering your weapon first?" he asked Peter. "Just for my peace of mind."

Peter nodded and holstered his handgun. He walked over to Slade, who regarded him warily.

"Stay away from this town," Peter said coldly. "Don't let me see you again."

"Fine with me," Slade said. He jerked his head over to John. "I never liked him anyway. I'll probably ride out West, try my luck as a deckhand. I always wanted to sail."

Peter didn't care much where Slade went, and he didn't respond. He left the outlaw and returned to Lydia, who still wept next to her father's lifeless body.

He sat next to her and wrapped her in his arms. She clung to him, sobbing into his shoulder. He tightened his arms around her, hoping to share what strength he could.

It was over now. John Smith was gone. Greg Gutenberg had died a hero. Isaac Slade and his men would leave Stevensville never to return. Sheriff Roberts would step down for a man more worthy of the job. They would bury Greg, and they would slowly but surely move on from this and build a life for themselves.

But right now, they would grieve.

Peter closed his eyes and for the first time since before the war, he wept.

Chapter Thirty-Five

Lydia stood next to her mother, her arm around her. Dorothy stood on Mary's right, also lending a comforting arm to the older woman. Eugene stood on the other side of Dorothy, hat in hand as he stared solemnly at the scene ahead.

Peter stood next to Lydia, keeping a steadying arm around her waist. She looked up to see the same solemn expression Eugene wore, but behind his eyes was a weight of loss that perhaps only the two of them could really understand.

Looking around at the gathered crowd, Lydia decided she was wrong about that. The gathered mourners all wore the same haunted expressions. She supposed the one thing everyone shared, regardless of who they were, was grief.

She turned her attention back to Reverend Whittier, who stood next to her father's casket, looking far older than his years. He cleared his throat, then said, "Friends, there really is nothing to say. Nothing that can ease the burden we must all bear. Our friend and neighbor has been taken cruelly from us by a man who may have been a neighbor but was surely no friend. I know some of us may see some justice in the fact that his murderer lost his life as well, and I am not such a saint that I don't feel the same sense of triumph at the removal of the scourge that has plagued our town.

"Today, though, I encourage you not to think of John Smith. He has had his moment, and if any yet live who mourn him, they will have theirs as well. This moment is for Greg, and I would not have it sullied by thoughts of anger or triumph or hate."

He looked squarely at Lydia. "I would not have it sullied by regret either. Greg died a man, protecting the ones he loved from the predations of the wolf. I guarantee you he went into the arms of his Creator without the slightest ounce of regret for the path that led him there. Let's not taint his sacrifice by thinking, even in part, that his actions were wasted on someone undeserving, even if that someone may be our very selves."

Lydia thought she had released all the tears she could cry, but when the Reverend said those words, her vision began to swim. She didn't feel guilty for her father's death, but part of her still wondered–if she had acted differently, could they perhaps have avoided his loss?

As though he were standing next to her, she heard her father's voice in her head. *Don't start with that, Lydia. I won't have you carry guilt for me.*

The reverend echoed her thoughts as he said, "So let us mourn our friend, but let us not blame ourselves for his passing. Let us grieve without guilt and remind ourselves that one day, we will all meet again in the arms of the Savior who even now welcomes His child home."

So saying, he nodded to Eugene and Peter. They stepped forward, taking their place at either side of the head of Greg's casket. Mr. Sorley and Doctor Anderson followed after them and Colton Bowers and the reverend took the rear.

The procession left the church house, moving slowly as they walked to the cemetery adjacent to the church. The journey was short, too short, and when they reached the freshly dug grave where her father's body would be laid to rest, Lydia's strength failed her. She collapsed to her knees, buried her face in her hands and wept.

She heard someone stoop next to her, and a moment later, a small but strong hand lifted her to her feet. She looked up, and her eyes widened when she saw her mother, teary-eyed but with a calm strength behind the tears.

"It's all right, Lydia," she said, gently but firmly. "Come say goodbye to your father with me."

Fresh grief rolled through Lydia at her mother's command but fresh strength filled her as well. She stood, took a breath and continued to walk with her mother.

They set her father's casket next to the grave and the mourners said their goodbyes in turn. When it came Lydia's turn, she knelt next to the grave and put her hand on the casket.

She was silent for several moments. She didn't know what to say. What could she say that would mean anything in the face of such loss?

Then she thought of something. She took a breath and said, "Thank you so much, Pa. Thank you for taking such wonderful care of me for so many years. You fought so hard to give me a good life. I want you to know you succeeded. My life was hard, but my life was joyful and full of love. That's all that anyone can ask and more than many receive. Thank you."

She took a shuddering breath and added, "Now it's time for you to take care of my brother. When you see him, tell him we all still love him, and we all still miss him. Tell him not to worry about us. Tell him God sent us an angel with the perfect name and that angel will make sure that his sister and mother never want again. Make sure you tell him how his brave father rescued his sister from an evil man. Make sure he knows that in the end, you stood tall and proud against those who would hurt your family and you won.

"I love you, Pa. I always will. Rest easy and rest well. I'll see you in Heaven one day."

She stood and returned to her mother. They held each other as the pallbearers lowered her father's coffin into the ground. She held her tears once more as they began to spade the dirt back into the grave.

She remained long after the last of the dirt was packed over the grave and the headstone was raised in front of it. The other mourners left one by one, until only she, her mother and Peter remained.

Peter walked to her side and placed a hand on her shoulder. The three of them stood in silence for several minutes.

Mary was the one to break the silence. She took a deep breath and said, "Well, if I know my husband, I imagine he's going insane over the fact that his family's standing here crying like fools. What do you say we go home and take turns telling our favorite stories about Greg over dinner?"

Lydia couldn't resist a chuckle. "I'm not sure that will help the crying, Mother."

"No," Mary said, "but it will remind us of the good. Life will always carry grief, but if we're fortunate, the good outweighs the grief. For thirty-two years with the most wonderful man I've ever known, I consider myself fortunate."

"Yes," Lydia said, "me too."

She looked up at Peter, who nodded through his own tears. He turned to her and smiled tenderly. "Me too."

The three of them said a final goodbye to Greg, then left to enjoy an evening of laughter and love with their friends and each other. As the wagon carried them away from the cemetery, Lydia looked ahead to the horizon. For the first time in years, she didn't fear what she'd find on the other side.

AVA WINTERS

Chapter Thirty-Six

Lydia walked slowly through the house, admiring the freshly hewn timbers that formed the walls and the lushly upholstered tables and chairs that furnished the parlor and kitchen. The stove was new as well, the copper of the pipe polished to a shine. She walked to the bedroom and gasped when she saw the ornately carved four poster bed.

"Oh, it's beautiful!" she exclaimed.

"Isn't it just lovely?" Dorothy gushed. "I told Pa that you would like it. He said it was too fancy, but I said that Lydia could use some fancy in her life after everything she's been through."

"But Dorothy, it's too much!" Lydia protested. "Surely your father can't afford this."

"Oh, he didn't buy it, silly!" Dorothy said, "Peter built it."

"He *built* it?" Lydia said.

"Of course he did. You know he was a carpenter before he moved here, right?"

"Well, yes, I knew," Lydia said, "but I thought he just built barns and stables."

Dorothy planted her hands on her hips and offered a tolerant sigh. "You really need to talk to your husband more."

"Well, he's not my husband yet," Lydia said. "I don't marry him until tomorrow."

Dorothy rolled her eyes. "Oh for heaven's sake. Fine. Starting *tomorrow*, you need to talk to your husband more."

Lydia giggled. "Sure, I'll do that. So Peter built the bedframe. Who gave us the mattress?"

"Oh, that was me!" Dorothy said brightly. "Colton's cousins helped."

"Ah yes, the wonderful Colton," Lydia replied, grinning. "And how is our knight in shining armor?"

"Shining and knightly," Dorothy replied with a grin. "Don't look so disappointed, Lydia. You know I'm a hopeless romantic. I'm not afraid of my sentimental side the way you are."

This time it was Lydia's turn to roll her eyes. "You can't throw that in my face anymore," she said, "I'm marrying him, aren't I?"

"So you are," Dorothy said with a smile. "I can't believe it's already been six months since he arrived here. It feels like only yesterday our tall, dark and morose stranger shuffled into our lives with his hat in his hand and his eyes looking anywhere but at whoever was talking to him."

"Be nice," Lydia said, "He's my husband, you can't talk about him like that."

"He's not your husband until tomorrow," Dorothy said impudently. "Besides, he knows I love him." She sighed and laid her hand softly across her brow. "Oh, if it weren't for you, Lydia, Peter and I would have had such a lovely romance."

"I'm sure," Lydia said wryly. "Does Colton know you feel this way?"

"Oh, of course he does," Dorothy said flippantly. "The first thing I told him when I met him was that I was only allowing him to court me because Peter was already in love with you."

"I'm sure you did," Lydia said with a laugh.

The front door opened and Mary and Eugene walked in. "Mary!" Dorothy cried, rushing to the older woman and wrapping her in a fierce embrace.

Eugene lifted his hands. "What, your Pa doesn't get a hug?"

Dorothy reached up and patted Eugene on the top of his head. "Hi, Papa," she said breezily.

Lydia started to giggle, and Eugene shook his head. "You took too much after your mom," he groused. "Never taking anything seriously."

Dorothy released Mary and said, "Pa, you're far too kindhearted of a person to get away with the grouchy old man act. Peter can pull it off when he's older if he wants, but not you."

"Yet another thing that Peter can do better than me," Eugene said, shaking his head.

"You can make better lamb stew than he can," Dorothy offered.

"Well, I should hope I'm at least a better shepherd than he is," Eugene said, "considering it's how I make a living."

While the Flisters bantered, Lydia embraced her mother. Mary squeezed tightly for a moment, then held Lydia out at arms' length. She shook her head and said, "How can you be so grown up already?"

Lydia laughed. "Mother, I'm thirty-one. I've been grown up for a while."

"I know," Mary said, caressing Lydia's cheek, "but you'll always be my baby girl."

Tears misted Lydia's eyes. "I know, Mother," she said softly.

Mary beamed, then stepped past her daughter. She exclaimed when she saw the stove. "Oh, Lydia! Lydia, have you seen our kitchen?"

"I've seen the whole house, Mother," Lydia said, "it's impressive."

"It's better than impressive," Mary said, "it's miraculous. And to believe I thought our neighbors didn't like us."

"Fear will freeze even the kindest of hearts," Eugene offered.

Mary looked at him, impressed, "Why Eugene," she said, "that was beautiful. You should be a poet."

"Well, I can't take credit for that one," Eugene said. "That's one of Peter's."

"Peter wrote that?" Lydia exclaimed.

Dorothy sighed in exasperation. "Lydia, you really *must* talk to him more."

"I talk to him!" she protested. "I *know* he likes to write poetry. I just hadn't heard that one yet."

"Well, to be fair, it's not finished yet," Eugene said. "he only started writing it yesterday."

"Well, I'll have to make him read the rest of it on our wedding night," Lydia said.

"I'm sure you'll find better things to do on your wedding night," Dorothy said.

"Dorothy!" Lydia exclaimed, reddening, "Don't talk like that!"

Dorothy giggled. "Oh, Lydia, I'm only teasing you because I'm happy for you. You know that."

"Well, you can be happy for me and still leave some mystery."

"If you insist, oh mysterious one," Dorothy replied.

The four of them finished the tour of the new house and the barn.

The new barn was equally impressive, as strong and sturdy as the one Peter had rebuilt, but larger, able to handle the expanded size of the ranch.

Most impressive, of course, was the herd. After John's death, their neighbors, –who, as Peter's poem suggested, had been frozen with fear–showed their true colors. Not only did they rebuild the ranch, they bought the Gutenbergs new breeding stock to start again. The ranch was now four times its original size, allowing for up to twice that number of cattle should they choose.

Well, they had all the time in the world to think about that. Right now, Lydia was happy just to have a home. Her smile faded as she thought of her father. Greg would have loved to see the ranch like this. More than anything, he would have loved to see Lydia marry Peter.

Mary put her arm around her daughter. "He would be proud," she said softly. "He would be so proud of you."

Lydia turned to her mother and smiled. "I know. I just miss him so much sometimes."

Mary pulled Lydia into her arms and softly stroked her hair. "I know, sweetheart. I miss him too."

They held each other for a moment, separating when Dorothy announced that she was making cornbread and if Lydia didn't come to help her she would pour in an entire gallon of maple syrup.

"I'd better go save us," Lydia said, pulling away from Mary.

They reached the house and Lydia just managed to intervene before Dorothy added too much syrup to the cornbread. Peter was noticeably absent from dinner, having been warned firmly by Dorothy that he was not to see Lydia until after the wedding.

"I thought he just couldn't see me in my wedding dress," Lydia asked.

"Oh come on," Dorothy said. "Won't it be so exciting to be deprived of him for so long only to see him suddenly, waiting for you at the end of the aisle, all handsome and dressed up in his finest suit, smiling that smile that belongs only to you?" Seeing Lydia's expression, she giggled. "See? I knew you'd see things my way."

"You're lucky you're so adorable," Lydia said.

Dorothy preened, prompting a round of laughter from everyone at the table. It felt good to laugh. It had been a while since Lydia had laughed. Peter was right. Grief would be her companion sometimes, but with the love of her friends and family, it would not be her master.

***

Lydia's wedding day dawned bright and unseasonably warm, despite the snow that blanketed the ground. Dorothy, who had initially protested the decision to marry in January, practically floated around Lydia, exclaiming at her dress, her hair, her shoes, her coat, and oh, her smile! Peter would be absolutely dumbstruck by the sight of her.

Lydia managed to smile and laugh and converse with her friend and her mother, but inwardly, her heart was pounding. She couldn't understand why she was so nervous! After all, this was what she'd wanted since she was a girl, and anyway, Peter had asked her to marry him, so he must want her as well.

She decided she wasn't nervous about that. Maybe she was nervous because...well, she didn't know why. As they drove toward the church where Reverend Whittier waited to marry her to Peter, she only knew that she was anxious somehow.

"Don't worry," Dorothy said, taking her hand and patting it. "It's okay to be nervous. Everyone's nervous when they get married."

"Really? Were you nervous when you married?" Lydia asked.

"Oh, I'm sure I'll be terribly nervous," Dorothy said, "but it will be worth it in the end."

"Does Colton know this?" Lydia asked.

"Of course he does," Dorothy said. "He's only waiting to ask me because he's far more nervous than I am. He thinks I'm too good for him."

She smiled as she said this, and Lydia commented wryly, "I'm sure you've done absolutely nothing to encourage that thought."

Dorothy giggled and said, "Well, you have to keep men on their toes. You can't let them know how much you care. Not all the time, anyway."

"Why are we talking about you?" Eugene asked, turning in his seat. "Lydia's getting married, not you."

"Not yet, Papa," Dorothy said, grinning, "but one day you'll have to let me marry my handsome prince."

"Oh, and Colton's a prince now, is he?"

"He is!" Dorothy said. "hHe's so sweet! I know you'd like him if you gave him a chance!"

"Who said I didn't like him? I just don't like thinking of you marrying and leaving me all alone."

"You won't be alone, Papa," Dorothy said, "I'll visit you every day. Besides, I'm sure you and Peter will practically live together the way you and Greg did."

At the mention of his friend, Eugene's smile faded slightly. Mary squeezed his hand briefly and he said, "Oh, I'm fine. I should be comforting you anyway, not the other way around."

"Grief is a constant companion, but only a master if I allow it," Lydia said.

"Is that another one of Peter's?" Eugene asked.

"Yes," Lydia said. "Not a poem, just good advice."

"He really is charming," Dorothy gushed. "I'm so happy for you, Lydia."

"Thank you," Lydia said, "I'm happy too."

She was also nervous, and she still didn't know why.

When they reached the church, her anxiety reached a fever pitch as seemingly every woman in town wanted to poke and prod and pinch and embrace her, all the while exclaiming about how beautiful she was and how lucky she was and how handsome Peter was and how happy they were for her.

She endured the well-wishing and gushing and giggling until finally, Reverend Whittier announced the start of the ceremony and everyone rushed to their seats. Dorothy led Lydia away to the bridal chamber and left her alone with her anxiety.

"Well, Lydia," she said, "today's the day."

Her voice echoed in the small room, and she sighed. "Why am I so nervous?"

That question remained unanswered for the moment. There was a soft rapping on the door, and Lydia called, "I'm ready."

The door opened and Eugene said, "Okay, Miss Lydia. He's waiting."

Lydia stood and put her hand in Eugene's arm. The older man smiled, and Lydia was surprised to see tears in his eyes. "Why are you crying?" she asked.

"Because I'm a sentimental old fool," he said, wiping tears from his eyes with his other hand. "That's what Dorothy says at least." He softened his voice and said, "I just wish Greg could be here to see you."

"I know," Lydia said. "me too."

She squeezed Eugene's hand and then turned to face ahead. They stopped in front of the big double doors that led to the auditorium.

"Well," Eugene said, "here goes."

The doors opened and when Lydia saw Peter standing at the end of the altar waiting for her, she realized she wasn't nervous at all. She was only anticipating this moment.

Peter was, as Dorothy had promised, absolutely breathtaking. He wore a newly fitted woolen suit with a bowler hat. His boots were polished to a high shine, and he did indeed wear that special soft smile that Lydia had never seen him smile for anyone else.

A smile lit up Lydia's own face as she walked the aisle toward him. In the front row, her mother smiled and wept happy tears, dabbing at her eyes every few seconds with a handkerchief. Dorothy sat next to her, her hand in Colton Bowers' decidedly nervous arm. Lydia thought wryly that the poor boy had better be serious about Dorothy because he would never hear the end of this wedding.

She looked back to Peter and the rest of the world faded away. She climbed the steps and stood next to him, and when she placed his hand in his, she knew that everything would be all right, now and for the rest of her life.

The ceremony passed in a blur. They recited their vows, but Lydia knew this was only a formality. They had already proven their commitment to each other. The words were only an announcement to others of their love.

Then the Reverend said, "You may kiss the bride."

Peter lifted his hand to caress Lydia's face. Lydia stared into his eyes and lifted her own hand to his face. She leaned forward and when their lips touched, warmth spread through her entire body.

The kiss seemed to last an eternity, and when it ended, Lydia was almost disoriented. She looked at Peter, briefly confused, and it wasn't until he turned her to face the crowd that she remembered that everyone had just seen her marry Peter. She giggled at her ridiculousness and said, "I hope for your sake I'm not so scatterbrained all the time."

"As long as one of us can think clearly," Peter said, "we'll be all right."

"Yes," Lydia said, regarding him. "I think we will."

The rest of the day was spent enduring congratulations from literally everyone in town. They only managed to enjoy some of their own wedding feast when Dorothy rather insistently shooed everyone away and stood guard like a soldier in front of their temple.

Eventually, though, the day ended, and Peter and Lydia found themselves heading home. At Dorothy's insistence, they rode in their own wagon while Mary and the Flisters rode in the Flisters' wagon. Dorothy promised to take good care of Mary for the evening, allowing Peter and Lydia the night alone.

They reached the house, but Lydia didn't want to go inside just yet. Anxiety, it seemed, had caught up to her again.

Peter smiled and said, "Shall we sit on the porch?"

"Yes, I'd like that," Lydia said, "thank you."

Peter laughed, "You're very welcome."

Lydia detected mirth in his tone and reddened. "Stop poking fun at me! I'm your wife now, you have to be nice."

"I'm the one who should be worried about you," Peter said, "I've seen your mean streak."

"Oh you haven't seen anything yet," she said, sitting next to him on the newly built porch swing—a gift from Doctor Anderson.

"Well," he said, "I can't wait to find out."

She giggled, "You say that now."

"I'll say it every day for the rest of my life," he promised.

She smiled and kissed him softly. When she pulled away, she leaned against his shoulder and gazed up at the sky. A breeze blew, and she shivered. Peter wrapped his arm around her and pulled her close, and she smiled as his warmth suffused her.

The sky was beautiful. The stars were a canopy of white and blue, shining brightly in spite of the full moon.

They sat in silence for a long time. As she leaned against her husband's chest, Lydia realized that she would have many more nights like this one. She would sit on her porch with her husband and watch the stars as they shifted from season to season, and there was no John Smith to crowd her mind with fear and despair.

There was only love.

She stood and turned to Peter. "Shall we go inside?"

"Already?" he asked, showing for the first time a little of his own anxiety.

Lydia smiled and held her hand. "Let's go inside, Mr. Kerouac."

He returned her smile and took her hand, standing from the swing. "Lead the way, Mrs. Kerouac."

Lydia did so, thinking to herself that this was what the stories meant when they said happily ever after.

Epilogue

Two Years Later

Lydia struggled to stifle laughter as Dorothy paced across the room. "Dorothy, relax," she said, finally releasing her laughter. "You're making me nervous."

"That's easy for you to say!" Dorothy said. "You have a built-in excuse to relax!"

Lydia grimaced and put her hand on her stomach to calm the baby kicking around inside. "I have a feeling you'll see this differently when you have one of your own."

Dorothy stopped dead in her tracks, a look of horror on her face. "Oh!" she cried, "I'd forgotten I'll have to have Colton's children!"

"Well, it's not as though you have to have them right away," Lydia said. "Besides, would it be so terrible if you had children?"

"No, I suppose not," Dorothy said, "and Colton *is* very handsome." Colton was working for them now, the chief stable hand at the ranch. Peter still did the work of foreman and chief wrangler, but at Lydia's insistence, he had hired Colton to care for the horses and tack. The boy—man—the man had proven quite handy and hardworking, and Peter had grudgingly admitted to Lydia a few weeks ago that it might be time for him to give him more responsibility and step back a little.

Lydia nodded and sipped her coffee without saying anything.

"I just…I just feel so grown up. But at the same time, it just feels so…the same."

Lydia smiled. "Growing up doesn't happen overnight, Dorothy. It's a lifelong process."

"I know, but…Well, how did you deal with it? When you realized you were in love with Peter, I mean?"

Lydia laughed, "Well, as I recall, a certain flighty friend of mine conspired with my parents to browbeat me with my attraction until I finally acquiesced merely to shut her up."

"I heard that," Peter said, walking into the room. "Don't scare Dorothy. It's bad enough she has to spend the rest of her life with that mopey-faced Bowers boy."

"Hey!" Dorothy cried, slapping Peter on his shoulder. "He is *not* mopey-faced! He only looks that way because he's earnest!"

"My mistake," Peter said with a laugh.

"*You're* mopey-faced," Dorothy jibed.

"Now that's enough of that talk," Mary said, walking into the parlor. "I promised Dorothy's father we'd bring her to the church in one piece. No more teasing. Honestly, Peter."

"What?" he said, "What did I do?"

"You called Colton mopey-faced!" Dorothy tattled.

"I meant that as a compliment! You know I like him."

The drive to the church was more of the same. Peter and Eugene competed to see who could be the grouchiest old man, all the while grinning like fools. Lydia watched them with a dry smile. Men couldn't admit to themselves that they enjoyed weddings as much as women did. Dorothy was a complete wreck by the time they reached the church, and it took the combined efforts of Lydia and her mother to coax her through the door. But like Lydia, her anxiety disappeared the moment she saw Colton standing at the altar waiting for her. His smile outshone any possibility of mopiness.

She whispered as much to Peter. "It's his hair," Peter said. "I told him to brush it today."

Lydia regarded him approvingly. "Well, look at you, thinking of his appearance like that. Why don't you brush your own hair?"

He lifted a sheepish hand to his hair, which as usual was an unkempt mess, and said, "Well, you usually do that for me."

"You're a grown man," Lydia said, "you can comb your own hair."

"I'll try."

Lydia rolled her eyes. She knew that meant he would do it once or twice, then stop, probably not even remembering this conversation. She looked at him sideways and said, "You're lucky you're so mopey-faced."

"What?"

"Handsome," she said. "You're lucky you're so handsome."

He smiled and leaned over to kiss her. She kissed him back, then turned ahead to watch her friend share her own kiss with the man she loved. The Reverend announced them man and wife and the crowd leapt from their seats to congratulate the new couple.

Peter and Lydia waited for the crowd to die down. While they sat, the baby kicked inside her, and she winced. "More energy than you know what to do with, little one," she said, looking down. "If you're a girl, we know you'll take after your namesake."

If they had a son, she and Peter had decided to name the baby after her father. Lydia had threatened to name a girl Dottie, over Dorothy's emphatic protests, and she had every intention of following through. Lydia thought that Mary would be about the happiest grandmother there ever was. She was pretty sure her mother was born to be a grandmother.

"You guys!" Dorothy cried, "Hurry up and follow me. Colton's mother made chocolate cake!"

"Chocolate cake," Peter repeated. "Well, I can't say no to that."

"Nor me," Lydia said.

Peter helped her stand and the two of them followed the newlyweds from the church to the outdoor pavilion where Colton's mother, as promised, had chocolate cake waiting for them.

Lydia smiled as she savored her dessert under the brilliant summer sun. All of her dreams had come true. She had a home, a husband, a family and wonderful friends. What more could anyone ask for?

THE END

Also by Ava Winters

Thank you for reading **"Second Chances and Sunsets for their Lonely Hearts"**!

I hope you enjoyed it! If you did, here are some of my other books!

My latest Best-Selling Books

#1 An Uninvited Bride on his Doorstep

#2 Once upon an Unlikely Marriage of Convenience

#3 Their Unlikely Marriage of Convenience

#4 An Orphaned Bride to Love Him Unconditionally

#5 An Unexpected Bride for the Lonely Cowboy

Also, if you liked this book, you can also check out **my full Amazon Book Catalogue at:**
https://go.avawinters.com/bc-authorpage

Thank you for allowing me to keep doing what I love! ❤